PANDORA DRIVE

TIM WAGGONER

LEISURE BOOKS NEW YORK CITY

A LEISURE BOOK®

April 2006

Published by

Dorchester Publishing Co., Inc.
200 Madison Avenue
New York, NY 10016

ISBN 0-8439-5625-9

Visit us on the web at www.dorchesterpub.com.

THE GRASPING HAND

"You're open, Mara. Wide open…"

Damara had no idea what the voice was talking about, but the words nevertheless chilled her.

The *scuttle-scratch* of claws was louder now, and though the shower was still running, Damara could no longer hear water falling. All she could hear was the sound of sharp nails on metal.

"You have to stop, Mara…stop now."

The round metal cover flew off the drain as a green clawed hand covered with spikes thrust upward. It didn't matter that the opening was too narrow for a normal hand and forearm to pass through, let alone one that sprouted wicked-looking black barbs. Jack Sharp could reach up through the drain because her little brother had once imagined he could, simple as that.

Damara reached for the shower door, but she only managed to slide the door a few inches before the spiny green hand took a swipe at her legs. Damara screamed as ebony needles raked her skin, lay open her flesh, scraped against bone…

Other *Leisure* books by Tim Waggoner:

LIKE DEATH

PANDORA DRIVE

Prologue

A cloudless night sky, stars spread out against the blackness from one horizon to the other. The air humid and sticky, cool instead of hot, though the ground beneath her sandaled feet still felt warm, as if it hoarded the heat it had absorbed during the day and was reluctant to give it up. The stars were alone in the sky, for tonight was a new moon. The name had never made any sense to Damara. How could something be *new* if you couldn't see it? She knew the moon was still out there somewhere, but instead of being a glowing blue-white, it was completely black. She supposed calling it a "dark moon" wouldn't sound as nice, but it would be more accurate.

A small dark form flew above Damara's head, dipping and darting in a zigzag pattern. But she wasn't afraid. She loved bats, thought they were cool . . . at a distance, anyway. As she watched the bat—at least she assumed it was a bat; she couldn't really tell for sure in the dark—a delicious shiver

1

ran though her body. She couldn't believe that she'd really done it, that she really was *here*. Tristan and she had talked about sneaking into Riverfork in the middle of the night at least a million times. But neither of them had ever done anything about it. Until now.

You'd never do it, Mara, so don't pretend like you would. You don't even like to go any farther than your backyard if you don't have to. You'd never really go into a deserted amusement park at night. Never ever.

That's what Tristan had said this afternoon on the school bus when Damara had started talking about visiting Riverfork again. She wasn't certain why he'd suddenly become such a butt-head about it and refused to play along like he always had. Maybe it was because he was a year older than she was and would be thirteen next year. Maybe he'd decided to get a head start on being a stuck-up, obnoxious teenager. Whatever the reason, she was looking forward to seeing Tristan tomorrow and telling him about her adventure— *and* showing him some souvenir that she'd bring back. A sign, maybe, or some piece of abandoned equipment. Anything would do, as long as it was proof.

She could hear Tristan now.

No freakin' way!

Tristan always replaced swear words with less-harsh substitutes, as if he wanted to talk like an adult but couldn't quite bring himself to.

You gotta be shishin' me! You really did it . . .

snuck out and went down to Riverfork—in the middle of the night—all by yourself. No freakin' way!

And then, best of all: *Geez, Mara, I'm really sorry for what I said yesterday. I guess I was wrong about you.*

Damara giggled at the thought of Tristan's grudging apology, her laughter sounding louder than it would've during the day, brittle, echoing, and with the slightest edge of hysteria to it.

Okay, so maybe she *was* afraid of being here . . . in the dark. Just a little, anyway.

Framed against the night sky, the silhouettes of Riverfork's ghosts surrounded her: the dark circle of a Ferris wheel, the twisting artificial canals of a log ride, the support beams and undulating track of a roller coaster, and many more. Surely they had once had names . . . Round-and-Around, Lumberjack Falls, the Whipcrack . . . But whatever they had once been called, whatever names had been used to thrill and entice kids both young and old to buy a ticket they could exchange for a five-minute thrill had long ago been lost. Riverfork—so named because it was built on the western bank of the Clearwater River that flowed through town, a river that forked into two smaller branches just south of the park—had been closed since before Damara was born. And since she, like any eleven-year-old, couldn't conceive of a world that had existed without her, that meant the park had been closed always and forever.

No one knew why Riverfork had been shut down. At least, none of the kids she knew, which to her young girl's mind was pretty much everyone in the world. Some said it was because the river overflowed its banks one exceptionally rainy spring and flooded the park. The water damage had been so severe that the owner couldn't afford to fix it and had instead shut the park down. Other kids said it was because Riverfork couldn't compete with Kings Island once it was built in the late sixties (right after the dinosaurs went extinct). Kings Island was only a forty-minute drive away, if that, and it was a zillion times better than Riverfork, which mostly had a bunch of kiddie rides anyway. But Damara's favorite story, one that Tristan and she told each other often, was that Riverfork had been the scene of a grisly roller-coaster accident that had forced the park's closure. An entire set of cars had jumped the track, sailed through the air, their riders' screams changing from cries of delight to shrieks of pure terror as the cars plunged down toward the fully occupied Ferris wheel. The crash, of course, had been spectacular and the causalities high.

Whatever the reason, mundane or sensational, Riverfork was closed and had stayed closed, its only visitors teenagers looking for a place to get drunk, get stoned, and get laid (though not necessarily in that order). Unless the spirits of all those people who died on the roller-coaster accident still wandered the park in a ghostly daze, trying to figure out how their day of fun had turned so bad so fast.

Stop it! she told herself. *You know you shouldn't think things like that!*

4

Damara wished she'd brought a different flashlight from the one she carried stuck handle-first in the back pocket of her shorts. She'd gotten it out of the junk drawer in the kitchen before going to bed, and she'd hidden it under her pillow while she'd waited for her mom and dad to finish watching the evening news, brush their teeth, and go to bed. She'd waited a whole other hour, lying in the dark, staring up at her ceiling and glancing at the digital alarm clock on her dresser every few minutes. When she couldn't stand waiting any longer, she got up—still dressed in T-shirt and shorts—slipped on her sandals, grabbed the flashlight, and opened her bedroom window just high enough for her to squeeze through.

The flashlight had worked just fine at first, but soon after she'd crawled over the chain-link fence that enclosed their backyard, the light had begun to flicker, and it continued flickering as she made her way through the short stretch of woods that sloped downhill from her house toward the river—and Riverfork. By the time she reached the rusty locked gate that closed off the entrance to the park, she was smacking the flashlight every few seconds to keep it illuminated, and after she found the loose board in the wooden wall that surrounded the park—a board Tristan and she had tugged on experimentally many times, though always during the day, and never had they gone further than prying the board back and peeking inside—the stupid flashlight had died on her. She didn't know if the batteries were weak or if there was some kind of loose connection, or if she'd broken the little bulb inside by smacking the flashlight so hard in her attempts to keep it lit. It didn't really matter, though. She'd made it inside Riverfork. So she'd stuck the useless flashlight in her pocket and began exploring the park by starlight, the flashlight handle bumping into her right butt cheek as she walked. She hoped that if she left it off long enough, maybe the batteries would recharge or something, and she'd have some light to see by so she could make her way home. She knew she was bullshitting herself (*bullshishing*, Tristan would say), that batteries didn't work like that, but the thought made her feel a little better nevertheless.

A breeze blew through the park, and Damara folded her arms over her chest. Though she was only eleven, she was already beginning to develop breast buds, and the cold night air had hardened her nipples. So when she brushed them while folding her arms, the sensation was so tickley-shivery that she yelped as if she'd been pinched. She wished she'd brought a jacket or even a light sweater. Though late August in southwestern Ohio could be (and often was) hot and humid as a motherbucket, as Tristan would say, the nights could feel more like September or even October. For all the warmth provided by her Wonder Woman T-shirt, shorts, and sandals, she might as well be wandering around the park naked.

The thought made her giggle and this time her nipples felt tingly-warm. For a moment, she was tempted to really do it, to take off her clothes, toss them to the ground, and let the night air caress her skin. She imagined the air's kiss making her nipples so swollen that they ached. She felt heat spreading through her vagina (her *virginia,* Tristan might say), burrowing inside her as if something warm and furry were exploring the hidden recesses of her body. She got as far as lifting her T-shirt up over her taut belly before a piece of the night swooped down toward her.

She squealed, let her shirt drop back down, and ducked. She could feel a swoosh of air as the bat traced the course of her spine, arced upward, and soared off to rejoin the darkness. Except maybe it *wasn't* a bat. Maybe it was something else, something . . .

She straightened and looked up at the sky, trying to find the bat (or whatever it was), flying somewhere above her. After a moment's searching, she saw a shadowy form circling in the air, but the bat seemed larger, its flight slower, its wings—were there four of them now?—beating the humid air more heavily. And it was making a noise that sounded nothing like the bat screeches she'd heard on Scooby-Doo cartoons. This sound was a combination of a sheep's bleat and fingernails being dragged across sheet metal.

She felt a tingling at the base of her skull, as if someone were lightly brushing fingers across her skin. Fear hit her like a punch to the stomach, and she began whispering aloud.

"It's a bat, just a bat, nothing else, just an ordinary furry, pug-nosed, beady-eyed, leather-winged bat-bat-bat . . ." And as she said this in a breathy whisper that was almost a chant, she thought of a polar bear standing in a blizzard. An image that was white, whiter than white, blank, nothing.

The bat was bat-sized again, flying fast and silent as it continued on its nightly mission to keep the insect population in check.

Damara let out a shaky breath. She'd kept *it* from happening again.

Maybe she shouldn't have come here. The dark, the shadows, the shapes . . . They were like black construction paper, black Play-Doh, black paint . . . just waiting for her to reach out, take hold, and work, mold, *use* them to make something different, new, and special. The shadowy forms of the park attractions seemed to lean in closer toward her, as if they were listening to her thoughts, eagerly waiting to find out what she would do with them.

Damara squeezed her eyes shut. "Polar bear, polar bear, polar bear, polar bear . . ."

White . . . blank . . . nothing.

She could hear her father's voice, half angry, half scared.

You have to be more careful, Dee. You could . . . could hurt someone. Not that you'd ever do it on purpose, sweetheart. You wouldn't, you're a good girl, your mother and I know that. But if you're not careful, what happened to your brother . . .

That was *definitely* a polar-bear thought, and Damara squashed it good and hard. She shouldn't have come here, shouldn't have let her fight with Tristan get to her like that. She should—

She heard the scrape of a shoe on gravel coming from somewhere out in the darkness. Damara's first thought was that Tristan had somehow figured out what she'd planned tonight, that he'd been watching from his bedroom window across the street, saw her crawl through her own open window, and snuck out after her. It would be just like that buttwipe to follow her and ruin her chance to rub her adventure in his face tomorrow.

She turned toward the sound—though in the dark it was hard for her to tell exactly which direction it had come from—and was about to call out to Tristan, when she heard a voice.

"Dee? Where are you? I know you're here somewhere! I heard you sneak out!"

She took in a small gasp of air, and her heart—which was already pounding fast—began to race. Omigod! It was Daddy!

"You know you're not supposed to leave home, Dee. Not unless you have to. You know what can happen."

Damara wanted to run, but her feet refused to move. Normally, she wasn't afraid of Daddy. He was kind, sweet, funny . . . until he thought that there was danger of her doing *it* again.

"I was going to call out before you left the yard, but I decided to wait and see what you were up to."

His voice sounded closer now, but Damara didn't see any sign of him in the darkness. She wondered why he didn't have a flashlight, but then she realized that since she'd taken the one in the junk drawer, Daddy probably hadn't had enough time to look for another before setting out to follow her. That was a lucky break, for if he didn't have a light to shine on her, if she were quiet enough and fast enough, maybe she'd be able to get away and hide from him, maybe even sneak past him and head back home, take off her clothes, hide the flashlight, and crawl back into bed before he got back. Then she could try to pretend that she'd been asleep all along. She didn't really think it would work, knew that Daddy had probably checked her bedroom before going outside, but it was the only plan she could come up with to escape his anger—and the punishment he was certain to dole out for her midnight expedition—and she had to go with it, regardless of how slim her chances for success were.

"What you're doing is dangerous, Dee. For any kid, not just you. Hell, it's dangerous for an adult to be wandering around here in the dark." He chuckled then, the sound so close that Damara thought she could almost feel her father's breath on her face. "People's imaginations can run wild in the dark, sweetheart. They can get really scared and do some foolish things that might get themselves hurt. But we know what happens when *your* imagination runs wild, don't we, Dee?"

She could tell that Daddy was fighting to sound calm, but she could hear suppressed anger in his voice, alongside fear. Fear of her, of what she might do.

"C'mon, Dee. Just tell me where you are so I can find you and we'll go back home together. I won't even tell your mom about tonight. It'll be our little secret, okay?"

Damara heard another scrape of shoe on gravel, and she was certain Daddy was real close now, maybe close enough to reach out and grab her if he knew which direction to reach. Damara took hold of the flashlight and pulled it out of her pocket. She guessed which direction her father was and threw the flashlight the opposite way. A couple of seconds later, plastic clattered on asphalt, and without waiting to see whether Daddy took the bait, Damara started running. Her sandals made a *thwop-thwop-thwop* sound as she ran, and she wished she'd thought of taking them off before she'd started running. Too late now.

She'd been inside the park long enough for her eyes to adjust somewhat, and she headed toward what she guessed was a building of some sort. She had no idea whether the door would be locked or not—assuming she could even find the door in the dark—but since Daddy didn't have a flashlight, even if he figured out which direction she'd run, she wouldn't have to go inside to hide. She could go around the side of the building, flatten herself against the wall, and wait until Daddy got tired of looking for her and gave up. All she had to do was reach the building. . . .

And that's when Daddy turned on his flashlight.

Jerry Ruschmann saw his daughter scamper away from his flashlight beam as if she were some manner of nocturnal animal that he'd startled. He

11

started to call out to her again, but he stopped himself. If words were going to make her come to him, they would've done so by now. He tried to track her with the flashlight—one he kept in his nightstand drawer in case the power went out in the middle of the night—but she was moving so fast, all he caught were glimpses of her long brown hair flying in the wind, skinny arms, and legs pumping as if her life depended on her mustering all the speed she was capable of.

He felt a pang of guilt then, for he knew that Dee (he never thought of her as Damara; that was the name her mother had insisted on), ran because she was afraid of *him,* afraid of what he might do to punish her. Jerry didn't want to punish her, nor did he want to be out here with her alone, in the dark, in an abandoned amusement part that he had visited so many times as a child back when Riverfork had been a going concern. In truth, though he never would admit this to anyone—had never even told his wife, though he was certain she suspected—he was scared of Dee. Oh, he loved her plenty, too, as much as he could imagine loving anyone. And that was why, despite his fear, he had followed her tonight.

He started jogging after Damara, keys jingling in the pocket of the jeans he'd hastily pulled on before leaving the house, gut bobbling beneath the too-small T-shirt he slept in. He'd put on some weight in the last year or so, drinking too much beer, eating too much crap, and just getting older, he figured. But he regretted every extra ounce now, and he was gulping for breath and hoping that his pounding heart wasn't going to explode on him in protest for making it work so hard.

Goddamn, better get myself a gym membership for Christmas, Jerry thought. *And maybe start cutting back on the quarter-pounders, too.*

The flashlight bounced around in his grip as he ran, making it even harder to keep track of Damara. But he was able to see that she was heading toward a building with dingy, cracked mirrors covering the outside walls. There was a faded sign over the entrance, and though the letters had been worn by wind, rain, and time, he could still read them. ALACRITY'S SPECTATORIUM. It was a hall of mirrors, and Damara was running pell-mell toward the entrance.

"Don't." He tried to shout, but the word came out as a whisper. He continued running toward the building, momentarily losing sight of Damara in the darkness. He came to a panting, sweating, pulse-throbbing stop outside the building's mirrored doors, then bent over and struggled to catch his breath. Though he couldn't count the number of times he'd come to Riverfork as a kid and later a teen, he had no trouble recalling how many times he'd been inside this place. Exactly once. He wasn't sure what "Spectatorium" meant, or who or what "Alacrity" was, but it was just a fancy name for a hall of mirrors. And it had scared the holy living shit out of him when he was little. The confusing maze of mirrors, the distorted nightmarish images looking out at him from behind the glass ... The

13

thought of going back in there after close to thirty years, going back in there with *Dee,* was almost enough to make him piss his pants. But regardless of whatever else she might be, Damara was just a little girl, and he was her daddy. He couldn't let her run around in there, alone, in the dark, no matter how much he might have wanted to.

He straightened, sweat cold and clammy on his skin. He took in a last shuddering breath and, flashlight held tight, pushed open the door and entered Alacrity's Spectatorium. And if someone had told him that he would never walk out again, he wouldn't have been surprised. Not in the slightest.

Chapter One

Damara sat on a folding chair in front of her bedroom window. The chair wasn't especially comfortable, but since she could fold it up and slide it under her bed, she could keep her mother from knowing how much time she spent sitting here, looking out at the world. She used to have a more comfortable chair, an old recliner that had once belonged to her dad, but her mother had given it away to Amvets last year, saying, *It's not good for you to sit and stare out the window all day,* but meaning so much more.

Damara had been forced to stand or kneel in front of her window after that, until one day when Mom was taking a shower, and Damara decided to go down to the basement. Tucked away in one musty corner she found an old card table and a couple chairs. On impulse, she'd carried one of the chairs upstairs and quickly hid it beneath her bed before Mom could finish her shower. Damara had felt foolish at the time, sneaking around like a little kid. After all, she *was* twenty-eight. Still, she knew that if Mom ever found out about the folding chair, she'd take it away, just as Damara knew that she'd do nothing to stop her.

Mom had gone grocery shopping this afternoon, though, and Damara could sit and look out the window all she wanted. Mom often ran other errands when she went out, sometimes even had lunch with friends or went out to a movie. Damara wondered what it would be like to see a movie in a real theater. She hadn't gone to a cinema since she was quite young, and she had no memory of the experience. But she didn't need a theater, did she? She had her window.

Two of them, actually: one that faced east and one that faced south. Through the east window she could see across the street and had great views of the Ledfords' house and the Marcinos'. Out the south window was the next-door neighbors' house, and she had a decent view of both the Coltons' front and back yards. But she had to be careful using the south window, for it lined up almost perfectly with the Coltons' bedroom. Emma Colton was quite the neighborhood busybody and spent more time peering through windows than Damara did. Plus, her husband Kenneth gave Damara the creeps. A couple of years ago, Damara had knelt in front of the south window (she'd kept the recliner in front of the east window, and it was too heavy to move easily). She craned her head to see the Coltons' front yard, and when she saw that nothing was happening, she started to turn to view

the back. But as her gaze passed over the Coltons'
bedroom window, she saw Kenneth there, staring
out at her with a blank expression. She froze, unable to tear her gaze away from the old man's, unable to do anything save watch as a slow smile
stretched across his face, revealing two rows of
yellowed, crooked teeth. It was a smile without
humor or joy, and it didn't reach his eyes. They remained cold and expressionless.

As if shrugging off a hypnotic spell, Damara had
stood, reached for the curtain cord, and closed the
curtains. Afterward, she'd sat on the side of her
bed and trembled for the better part of a half hour.
Since then, she hadn't used the south window
much. Sometimes when she passed by it, regardless of whether the curtains were open or closed,
she felt Kenneth Colton's gaze on her, but whenever she got up the courage to look (which wasn't
often), she never saw him.

So this afternoon, as on most days, it was the
east window through which Damara viewed the
world—or at least, her little corner of it. Though
Pandora Drive wasn't the busiest street in town,
she usually found enough to keep her entertained.
The street ran through a suburban neighborhood
whose best days were behind it. The houses had
been built in the forties and fifties, all of them two-
story Cape Cods with red brick and green- or
black-shingled roofs and shutters to match. The
yards were small and devoid of any landscaping
except for the occasional flowerbed. There were
few garages in the neighborhood, so most resi-

dents parked in their driveways or on the street. About half the houses on the street needed some sort of improvement—new roof, new shutters, new porch—and most of the cars were used, with dents and scratches, rust-nibbled frames, patches of primer and smears of Bondo.

Once, this had been one of the nicer neighborhoods in town, especially back when the amusement park had been thriving. But after Riverfork had closed down, the neighborhood had begun a gradual process of decay, as if the park's dissolution were slowly spreading. Pandora Drive wasn't a dump, and it was still safe enough, but it wasn't what it used to be, either.

It was early October, and the leaves on the oak and elm trees that lined both sides of the street were beginning to change color, from shades of green to a riot of oranges, reds, browns, and yellows. Before too many more days passed, Kenneth Colton would be outside with his leaf blower, battling the season to keep his yard as immaculate as possible. Across the street, Anne Marcino would wait until her yard was completely covered. Then she and her young daughter would go outside, rake the leaves into one big pile, and both of them would take turns jumping into it until the leaves were scattered all over the yard, and they'd laugh, pick up their rakes, and start the process all over again. Damara's mom would just pay one of the teenage boys who lived down the street to rake for them, just like Mrs. Ledford always . . .

Damara paused in mid-thought. She'd been about to think, *Just like Mrs. Ledford always does,* except that wasn't the proper verb anymore, was it? Poor Mrs. Ledford had lost her battle with cancer less than a month ago, and right now a For Sale sign was displayed in her yard, leaves lazily drifting down around it and forming a small mound at its base. Damara hadn't gone to the funeral. She'd wanted to, as much to see Tristan again as to say goodbye to his mother, but her own mom had insisted she stay home. "Just to be on the safe side." Damara had been so ashamed at missing the funeral that she hadn't even tried to go across the street to tell Tristan how sorry she was (not that her mom would've let her), and she'd felt even more awkward about calling. Tristan had only remained in Zephyr for a couple more days before getting back into his rental car and, she presumed, heading to the airport. A real estate agent had stopped by the next day and put up the For Sale sign.

Thinking about Mrs. Ledford and Tristan depressed Damara. She was about to give up on window watching for the day when she heard the distant rumble of the school bus coming down the street. She stayed where she was, hands folded in her lap, and waited. Before long the bus came hissing to a stop in front of the Marcinos'. The bus pulled away, a couple of children looking out their own windows at Damara, so used were they to seeing her sitting there. A couple waved and a few more stuck out tongues or made similarly rude gestures. Damara, as she always did, ignored the rude ones and waved back to the nice ones.

When the bus pulled away, Damara could see Autumn, who hated her name, especially at this time of the year. But whether she liked it or not, the girl certainly fit the season. Her hair was a rich, deep auburn, and she wore a white top, brown skirt, orange socks, and brown shoes. She was a pretty girl, and with the way she was dressed and the leaves on the ground and in the trees, she looked as if she belonged on the cover of a JCPenney catalog.

Carrying a heavy backpack, Autumn kicked through the leaves as she crossed the yard (she never used the walkway) toward the front porch. Even with the window closed, Damara could hear the leaves rustle, and she leaned forward and rapped her knuckle against the glass three times. Autumn stopped, turned around, saw Damara sitting at her window, and broke into a huge grin. She dropped her backpack to the ground and ran across the lawn toward Damara's house. As usual, the girl didn't bother looking before she darted into the street, and Damara held her breath and prayed that the child wouldn't be struck by a car. Autumn survived the crossing and came skipping up to Damara's window. Damara opened it so the two of them could talk.

"You're going to get killed if you don't start looking before you cross the street," Damara said.

Autumn made a face. "You sound just like my

mom. Next you're probably going to tell me not to carry so many books in my backpack." Autumn had a bad habit of taking out a dozen books at a time from the school library and carrying them around in her backpack every day. Autumn's mom, Anne, was always worried that her daughter was going to strain a muscle or develop back problems.

Damara laughed. "And you sound just like I did when I was your age. So how was school today?"

"It was all right. Evan chased me on the playground again. He wouldn't stop until I threatened to kiss him." Autumn frowned. "Why are boys like that, anyway?"

"Like what?" Damara asked.

"Stupid."

Damara smiled. "Who knows? Maybe they think that we're the stupid ones."

"C'mon, Damara—everyone *knows* that girls are *way* smarter than boys!"

Everyone knows. Such a simple phrase, so common as to be almost meaningless. But when it came to relationships between the genders, Damara had almost no experience to draw on, and thus she had no advice to offer Autumn on how to deal with the attentions of Evan Dorr. The only boyfriend she'd ever had was Tristan, and it wasn't like they'd officially dated or anything. Not for the first time, Damara was struck by the fact that her closest friend these days—her only friend, really— was a ten-year-old girl. But it made sense, didn't it? In terms of experience, Damara wasn't all that older than Autumn, and she wondered how long it would be until the girl had learned more of life than someone like Damara, someone who didn't go *out,* would ever know. How much longer until Autumn started feeling awkward in her presence and began looking at her funny? Before she stopped visiting the creepy woman across the street, ceased waving to her, and eventually avoided so much as looking toward the woman's window as she got off the bus? Not long enough, Damara feared.

"Did I say something wrong?" Autumn asked. "You're awful quiet."

Damara realized that she'd gotten so caught up in her self-pity—something that happened too often—she'd momentarily forgotten about Autumn. "Sorry," she said with an apologetic smile. "I guess my mind wandered there for a minute. Maybe you should just tell Evan how you feel. Maybe he thinks you like it when he chases you."

"But I do. I mean, kinda. I mean . . ." She trailed off and glanced to her left. Her eyes widened and she paled. "Oh, no."

Damara felt a cold twist of revulsion in her stomach, and though she had a pretty clear notion of what was bothering Autumn, in a soft voice she asked, "What is it?"

Autumn replied in a whisper, "Mr. Colton. He's watching me out his front window right now, and he's . . . smiling." Autumn shuddered.

"There's nothing wrong with someone looking out a window," Damara said, more to comfort her young friend than because she believed whatever Kenneth was doing was innocent. "Look at me; I do it all the time."

Damara hoped that last line would at least elicit a smile from Autumn, but the girl didn't react, didn't take her gaze off the Coltons' house.

"It's hard to tell, but I . . . I don't think he's wearing a shirt."

Damara's revulsion grew stronger, and now it was mixed with anger as well. She balled her hands into fists and pressed them against her sides, but when she spoke, she fought to keep her voice calm. "Maybe he's just hot or something. I'd ignore him. Besides, if I know Mrs. Hamilton, you probably have some homework to do."

It took an effort, but Autumn pulled her gaze away from the shirtless Kenneth Colton and looked at Damara. "Some history and math. But Mom always lets me wait until after supper to do my homework."

"And who was telling me the other day how much she hates doing homework late because she gets so tired?"

Autumn looked sheepish. "Me."

"So why don't you go on home and do your schoolwork now? That way you'll be finished by the time your mom gets home and you'll have the rest of the night to do whatever you want."

As Damara spoke, she tried not to imagine Kenneth standing at his front window, looking at Autumn and leering at the little girl (he wasn't just smiling, Damara was sure of that), wearing no shirt . . . and maybe not wearing anything else, either.

"Oh, all right," Autumn said, but despite her words, there was no protest in her voice. Only relief at having an excuse to get away from Kenneth Colton's leering gaze. "See you tomorrow, Damara!"

Before Damara could reply, Autumn turned and ran. Once again, she didn't look before crossing the street, but this time Damara didn't blame her. She leaned her head out the window and looked over at the Coltons' house, but she still couldn't see Kenneth from this angle. She shook her head in disgust. She could just imagine what that horny old bastard was thinking. . . .

But she wasn't supposed to imagine, was she? It wasn't safe.

Damara leaned back inside, closed the window, shut the curtains and ran to her bed. She crawled under the covers, lay her head back on the pillow and concentrated on summoning the mental image of a polar bear in a blizzard.

Kenneth watched Autumn grab her backpack off the ground, carry it onto her front porch, fish out her house key, open the door, go inside, and slam the door shut. His window was closed, so he couldn't hear whether she locked the door, but he'd bet his left nut that she did.

Speaking of his left nut, Kenneth held it in his hand, along with its matching counterpart, working them both as it they were rubber exercise balls: squeeze, release, squeeze, release, squeeze, release . . . The sensation wasn't pleasurable exactly, but it was enough to make the tiny shriveled nub of flesh that was his penis twitch, which was just about all the old boy was capable of these days. A year and a half ago, Kenneth had traded his ability to get an erection for having his cancerous prostate removed before it could spread its poison throughout the rest of his body. At the time, he'd thought it was a fair trade. Now he wasn't so sure.

Even though he couldn't see Autumn anymore, he stood at the window for several moments longer, squeezing his balls and thinking about how pretty that little girl was. She was a piece, all right, and if she kept on going like she was, before too long she'd be even sexier than her mamma. One of the many things he regretted about losing the lead in his pencil was that he'd never had the chance to beat off while Anne Marcino was out front doing yard work in her cut-off jeans and bikini top. But she and her little girl had moved in only a couple of weeks after he'd gotten home from the hospital. Talk about lousy fuckin' timing.

Kenneth was tempted to go into his bedroom, pull up the blinds, and see if Damara had moved from her front window to the side one. She wasn't as pretty as Anne—a bit too pale and bony for his taste—but beggars couldn't be choosers, right? He decided against it. Damara hardly ever opened the curtains on that window anymore. Besides, he'd been just about to go online when he heard the school bus coming down the street. Emma usually stayed a half hour after school let out to prepare for the next day, and even though she had only two years to go until she retired, his wife worked just as hard as ever. So if he wanted to have himself a little virtual fun, he'd better get to it. Emma didn't seem to mind that he was a Weak Willie these days—she'd never cared too much for sex as it was—but she could be one jealous hellcat if he so much as glanced at another woman. If she came home and found him squeezing his balls in front of the computer screen, she'd probably pick up the monitor and hurl it at the wall—and he'd be lucky if that's all she'd do.

Kenneth padded out of the living room and down the hall to the computer room, flaccid dick bobbling all the way. Emma and he had never had children—kind of hard for a woman to get pregnant if she only wanted to have sex once a month—and so they used their second bedroom as a small rec room. The computer table was in one corner, and Emma had a chair near the window that she sat in when she did needlepoint and cross-stitch. Since neither Emma nor Kenneth had any friends to speak of, the banal samplers she liked to make were framed and hung up throughout the house. In here, there were three. A picture of a rainbow above the saying "Miracles Happen"; a scattering of balloons against a sky-blue background and a single word, "Joy"; and hanging above his computer, a cartoonish man in a flannel shirt and hip waders standing in the middle of a stream fishing (though Kenneth hated fishing), fish leaping out of the water, the man's line stretching from the tip of his pole to the fish's mouth. Beneath the picture, this saying: "I'm hooked on you!" complete with overlarge exclamation point. Kenneth would've liked nothing better than to take all Emma's stupid samplers—especially the fishing one—and toss them in the fireplace and flame on! But as satisfying as that might be, he knew it would bring him more trouble than it was worth.

So he sat down at the computer, turned it on, and squeezed his balls some more as he waited for the machine to boot. He was trying to decide whether to go into the bedroom and get his penis pump, and whether he'd have enough time to make use of it before Emma got home, when the screen finally flickered to life. He worked the mouse with one hand while he kept working his balls with the other, and soon he was online and ready to hit one of his favorite porn sites. But as he started to type in the URL (typing one-handed, of course), he changed his mind and decided to check his e-mail. It was a special account, one that Emma didn't know he had, and he only received special e-mail there. He reached the site, logged on, and saw that he had three messages waiting.

The first two were junk—one for a male-enhancement drug that didn't work (as Kenneth knew from firsthand experience) and one for cheap prescription drugs. He deleted them both, then checked the third. It was from NOT-E-DD.

Naughty Double-D, Kenneth thought, recognizing the screen name from an adult site he frequented. He opened the e-mail, repressing a surge of excitement. He'd gotten enough of these sort of messages to know better than to get his hopes up.

Dear Rawdog:

Thanks for viewing my profile and sending me a message! And thanks for the compliments on my picture! I have even better ones to share with the right person! Here's a sample:

There was an icon all by itself on the next line, a tiny image of a camera. Kenneth was by no means a computer expert. He'd worked in sales his entire adult life until retiring after his prostate removal. But he'd surfed the seamier side of the Web often enough that he was quite familiar with the endless and ever-changing scams out there in cyberspace. He knew there was a good chance that if he clicked on the icon, he'd end up downloading a virus onto his computer, so he hesitated, cursor-arrow next to the little camera, index finger resting lightly on the mouse button. But then he figured he'd come this far, so what the hell?

He clicked on the icon.

The monitor screen went white for a second, and Kenneth feared that he'd gambled and lost, that a virus was beginning to spread like wildfire through his PC's files. But then a picture appeared, and he knew his risk had paid off.

He remembered the woman at once. He spent a lot of time on the Adult ConnXtions site, usually when Emma was at school or after she'd gone to bed. He'd viewed a lot of profiles of female members ages eighteen to sixty, searching for what the site euphemistically termed a "friend with benefits." Most of the profiles he viewed were unsuitable for one reason or another. Either the women lived too far away, weren't interested in someone his age (though his own profile claimed that he was forty-eight instead of sixty), or they were fake profiles set up by the male-enhancement/prescription-drug scammers and their ilk. But this woman, NOT-E-DD, lived right here in Zephyr. Though her profile listed her age as fifty-two and her body type as "ample," he'd found her attractive and had sent her an e-mail saying so, though he'd colored his admiration with somewhat raunchier terms.

This new picture she'd sent put the one displayed on her site profile to shame. The other picture showed NOT-E-DD from the waist up, wearing a tight red sweater, bending low to reveal a generous amount of cleavage. Curly red hair spilled down over her shoulders, and for some unknown reason she was wearing a Santa hat. She had a pretty, if somewhat plump face and a nice smile. One that was inviting without being too slutty (not that there was anything wrong with slutty as far as Kenneth was concerned). But this new picture . . .

She sat in an old-fashioned clawfoot bathtub, surrounded by mounds of bubbles. But the bubbles didn't cover her large breasts. She held them cupped in her hands, as if she were presenting them to the viewer—to Kenneth—to do whatever he wanted with them. She had no Santa hat this time, but her makeup was more pronounced, more exaggerated, more *slutty* in the best possible way. Best of all was her lipstick: bubble-gum pink with an overlying sheen of lip gloss, the sort of thing a horny teenage girl might wear, thinking it made her seem grown-up and sophisticated when in truth it made her look like a dumb whore. And though NOT-E-DD was supposed to be fifty-two, in this picture, she seemed ten years younger.

Kenneth squeezed his balls so hard he thought they might burst like the yolks of a couple soft-boiled eggs. God-*damn,* that was one hot picture! He wished like hell that he'd seen it before his cock became permanently deflated. He'd give anything to be able to splooge all over those gigantic tits.

And then Kenneth felt a warmth spread through his groin, a warmth that he knew well, though it had been several years since he'd last experienced it. He stopped squeezing his nuts and pulled his hand away so he could get a better view of his dick. As he watched, his penis twitched once, twice, then began to thicken and swell, the flesh growing darker as blood rushed through the capillaries. The head of his cock became shiny and purple, and the veins lining the shaft became thick and ropy. He couldn't believe it; he had achieved his first erection in more than two years. And as if his dick were making up for lost time, his hard-on was better than any he'd ever had, including when he'd been a teenager and it seemed like he sported a continuous boner twenty-four hours a day. His cock got so hard it hurt. The skin seemed stretched so tight he thought it had reached the limits of its elasticity and would tear any second. And though he wasn't sure, he thought that his erection was larger than it had ever been, by as much as an inch, maybe two.

Tentatively, as if afraid he might do something to spoil his erection if he touched it, Kenneth reached for his penis and slowly wrapped his fingers around the shaft. The simple act of putting pressure on his cock, however light, sent waves of pleasure rippling along his nerve endings, and he thought he was going to cum like a shotgun right then. But he gritted his teeth and did his best to hold back. For all he knew, he might never get another erection in his life, and he wanted to make it count.

He fastened his gaze on the picture of NOT-E-DD in the tub, offering her large, water-slick breasts to him, and he began to stroke his cock, slowly and gently at first, and then with increasing speed and pressure. Even though he was only jacking off, the sensations were more intense than anything he'd ever experienced with Emma, anything he'd ever experienced with any woman, including all the prostitutes he'd visited to help him endure the years of sexual drought that was his marriage. Despite his intention to hold off as long as he could, he soon found himself building toward orgasm. The internal pressure was incredible, as if all the semen he had stored up for the last two years was going to come out in a single blast. How much would it be? Enough to cover the keyboard, maybe obscure the monitor? Enough to spread across the whole damn floor, fill the room, the house, inundate the whole goddamned world like some triple-X version of Noah's flood?

"Goddamn, son," he whispered to himself in a thick voice as he worked his cock with increasing vigor. "You're a machine, a goddamn sex machine!"

Almost there . . . just another few seconds . . .

And then Kenneth heard the sound of Emma's car pulling into the driveway.

As if a switch had been flipped somewhere inside him, his dick rapidly began to deflate, shrinking, turning pale and yellowish, withdrawing like a wrinkled turtle head into his body until it was barely visible in the nest of his white pubic hair.

"Fucking bitch!" Kenneth swore, almost shouting. But he didn't have time for anger right then—he needed to shut down the computer and get dressed before Emma came into the house and caught him.

He didn't bother logging off the Internet or even hitting the power switch. Instead, he grabbed the power cord and yanked it out of the wall. The monitor screen died, and Kenneth dropped the cord, jumped out of his chair, and started running for the bedroom where he'd left his clothes. As he ran, he caught a glimpse of the sampler Emma had made with the rainbow on it and once more he read the words "Miracles Happen."

I guess sometimes they do, he thought, then forgot about it as he hurried to the bedroom.

Chapter Two

"Don't put that peanut butter in the cupboard, dear. It goes in the refrigerator."

Damara held the jar closer to her face and squinted so she could better read the label. She'd become a bit nearsighted over the last few years, but she hadn't said anything to her mother about it. She didn't want to go to the eye doctor—or anywhere else, for that matter—unless it was absolutely necessary.

"How come?" she asked. "It looks like regular peanut butter to me."

"It's unhydrogenated," Claire Ruschmann said. She was busy putting cans and boxes into the kitchen cupboards and didn't turn to look at her daughter as she spoke. "It's healthier, but it'll spoil if it's not refrigerated."

"Probably tastes like peanut butter–colored mud," Damara muttered, but she opened the fridge and put the jar on the top shelf.

"And don't use the top shelf," Claire said. "I still

Tim Waggoner

have to put the milk and juice away, so I'll need the room."

Damara almost told her mother that she could put her own damn unhydrogenated peanut butter away if she was going to be so picky, but she managed to hold her tongue. She moved the peanut butter to the second shelf, then closed the door. She knew that she was irritable this afternoon. It was all she could do to keep from biting her mom's head off at the least provocation. But she wasn't sure why. Her period was still a couple of weeks away, and she never had real bad PMS anyway. Sometimes she got a little stir crazy hanging around the house all day, but she didn't think that was her problem. Not for the first time she wondered whether she was simply getting tired of living with her mother. Though Mom wasn't particularly bossy, she did like things in her house to be a certain way. And though Damara had lived here all her life, it *was* Mom's house. Damara was twenty-eight, but she'd never lived on her own, and though she did help out by doing most of the cooking and cleaning, this would never be *her* house, not even once her mom passed away.

Thinking about Mom's eventual death (which she hoped was many years away) made Damara feel guilty for feeling so irritable.

"Why don't you go sit down? I'll put the rest of the groceries away," she offered.

Claire finally turned around to face Damara. "Are you sure?" But though she was looking in her daughter's direction, Claire's gaze didn't quite

34

meet Damara's eyes. She always looked slightly off to the side or above or below Damara's eyes. Mom had been reluctant to make eye contact with her ever since Jason had . . . gone away.

Claire looked at her then, really *looked,* gaze meeting gaze, and Damara was struck by how little she had changed over the years. Sure, she'd put on some weight, but since she was short, she looked heavier than she really was. Her short straight hair was still blond, though Damara knew she colored it. She had tiny crow's feet at the corners of her eyes, and the flesh beneath her chin sagged and wobbled when she laughed—not that she laughed very often. But otherwise her mother was just as Damara remembered from her childhood. Even the clothes she wore—gray Ohio State sweatshirt, jeans, and sneakers—seemed the same. Damara thought she could find pictures of her mother dressed exactly the same way if she looked through the family photo albums. It seemed that Claire hadn't changed since Damara was eleven, since the night Jerry Ruschmann had disappeared. It was as if Claire were determined to keep herself looking exactly as she had when her husband vanished, just in case he came back one day.

Another wave of guilt crashed into Damara, but she withstood it. She'd had a great deal of practice over the years.

"C'mon, you've got to leave for work in a few hours," Damara said. "You *should* take a nap, but if you won't, then at least sit down and rest."

Claire laughed and raised her hands in surrender. "All right, all right! You win." She shook her head, smiling. "You know, sometimes I can't tell which one of us is the mother and which is the daughter."

Damara returned her mother's smile, but she thought, *I can tell, Mom. I never forget.*

By the time Damara had finished putting away the groceries, Claire had hopped in the shower to get ready for work. She ran the front desk at the Econo Inn over in Waldron, and she left home when most folks were finishing their dinner. The arrangement suited both of them, since they were both night owls, and Damara normally did the housework while Claire was at work.

Damara took a couple of microwaveable meals out of the freezer and set them on the counter to thaw for a few minutes. She needed to go to the bathroom, but Mom was still in the shower. If all she had to do was pee, she'd have gone ahead and entered the bathroom, relieved herself, closed the lid, and asked Mom to flush it for her when she finished with her shower (otherwise, the shower water would turn instantly scalding when Damara flushed the toilet). But Damara had to do more than pee, and though she had lived with Mom her whole life, she wasn't comfortable defecating in her presence. The idea was just too embarrassing.

There was another option: the house had a second bathroom, next to Damara's room. But neither Damara nor her mother used it. They kept the door closed, though not locked, and Damara cleaned in there rarely, maybe once, twice a year at most. The plumbing was still functional—at least, it had been the last time the bathroom had been cleaned—but Damara would rather wait for Mom to finish in the other bathroom if she could. Hell, she'd almost rather soil herself than use the second one.

She went into the living room, sat down on the couch, and turned on the television. She flipped through the cable channels, trying to find something good. She skipped movies, drama and comedy series, kids' cartoons, and finally settled for a nature documentary on the Discovery Channel. Damara avoided fictional stories of any sort, whether written or visual. She didn't want to risk any possible stimulating effect they might have on her imagination. News, documentaries, and the tamer reality shows were all safer choices.

An image of a river appeared on the screen, accompanied by a disembodied narrator's voice.

"The environmental effect on the fish population downstream from where the chemical spill took place was absolutely devastating."

The scene shifted to a close-up of the riverbank. Dead fish bobbed in the water near the shore, surrounded by a thick foamy froth that had collected along the bank. The camera zoomed in on one of the fish until a single dead black eye nearly filled the entire screen.

The announcer droned on, but Damara didn't hear what he was saying. A painful spasm wracked her gut as her bowels threatened to unburden themselves right there on the couch. Despite her earlier determination not to use the second bathroom, Damara jumped off the couch, ran out the living room, down a short hallway, until she reached the closed bathroom door.

Her gut spasmed again, and she gritted her teeth against the pain and concentrated on holding on. But even so, she still hesitated at the door, hand halfway to the knob. She decided that she'd rather use the other bathroom and to hell with any embarrassment she might feel, but by then it was too late. Another cramp hit her and she passed some gas, and she knew she'd never make it to the other bathroom in time.

She grabbed the knob, opened the door, hurried inside, shut the door, lifted the toilet seat without bothering to turn the light on first, pulled down her pants and underwear, sat down, and waited for her body to do what it had to do. But now that she was here, sitting on a cold toilet seat in the dark, insides twisting and writhing as if her intestines were angry serpents desperate to escape the trap of flesh they were encased in, she couldn't go. The pain continued, increased, until tears ran down her cheeks.

And then she heard a soft gurgle from the direction of the tub, as if the drain were backing up.

"No," she whispered between clenched teeth. She tried to summon the image of the polar bear, but all she could see in her mind's eye was a bathtub half full of water and a naked little brown-haired boy sitting amidst a tiny fleet of plastic boats, rubber ducks, and toy fish that shot streams of water from their mouths when squeezed.

Damara moaned as her bowels finally let go.

Jason . . .

"Mara?"

"What?" Damara didn't look up from the book she was reading. She was in second grade and had just started reading chapter books. She loved reading, loved how grown up it made her feel, and she constantly had her nose in one book or another.

"Is he going to get me?"

That question got Damara's full attention. She looked up from her Boxcar Kids book and turned toward her younger brother. She sat on the toilet seat, the lid down, her legs crossed the same way Mom crossed hers.

"Is *who* going to get you?" she asked.

"You know . . . the sharp guy."

Damara frowned. She was almost seven while Jason was only four. She was well on her way to being a grown-up while he was practically still a baby. She was used to him saying weird stuff that didn't make sense, but it still irritated her. She wished that Mom hadn't made her sit in here and watch Jason while she put a load of laundry in the washer. Damara might be old enough to watch her little brother for a few minutes, but that didn't mean she wanted to.

"No, I *don't* know, Jason. But whatever you're talking about, it doesn't matter. No one can get you in the tub."

"But he jumps out of the water!" Jason insisted. "I saw it in the ABC book Mamma read to me!"

Damara wanted nothing more than for her brother to shut up so she could get back to reading her book, but despite herself, she was intrigued. "Which ABC book? You have a lot of them, you know."

"The Peter Rabbit one."

Damara knew exactly which one he was talking about. *Peter Rabbit's ABC, 123*. It technically was her book, but because she was much too old for ABC's, she let Jason keep it in his room and think it was his. She also knew who the "sharp guy" was that Jason had referred to. All the illustrations in the book were taken from various Beatrix Potter stories, and the page for the letter J had a picture of a frog in waistcoat and pants named Jeremy Fisher. He sat on a lily pad, holding a fishing pole, and he was shown jumping backward off the pad, froggy eyes wide with surprise, as a fish leaped out of the water. There was a big red J in the upper left-hand corner of the page, and the caption below the illustration said, "Splash! Jack Sharp, covered in spines."

When Damara had been Jason's age, she'd thought the picture was funny, though there was something about the fish's eye—Jack Sharp's eye—that bothered her. It was so black, with only a thin circle of white around it. It looked so cold, so alien . . . Damara used to touch that eye (only one was visible in the drawing) with her index finger, gently rubbing the smooth paper it was printed on and wondering if it was just her imagination that the paper was cooler and smoother there than on the rest of the page.

"I know what you're talking about now," Damara said. "But Jack Sharp's just a picture in a book. He can't hurt you. And even if he was a real fish, he wouldn't be in the bathtub. He'd be somewhere where there was a lot more water, like in a pond or a lake."

"But there's only a little bit of water on that page," Jason said. "And Jack Sharp jumps out of that. What if he jumps out of *this* water, with all his spines? What if he tries to *eat* me?" Jason shuddered and continued in a soft, frightened voice. "And what if one of his spines pokes my wee-wee?"

Damara almost laughed to hear Jason use such a baby word. Mom had told her last year that the real word for a boy's wee-wee was *pee-nus,* which sounded liked *peanuts* to her, and that was funny, too. But she didn't laugh. She could tell that Jason was really scared, and though he was scared for a stupid reason, he was still her little brother and Mom was depending on her to take care of him.

"That's not going to happen, Jason, because Jack Sharp is only pretend. And even if he wasn't, I bet he's a nice fish who'd never hurt anybody."

"Really?" Jason looked at her with wide, hopeful eyes.

"Sure. Besides, he's just a little fish. It's not like he's the Creature from the Black Lagoon or anything."

The water in the tub began to splash and roil, and Jason screamed as a clawed green hand covered with cactuslike spines reached up from somewhere beyond the bottom of the tub and grabbed hold of his throat. As the spines plunged into the flesh of his neck, Jason's scream was choked off. Blood bubbled over his lips, splattered onto the spiny green hand, ran onto his chest, down into the still-roiling bathwater and began to turn it pink.

Jason looked at her, his eyes filled with terror and pain, his lips working as he tried to speak, but all he could get out was, "Muh-muh-muh-muh . . ."

She knew he was trying to say *Mara*.

He held out a hand toward her, and though she was more frightened than she ever imagined she could be, she reached out to take it.

And that's when Jack Sharp pulled Jason under.

Damara sobbed as she wiped herself and flushed the toilet. She didn't know whether her mother was done in the shower yet. If not, Claire was probably screeching as the water suddenly turned hot on her, but Damara didn't care. She couldn't abide the thought of leaving her feces floating in the bowl any longer than she had to. But even more, she wanted to drown out the sound of gurgling water that came from the tub drain, along with a faint echo of a whisper that sounded like a scared little boy saying *Mara*.

Chapter Three

Emma Colton was outside pulling weeds from her flower garden when Anne Marcino came driving down the street in her red Camaro. The woman always drove too fast as far as Emma was concerned, and her car wasn't suitable for a respectable woman. Not that Anne worried about that, Emma figured. Not the way she always dressed to draw as much male attention as possible. Her shirts never quite came down all the way to her pants, allowing her pierced navel and part of the butterfly tattoo on her lower back to peek out. And though she was, quote unquote, a single mom, from what Emma understood, the woman wasn't officially divorced from her husband. He was just . . . elsewhere. Worst of all was how Anne let that daughter of hers stay alone in the house from after school until she got home from work. Hadn't the woman ever heard of day care? Sure, the girl didn't run around the neighborhood, and though Emma had never had her as a student, Autumn Marcino had a reputation as a good kid around Klyburn Elementary. But it was only a matter of time before the girl ended up a tramp like her mother. One thing that Emma had learned during nearly thirty years as a teacher: The acorn didn't fall too damn far from the tree.

Anne drove past the Markleys' house. As usual, the three Markley teens and a number of their white-trash friends were hanging out on the porch. Anne honked as she drove by, and the kids smiled and waved.

Emma frowned. *Birds of a feather...* She grabbed a fistful of dead dry weeds in her gloved hand and yanked them out of the ground.

The Markleys lived next door to Anne, and she slowed as she approached her driveway.

Don't look at me, you tramp, Emma thought as she shoved the weeds into a plastic trash bag. *Don't you dare look at me.*

Anne looked at Emma, smiled, and waved. Emma faked a smile and returned the wave. She hated to do it, but one had to maintain certain standards. The whole neighborhood had gone down the toilet over the last ten years or so, with more white trash and even some blacks and Mexicans moving in, but Emma refused to allow herself to be dragged down to the level of her so-called neighbors. So when someone smiled at her, she smiled back, and when someone waved, she waved. No matter how much she might loathe them.

Autumn came out onto the porch as Anne pulled into the driveway, and the girl ran down the front steps to greet her mother. Emma glanced over at the Markleys' porch. There were seven teens there. Three of them were smoking (including the Markley girl), and two of the remaining four (a boy and a girl, thank God for small favors) were kissing—*if* you could call ramming tongues into one another's mouth kissing. The other two were the Markley twins, Brad and Bobby, and they were looking at Emma and laughing. No, not at her, she realized. They were looking *past* her.

She turned and saw Kenneth standing at the front window, looking across the street, watching as Anne Marcino got out of her car in a too-tight sweater and a too-short skirt and gave Autumn a hug.

Emma heard one of the twins—she didn't know which since she'd never been able to tell them apart, even when she'd had them both as students years ago—say, "What a fuckin' perv!"

Warmth spread through her cheeks as she flushed with embarrassed anger. How dare those little bastards say that about her Kenneth! As if they were qualified to cast stones . . . She'd heard from Janice Connor down the street that one of the twins, who'd had their eighteenth birthday this summer, was dating a tawdry little piece of sixteen-year-old jailbait.

Anne popped open the truck of her car and lifted out a cardboard box full of files. She was an accountant and often brought work home with her. Probably because she was always too busy flirting at the office—or maybe doing a lot *more* than flirting— to get all her work finished during the day. Whore.

Emma looked back toward the front window of her house. She was too close for Kenneth to see her unless he looked down and to his left. She'd started working out back soon after getting home from school but had since moved around to the front. She doubted that Kenneth realized she was here. She watched him stare at Anne Marcino as she walked up the front steps of her house, her barely covered ass swinging back and forth with each step, Autumn following behind her. Kenneth's eyes shone with lust, and though his hands weren't visible, Emma saw his left shoulder moving up and down, back and forth, and she had a pretty goddamned good idea what he was doing.

She grabbed a dirt clod from the flowerbed and hurled it toward the window. It smacked into the glass and burst apart in a shower of dirt. Kenneth jumped, startled, and he looked around in confusion until he finally saw her. He smiled sheepishly and waved, but Emma just glared at him. His smile fell away, and he turned and retreated deeper into the house.

Anne and Autumn had already gone inside and closed their front door, but the kids on the Markleys' porch erupted into peals of laughter at the show Emma and Kenneth had just put on for them. Emma felt like flashing her middle finger at the little fuckers, but instead she ignored them and turned her attention back to her weeds. She was determined to maintain certain behavioral standards, even if she was the last one on the street, hell, in the whole damn world to do so. But as she yanked up another handful of weeds, she imagined she was instead pulling up the Markley twin who had made that perv crack about Kenneth. She tossed the weeds toward the trash bag without looking, then reached for another handful. But before she could pull it up, she heard a meaty *thud* and then one of the girls on the Markelys' porch screamed.

One of the twins lay facedown on the porch steps, thick dark blood running from his head, trickling over the last step and pattering onto the walkway like a grisly miniature waterfall.

"I just can't believe it. I mean, I drove past and waved only a few minutes ago, and now . . ." Anne's voice was choked off by a sob, and she pulled Autumn closer to her. Autumn wrapped her arms around her mother's waist, but she didn't take her eyes off the scene next door.

Paramedics knelt next to Bobby Markley, who now lay on the walkway where his brother had dragged him. The medics were doing their best to save Bobby's life, but there was so much blood all over, and his forehead was a ragged ruin of flesh, blood, and what looked like bits of brain. Damara didn't think much of Bobby's chances.

She stood on the Marcinos' lawn, along with her mom, Anne, and Autumn. Claire and Damara both stood with their arms folded across their chests as if they didn't know what to do with their hands, or perhaps to form a barrier—however inadequate—between themselves and the tragedy taking place next door.

"Is he going to be okay, Mom?" Autumn asked.

Anne opened her mouth to answer, but no words came out.

Damara stepped in. "We'll just have to wait and see, honey."

Claire nodded, but Damara wasn't sure what her mother meant to communicate with the gesture.

They weren't the only ones standing out in their yards watching the drama taking place in their midst. Up and down the length of Pandora Drive, people stood in groups of twos, threes, or more, some talking, some watching silently as the police and paramedics went about their work with professional efficiency.

Besides the paramedic van pulled up in front of the Markleys', there were three police cruisers and even a state trooper's car. Two of the officers stood with the other Markley children and their friends—neither of their parents had gotten home from work yet—trying to keep them calm, especially Bobby's twin Brad, who was sobbing so violently that he could barely catch his breath.

The boys' sister said to no one in particular, "He was standing there, right next to me, laughing, and then it was like he just took off. He didn't run, didn't jump, just . . . took off."

"The boy was probably high on one drug or another and slipped on his way down the stairs."

Damara turned to see that Emma and Kenneth

Colton had joined them. She hadn't noticed either of them cross the street, but then she'd been unable to take her gaze off the still form of Bobby Markley and hadn't been looking in the direction of their house.

"That's not a nice thing to say, Emma," Claire said. "Especially right now." Damara's mother was always cordial enough to Emma Colton, but she didn't have much tolerance for the woman's nonsense. It was one of the traits that Damara admired most in her mom.

"Maybe not," Emma said, "but that doesn't make it any the less likely to be true, and you all know it."

Claire pursed her lips as if she were fighting to keep her mouth shut.

Damara glanced at Kenneth. He stood next to his wife, hands in his pockets, but he wasn't looking at Bobby; he was looking at Anne. Damara didn't need to be able to read the man's mind to know what he was thinking. It was perfectly evident from the way he moved his hands about in his pockets. Damara was thoroughly disgusted. It was bad enough that Kenneth leered at the women in the neighborhood through the windows of his house. But it was another thing entirely for him to do it while standing a few feet away from the woman he stared at—*and* while playing pocket pool, no less! And as if that wasn't sick enough, he was doing it while paramedics struggled to save the life of a neighbor boy who might already be dead.

49

Damara was hardly the most sexually experienced person in the world. She'd only made love with another person once, and even then they hadn't completed the act. While in many ways it had been wonderful, ultimately it had turned out to be disastrous. But Damara didn't think she needed to be the most worldly person in Zephyr to recognize that there was something seriously wrong with a man who yanked his crank at an accident scene. If it hadn't been for Autumn's presence, not to mention the distraught teens next door, Damara would've publicly denounced Kenneth as the degenerate he was.

As if suddenly sensing she was looking at him, Kenneth turned to Damara and smiled. She could imagine what he must be thinking: *Yeah, I know you know what I'm doing, and not only don't I give a damn, I like that you know. Go ahead and take a good long look, honey. Bet you get off on seein' a real man like me tenderizing his tube-steak, eh?*

For an instant, it was almost as if she weren't imagining, that Kenneth were speaking in her head, and Damara felt suddenly weak and dizzy. She swayed and feared she might faint. Kenneth continued smiling at her while his hands worked their pocket magic, and she seemed to hear the faint echo of his thoughts.

Look at her . . . she's gettin' so hot and bothered she doesn't know what to do. I always thought that little homebody was really a slut-in-waiting.

Damara felt her throat constrict and her pulse

begin to race. She was vulnerable out here in the open, exposed . . . she needed to get back inside where she was safe, where she had walls and floors, a ceiling and windows to protect her. Darkness began to creep outward from the edges of her vision, and she knew if she didn't do something fast, she was going to lapse into unconsciousness. Or worse, perhaps she would die of a heart attack or a stroke.

But then Autumn said, "I hope Bobby's going to be all right."

Over at the Markleys', one of the paramedics shouted, "I've got a pulse!"

And that was the last thing Damara knew before the darkness swallowed her vision and swept her away from the world.

"Please, Mom, stop fussing over me. I'm all right."

Damara lay on the couch in Anne and Autumn's living room. She'd never been inside their house before, and though their living room didn't look all that different from hers—same basic layout, same basic furniture, though more modern—she couldn't get over how the place smelled: like a combination of Windex and boiled cabbage.

Claire knelt next to Damara and kept trying to press a wet cloth to her daughter's forehead, but Damara kept pushing her hand away. Anne stood watching, clearly amused.

"She's right, Claire. She's not the first person who's fainted at the sight of blood. My brother's a dentist, and every time he has to have his blood drawn, like for a cholesterol test or something, he's out like a light."

Autumn came back into the living room carrying a plastic cup filled with water. She held it out to Damara, and Damara took it with a grateful smile.

"Now *this* I can use." She pushed herself up into a sitting position and took a sip of water. It was cold, so much so that the first taste came as something of a shock to her, and she began coughing.

"Not too much at once now," Claire said. "Too much water too fast isn't good on a queasy stomach."

Damara waved away her mother's concern. "I'm fine. I just swallowed wrong, that's all." She looked at Autumn, and though the girl smiled at her, Damara could see that she was paler than usual and her hands trembled. Poor thing. First one of the neighbor boys gets injured, and then Damara faints right in front of the girl.

"Try not to worry, sweetie," Damara said. "Like your mom said, I just fainted. I'll be fine. And while one of the police officers was checking on me, didn't she tell you that it looks like Bobby's going to be okay, too?"

Autumn nodded.

"Well, there you go. Happy endings all around." Damara smiled and hoped that she sounded more certain than she felt.

She must have pulled it off, for Autumn responded with a grin. Damara took another sip of water without coughing this time, then handed the cup back to Autumn.

"Thanks for letting me lie down for a couple minutes. I'm feeling much better now." She pushed herself all the way up and sat with her feet touching the floor. She experienced a fresh wave of dizziness, but it was mild and passed quickly. "We should probably get back to our place. Mom has to go to work soon, and I have some chores to do." Damara stood up, and though she felt weak, she didn't feel as if she were in any danger of collapsing back onto the couch.

Claire stood and took hold of Damara's elbow to steady her. Damara wanted to tell Mom that while she appreciated the gesture, she didn't need the help, but the truth of the matter was she probably did.

"You're both welcome to stay for dinner if you'd like," Anne said. "I can whip up something fast, like spaghetti."

Autumn clapped her hands, making her seem much younger than she was. "Yes! Please say you'll stay, Damara!"

Damara glanced at her mother. Claire looked suddenly afraid, and she gave her head a slight shake.

"Thanks," Damara said, "but I don't think my stomach's quite ready for food just yet. Especially something as red as tomato sauce."

Autumn looked disappointed, but Anne laughed. "All right. Another time."

Damara was surprised to find herself sharing Autumn's disappointment. Staying for dinner actually sounded like fun, but her mother really did have to get to work, and Damara knew that Claire would drive herself to distraction with worry if Damara remained at the Marcinos' alone. So Mom handed the wet cloth back to Anne, and the four of them headed for the front door.

"I wonder if the police cars are gone," Autumn said.

"Probably," Anne replied. "The paramedics already took Bobby off to the hospital, so there's really nothing left for them to do here. But let's take a look and see." Anne opened the door, and the four of them stopped and stared. Standing there, hand raised to knock, was Tristan Ledford.

Damara suddenly felt faint again.

Chapter Four

"You sure you don't want something to eat? A sandwich, maybe? There's some cold meat in the fridge. Mom just went grocery shopping, so you picked a good time to visit."

"Thanks," Tristan said, "but coffee's enough for now. My internal clock is still on California time. It's not that long after lunch for me."

"Okay, but let me know if you get hungry."

"I will."

A silence descended between them then, and Damara tried not to look as uncomfortable as she felt. They sat at the dining table in Damara's house, mugs of fresh coffee in front of them, still so hot that neither of them had taken a sip yet. Damara was tempted to take a drink just to have something to do besides sit and stare at Tristan, not caring that she'd probably scald her tongue, but before she could, Tristan starting speaking again.

"It's weird coming home again and finding police cars pulling away from a neighbor's house, seeing blood all over the front walk . . . That's why I went over to Anne's—to make sure everything was all right."

Damara felt a surge of jealousy toward Anne Marcino. She was around the same age as Damara and Tristan, and not only was she very attractive physically, she was also a wonderful person. In addition, she lived next door to the house where Tristan had grown up. His family had owned the home on the south side of Anne's place, while the Markleys lived in the house on the northern side. Anne was far prettier than Damara, *and* she lived next door to Tristan's childhood home. How could Damara compete with that?

Damara's mother had left for work fifteen minutes ago, and while Damara had been excited, if nervous as hell, at being alone with Tristan, now she wished Claire were still there to form a buffer of sorts between the two of them. She hadn't talked face to face like this with Tristan for . . . God, close to ten years now. She had little idea what to say to him and absolutely no notion what to feel.

"It's a hell of a thing," Tristan said. He picked up his coffee mug, but he didn't take a sip right away. "Bobby Markley falling like that. You wouldn't think someone could get hurt so bad from a simple fall."

Damara feared that it hadn't been *simple* at all. She wasn't sure how she had caused the accident, or even *if*. She hadn't been thinking about Bobby when it had happened. But then, she hadn't been thinking of healing him, either. Autumn had put that thought into her head. Still, she couldn't escape the feeling that she had somehow been the spark for his accident as well.

"He *did* fall face-first onto concrete." Damara tried to keep the guilt and anxiety she felt out of her voice. What she had feared for so many years was finally beginning to happen . . . she was losing control. And she had let Tristan come into the house for coffee and conversation, exposing him to the danger of being in her presence. She knew she should tell him she still didn't feel all that well after fainting and needed to lie down. She should say anything that would get him to leave, for the sake of his own safety, if nothing else.

Tristan sat across the table from her, smiling, cupping his coffee mug in his hands as if to warm them, and though Damara knew she should make him get out of there, she couldn't bring herself to ask him to go. Not only didn't she want to be alone right then, she wanted to learn how her one-time friend had changed over the years, and why he'd returned to Ohio once more after burying his mother.

"Yeah," he said, "I suppose even a simple fall can kill if you hit your head on something hard enough." He paused to take his first sip of Damara's coffee, and she watched him closely to see whether he made a face. If he did, she'd make a fresh pot. But if Tristan had any feelings about the coffee— positive or negative—he didn't display them.

"Listen, Tristan, before we go any further, I want you to know why I didn't make it to your mom's funeral."

"There's no need to explain, Damara. Your mother was there, and she told me all about your rheumatoid arthritis."

"My what?" Damara didn't have arthritis, rheumatoid or otherwise. It didn't even run in her family, as far as she knew.

"Your mom said that it can hit people as young as us, and that the pain in your hands and feet gets so intense sometimes that you can't leave the house."

Damara knew she should be mad at her mother for lying, but right now she was grateful for the excuse.

"I'm surprised that you came back to town again so soon. I hope it's for a more pleasant reason this time." *Like to see me,* Damara thought.

"Afraid not. I took a leave of absence from work so I could come back and get Mom's house cleaned up and ready to sell. I don't know if you've been in the place recently, but Mom wasn't able to keep up with the chores and repairs during the last few years. And I wasn't much help, living clear on the other side of the country."

While both Damara and Tristan had graduated from high school—though Damara had been home-schooled for most of her junior and senior years—only Tristan had gone to college. He'd majored in music, gone on to get a Master's degree, and took a teaching position at a community college in upstate California. Damara was proud of him, but she was a little jealous, too. She wondered what it would be like to make a life for yourself, and a successful one at that.

"How long will you be staying?" Even as she spoke, Damara knew she'd been too blunt. Whatever social skills she possessed were rusty, if not completely calcified.

"I took off the rest of the semester, so I'll be here until the first of the year. I'm afraid it's going to take me that long to clear out all the junk and fix up the place so it looks decent. I tried to do some work on it when I was here for Mom's funeral, but I didn't get very far. For every mess I cleaned up or repair I made, it seemed like three more popped up to take its place. I swear, it's almost as if the house didn't want to be sold and was fighting me every step of the way."

Damara's hand twitched and coffee spilled onto the table. Some splashed onto her fingers, but it had cooled enough by now that it didn't hurt much.

"Are you okay?" Tristan asked, concerned.

"I'm fine. It's just my . . . arthritis. Makes my hands spasm sometimes." She carefully set her mug down and stood. "Let me go get something to wipe the table with. I'll be right back."

She hurried off to the kitchen, not wanting Tristan to see the look of panic on her face. She hadn't spilled coffee due to her nonexistent arthritis. She'd spilled it because she'd been startled by Tristan's words—*I swear, it's almost as if the house didn't want to be sold and was fighting me every*

59

step of the way. She went to the sink, turned on the faucet, and held her burnt hand under the cold water that came out.

Think of the polar bear, Damara told herself. She heard the words in her head accompanied by the tune to the old song, "Lollipop." *Polar bear, polar bear, puh-puh-puh-polar bear, polar bear! POP! Ba-dum, dum, dum!*

The water gurgling out of the faucet was so cold that her hand started to hurt, but she didn't pull it away. The pain was good, gave her something to focus on besides the polar bear and the stupid tune, and most of all besides the image Tristan's words had planted in her head.

. . . didn't want to be sold . . . fighting me . . .

The pain was slowly giving way to numbness, but Damara kept her hand where it was.

"I thought you said you were fine."

Damara jumped. She turned abruptly, yanking her hand out of the water and flinging droplets all over Tristan's light blue shirt. The water soaked in, turned the fabric dark blue, the spots increasing in size as more water was absorbed.

"Sorry," Damara said. She turned back around and shut off the faucet. "I didn't hear you come into the kitchen with the water running."

"Let me take a look." Without waiting for permission, Tristan took her hand and lifted it so he could examine it more closely. Though her flesh was still numb, she felt a thrill jolt through her body like an electric shock at his touch. He turned her hand one way, then the other, holding it gently as he checked to see how badly she was burned. The hand no longer felt cold to Damara. In fact, it was starting to feel quite warm. A similar warmth blossomed between her legs and began spreading throughout the lower half of her body.

Tristan looked up from her hand—though he didn't let go of it—and met her gaze.

"You're right," he said. "It looks just fine."

They stood there like that, Tristan holding her hand, Damara letting him, looking into each other's eyes. The warmth between Damara's legs was now accompanied by wetness, so much that she wouldn't have been surprised if she started dripping onto the kitchen floor.

"I . . . should probably go," Tristan said. "I got a lot of work to do, and the sooner I get started, the sooner I'll get finished." He still didn't let go of her hand, though.

"Okay. Well, I, uh . . . that is, will you . . ."

"Come visit again? Sure. And you're welcome to come on over to Mom's . . . well, I guess it's really *my* place now. At least until I sell it. Come over whenever you want. It'll give me an excuse to take a break from doing scut work."

"I will. Come over, I mean."

"Good."

Another few seconds passed, and then Tristan finally let go of her hand. She felt a sense of loss as he did, as if they'd forged some sort of connection that had just been broken.

"I'll see you to the door," Damara said. But as they started to leave the kitchen, she heard a thick, wet, gurgling sound coming from the sink, accompanied by a *skrittch-skrittch-skriiiiiiiiitch* as if claws were scratching metal. She then heard a small frightened voice say, *What have you done, Mara? What-have-you-done?*

Tristan stopped and frowned. "Did you hear something, Damara?"

All Damara could do was shake her head. She was afraid that if she opened her mouth she'd start screaming and never stop.

Tristan paused, listening more closely. Then he shrugged. "Must've been my imagination."

No, Damara thought. *It was mine.*

The first thing Tristan did was put a CD in the stereo he'd gotten his mom two Christmases ago—which he suspected she'd never used, if the dust on it were any indication. Diana Krall's voice drifted out of the speakers like honeyed smoke, perfect for his current mood. Melancholy, but with a touch of weary optimism. He wasn't looking forward to getting to work on the house. It seemed like just thinking about selling the place was a betrayal of his mother's memory, and his own childhood for that matter. He knew it had to be done; he just wished he didn't have to be the one to do it. But his sister was in the air force, stationed in Italy, and though she'd been able to get leave for the funeral, she had returned overseas and wouldn't be able to help him with the house. His only other relatives were some cousins in Michigan, but they hadn't even come to the funeral, so there was no way he could ask them for help.

But even though he had to get the house ready on his own and therefore should've been thoroughly depressed, he wasn't. In had been wonderful seeing Damara again, even though a terrible accident had been the catalyst for the reunion. She was more introverted than he remembered . . . quieter, more subdued. And it was a shame about her arthritis. He'd gathered that it had turned her into something of a shut-in. But the connection he remembered from when they were kids, the feeling that they were on the same wavelength, almost to the point of knowing what the other was thinking . . . that was still present, and still just as strong as he recalled. He couldn't ask Damara to help him with the house, not with her arthritis, but maybe she wouldn't mind coming over and keeping him company while he worked. As much as he loved Diana Krall's voice, he'd much rather have a real person to talk to—especially if that person were Damara.

The stereo was on an entertainment center in the living room, one of the few places in the house that didn't need much work. This had always been the place where his mother received visitors while he was growing up, and she'd done her best to keep it looking nice. The carpet needed cleaning— or maybe replacing—and the walls could use a fresh coat or two of paint. Right now, they were blue, his mom's favorite color. Though Tristan was no real-estate expert, he knew that a neutral color was best when trying to sell a house. "Relocation beige," he'd heard it called. The kitchen needed new tile—as did the bathrooms—and it could use new cabinets, too, but he wasn't sure he had the money, let alone the know-how, to do that work. Mom's bedroom (it had been Mom and Dad's eight years ago, before his father had died of a heart attack) needed carpet and paint as well, but the worst areas of the house were the bedrooms that had once belonged to his sister and him, and the attic. They were filled wall to wall, floor to ceiling, with junk. Cardboard boxes jammed with books, holiday decorations, old magazines, folded grocery sacks, empty plastic liter bottles that had once contained soda, clothes from the time that Tristan had been a baby up until the present, video tapes, broken appliances (he'd counted nine toasters and five television sets of various sizes), and on and on. His mom had always been something of a packrat, but after he and his sister had moved out, she'd gotten worse, it seemed. And without his dad to keep her from keeping too much, she'd stopped throwing anything away.

But the basement . . . that was an even nastier story.

Tristan left the living room, walked into the kitchen, and removed a key from the top of the refrigerator. He then walked to the basement door and stood in front of it. He held the key between his thumb and forefinger, rubbing it as if it were some sort of charm, but he made no move to insert it into the lock. The cracks around the door had been sealed with silver duct tape; he'd done the job the last time he'd been home, when he'd come to bury his mother. Though the tape held, the air was heavy with an odor like rotten eggs and overripe mulch. But that was no surprise, for as Tristan had learned during his last trip, his mom had been keeping her own little compost heap in the basement.

Like most of the rest of the house, the basement was crammed with boxes full of junk, but there was an additional problem. Sometime in the last few years—Tristan didn't know precisely when— his mother had stopped taking the trash out to the curb. Instead, she'd bagged it up, opened the basement door, and threw it down into the darkness. He'd heard about crazy old people doing things like that . . . who hadn't? But he'd never imagined his mother would end up as one of them.

Tristan sensed movement down at his feet. He saw that a portion of duct tape had come loose, and a thick grayish substance was slowly oozing forth.

"What the hell?"

He started to bend down to examine it, but then the smell hit him and he recoiled. It was a hundred times worse than he remembered from the last time he'd opened the basement door, and he wondered what had happened down there in the couple of weeks he'd been gone. Had some kind of nasty mold spread throughout the basement? Or had a sewer line somehow backed up and flooded the place, soaking into the trash bags and transforming a nasty mess into a hellish one? Whichever the case, he wasn't about to go down now.

He clapped his hand over his nose and mouth and backed away from the door. He turned and ran to the bathroom, lifted the toilet seat, and leaned over the bowl just in time to vomit up the coffee Damara had served him. As rank and acidic as the smell of his own sick was, it was like a bouquet of fresh flowers compared to that gray gunk in the kitchen. It didn't take him long to empty the contents of his stomach. Then he flushed the toilet and rinsed his mouth out at the sink. He opened the linen closet, grabbed a threadbare old towel, and returned to the kitchen, careful to hold his breath this time.

More gray gunk had oozed out of the hole in the tape, forming a puddle of glop about the size of a man's fist. Tristan rolled the towel up and shoved it against the bottom of the door, blocking the hole as the goop already released soaked into the towel. It wasn't much of a solution, but it would have to do for now. It was all Tristan could do to keep from dry heaving as it was.

Once the towel was in place, he opened the back door, stepped outside and sat down on the rear porch. The fall air was crisp and clear, and he allowed himself to breathe normally again, slow and even. Before long his nausea began to subside, though it didn't leave him altogether.

He'd been hoping that he could clean the house up on his own, but after seeing—and worse, smelling—that gray shit, he was having serious second thoughts. He didn't care if he made any money selling the house, but he'd prefer not to lose any. And if he needed to call in someone to clean the basement . . . like, say a hazmat team . . . he'd have to lay out his own money to pay for it, and community college music professors weren't exactly rich. Maybe if he got some coveralls, rubber gloves, and some kind of mask to filter out the stench . . . but if that crap was toxic, the safest thing to do would be to leave the clean-up to professionals.

Fuck. Maybe he should just have the god-damned place condemned and torn down. But he could just hear what his sister would say, and besides, he couldn't betray the memory of his parents like that.

Despite how strange his homecoming had been tonight—learning about Bobby Markley's injury and discovering the oozing gray crud—Tristan had had a good time over at Damara's. It'd been great seeing her again. She was even prettier than he remembered, and she still had the same sense of humor. Her manner was more reserved, though, and she seemed more emotionally guarded than he recalled. He wondered if it had something to do with being practically confined to her home due to her arthritis. Maybe, but when they'd talked, he'd sensed that something else had been bothering her, though he hadn't been able to tell what. But all in all, it had been good to spend some time with an old friend, and he hoped they'd see each other again soon.

One way or another, he'd get the basement cleaned up. But not tonight. He'd do some other work around the house while he considered his options, and then try to make a decision in the morning.

"Assuming the stink doesn't asphyxiate me in my sleep," he muttered.

He let out a deep sigh, stood, and went back into the house. He hurried through the kitchen, holding his breath and not even looking in the direction of the basement door. Which was a pity, because if he had, he might've noticed that the towel he'd placed against the bottom of the door was completely suffused with foul-smelling gray gunk, and that the duct tape was beginning to peel away in another half dozen places.

Chapter Five

Emma stood at the bathroom counter, brushing her teeth. The door to the master bathroom was open, and Kenneth sat on the edge of the bed, wearing only a pair of slightly yellowed underwear, watching his wife. Kenneth knew her routines just as well if not even better than his own, and he counted her brush strokes. One, two, three, four, five, six, seven, eight. Move the toothbrush to the next few teeth and repeat. One, two, three, four, five, six, seven, eight. Emma always brushed her teeth eight times: fronts, tops, and backs. Ordinarily the unwavering rigidity of her nightly ritual irritated him, but tonight for some odd reason he actually found it sort of sexy. Maybe it was the way her small breasts joggled inside her pale yellow nightgown as she brushed. Or maybe it was the way the sheer fabric clung to her ass and defined its curves. Or maybe he'd just gotten his engine so revved up today what with receiving NOT-E-DD's e-mail and watching the women (and girl) in the neighborhood. Whatever the reason, he was horny as a damn hoot owl, and he wanted to do something about it. Something that didn't require the pump or necessitate him squeezing his balls. He'd gotten an erection once today, and he intended to see if he could achieve lift-off for a second time.

Emma rinsed and spit—careful not to do so with too much force lest she splatter the counter—and then began to brush out her hair. She'd do one hundred strokes altogether: twenty-five each for the front, back, and sides. He heard her counting beneath her breath. "One, two, three . . . ," heard the soft *whissk-whissk-whissk* of the brush's bristles moving through her hair. Kenneth felt the little man downstairs twitch, and he knew the time had arrived at last. He stood up, padded across the bedroom carpet in his bare feet, and walked into the bathroom until he found himself standing behind Emma, looking over her shoulder at his own reflection peering back from the mirror above the sink. He put his hands on his wife's shoulders and gently began kneading them.

Emma stopped brushing and frowned at his reflection. The mirror Emma frowned at him as well. "What are you doing?" she asked.

"What does it feel like I'm doing? I'm rubbing your shoulders. Doesn't it feel good?"

Emma ignored his last question. "You only touch me whenever you want something. So what is it?"

Despite Emma's less-than-welcoming tone, Kenneth's penis was getting harder, making the front of his underwear bulge. He pressed his erection against Emma's rear. *That* ought to give her the message loud and clear.

Emma squawked, jumped, and dropped the hairbrush. It fell into the sink, plastic handle clattering on porcelain. She turned around and scowled at Kenneth. "What in the world was that?" she demanded. "Did you just poke me with one of your horrid toys?"

After Kenneth's operation and subsequent limp-dickness, he'd gone to a sex shop just outside of Waldron and bought an assortment of dildos and vibrators of varying designs and sizes. He'd figured that if he couldn't pleasure his wife with his natural tool, he'd settle for performing his husbandly duties via artificial means. But when he'd showed Emma his new collection of equipment, she'd only grimaced and said, *You can't possibly be serious, Kenneth.*

He'd put the toys away in the closet the next morning and hadn't so much as looked at them since.

He was disappointed, and more than a little hurt by Emma's reaction to his giving her a little pre-Christmas goose, but he grinned to cover up his feelings. "No plastic or metal that time, Emma. That was one hundred percent all-beef Kenny."

"What are you talking . . ." and then she trailed off as she looked down and saw the bulge in his underwear.

Kenneth hoped she'd smile in amazement,

71

throw her arms around him and shout, *It's a miracle!* But instead she pursed her lips in distaste.

"I thought it didn't work anymore."

Anger flared within Kenneth, and he fought to keep his voice calm as he replied. "I think the old boy's starting to get better. Why don't you help me try it out and see what it can do?" He didn't know why he bothered to persist. He knew what her answer was going to be.

"Kenneth . . ." She used her teacher-struggling-to-be-patient-with-a-slow-student voice—the one Kenneth despised. "It's late and I'm tired."

It was only 10:40 or thereabouts, but Emma was an early-to-bed, early-to-rise type, both by nature and from thirty years of getting up in the morning to teach.

She went on. "Maybe tomorrow, okay? But if you want to find out if it works, go ahead and play with yourself. I won't mind."

Kenneth stared incredulously at Emma. Had his wife just told him to go fuck himself?

Emma reached up and patted him on the cheek. "But not in here, okay? I'd really rather not hear you do it while I'm trying to sleep." She turned and walked out of the bathroom, leaving him standing at the sink, bulge in his underwear shrinking, like a balloon with a slow leak.

Kenneth's hands curled into fists so tight they shook. He wanted to go after Emma, grab her by the arm, turn her around and tell her what a frigid, dried-up old cooz she was. But he forced himself to stay where he was and keep quiet. Emma was

no pushover; she could give as good as she got . . .
better even. The best way to get back at her was to
find someone else who was willing to help him
field test his reborn dick. And he thought he knew
just the person.

Emma was already under the covers and breathing deeply when he walked into the bedroom. He
didn't know if she really was asleep or if she was
faking it so he wouldn't come on to her again—like
that was going to happen. But it didn't matter, just
so long as she stayed where she was and left him
alone. He'd dropped his clothes in a pile on the
floor by his side of the bed, as usual. He scooped
them up and carried them out of the bedroom,
closing the door behind him. If Emma weren't
asleep yet, with any luck she soon would be. He
went into the computer room, started the machine, then dressed while he waited for it to boot
up. When it was ready, he sat down in blue slacks
and red polo shirt, logged on to the Internet, and
opened his e-mail program. Screw Emma—or not,
as the case may be. He had other options, and they
didn't involve a date with Rosie Palm and her five
sisters.

He began composing an e-mail.

Dear NOT-E-DD:

(He wasn't sure whether to spell out her screen
name or type it the way she did, so he decided to
play it safe and went with the latter.)

*I got your e-mail and your pictures, and all I can
say is wow! You are one fine-looking woman!
How about you and I get together for coffee some-*

time (or maybe something stronger?). We can talk and get to know each other and see what happens from there. What do you say?

He signed it with his screen name, Rawdog, then clicked *Send*. The message vanished and began its trip through cyberspace. Kenneth hoped NOT-E-DD checked her e-mail regularly. If she were agreeable to meeting him—and why wouldn't she be after sending those pictures of herself, especially that bubble-bath one—maybe they could meet sometime in the next few days, or maybe sometime this weekend. He'd have to come up with some kind of excuse to tell Emma about why he wanted to go out alone, but it shouldn't be too hard to think of something. Maybe he could tell her he wanted to go see an action movie. Emma hated—

Kenneth was startled when an envelope icon appeared in the corner of his computer screen and a soft electronic chime sounded to tell him he had mail. There was no way it could be a reply from NOT-E-DD, not so fast. Still, he couldn't repress his excitement as he clicked on the envelope icon to download his new message.

He stared at the *From* line for almost thirty seconds before reading further. It *was* from NOT-E-DD.

Hey, Rawdog!

Guess we must both be online right now . . . what a happy coincidence, huh? I don't usually agree to meet with someone after only exchanging a couple of e-mails, but I'm feeling bored and

*lonely tonight, so what the hell? <g> How bout we
meet at Spinners? Do you know the place? It's a
bar on the north side of town, not too far from the
Wal-Mart. Send me a reply in the next fifteen minutes or so if you want to get together tonight,
sugar.*

*P.S.: I sure hope you're not a psycho or any-
thing! lol*

Kenneth read the message over again, his lips
slowly forming a grin. Talk about lucky! Not only
did she want to meet, she wanted to do so right
now. The problem was, he didn't know if he could
get out of the house, start his van, and pull out of
the driveway without Emma knowing. Sure, she
was a sound sleeper, but . . .

*If you want to find out if it works, go ahead and
play with yourself. I won't mind. But not in here,
okay? I'd really rather not hear you do it while I'm
trying to sleep.*

Fuck it. He clicked on *Reply* and typed a quick
message.

Dear NOT-E-DD:

*I know Spinners, and I'd love to get together to-
night. See you in about a half hour?*

Her response came even faster this time.

Sounds great! See you soon!

Still grinning, Kenneth logged off the Internet
and shut down the computer. No more time for
farting around on the Web—he had a date to keep!
He looked down at his crotch.

"All right, boy. Ready for your big comeback appearance?"

It was probably his imagination, but he thought he felt his cock twitch, almost as if it were answering him.

Emma was dozing, hovering in that drowsy pleasant state between sleep and wakefulness. She thought she heard a car engine start, but she was enjoying the sensation of being almost but not quite asleep too much to care. Soon, the sound of the engine diminished as the car traveled down the road, and then all was quiet once more. Still not all the way asleep, Emma found herself wondering if the car she'd heard had belonged to the Markleys, if perhaps they were headed to the hospital to visit their son and brother. It was too late for regular visiting hours, but then rules like that didn't always apply to immediate family.

Emma wasn't sorry at all that the little whitetrash bastard had split his skull open on his front walkway. But she *was* sorry that the paramedics arrived in time to save his life. As far as she was concerned, the world would be better off without trash like Bobby Markley around. If he lived, all he'd do was knock up some stupid girl who'd squeeze out a white-trash baby of his, and the whole damn cycle of ignorance and immorality would start all over again. They were like human weeds; pull up a few and a hundred more took their place. It was an inescapable law of nature.

Emma rolled onto her side and pulled the blanket up over her head. A petite woman, she was usually cold, no matter the time of year. As she wiggled her head in an attempt to find the most comfortable spot on her pillow, she began to slip more fully into sleep. Just before doing so, she had one last half-coherent thought.

Bobby Markley . . . hospital . . . weeds . . .

And then she descended completely into darkness—in more ways than one.

Bobby Markley had one motherfucker of a headache. He lay propped up on the hospital bed, head wrapped in what his sister had jokingly called a mummy bandage, saline IV in the back of his hand, the TV on but the volume turned low. The other bed in the room was empty, so he didn't have to worry about the TV bothering anyone else, but the noise made his head pound even worse. His pain medication had worn off, but he wasn't due to get more for another hour yet, and he knew the night nurses wouldn't give him anything until the appointed hour arrived. He'd already asked three times, each time receiving a polite but firm no. He had some good stuff at home that would probably kill the pain, or at least take enough of the edge off to allow him to sleep, but there was no way he could get hold of it. His parents would kick his ass if they found out about his stash, and his brother and sister would just claim it for themselves, so he was shit out of luck on that score.

He clicked the TV remote, surfing through the channels in yet another vain attempt to find something at least halfway decent to watch. But the hospital only had basic cable, and this time of night all that was on was local TV news with way too many commercials. There was a Playstation in the room that could be hooked up to the TV, but the assortment of games on hand was lame, mostly video tennis and simple Space Invaders–type games. Boring as hell. Besides, bad as his head felt, he wasn't certain that he'd be able to play a videogame right now. He was sure his parents would be shocked to hear *that,* since almost all he ever did at home was play video and computer games. He wanted to be a videogame designer someday, but his dad—who was an electrician—told him that fantasizing about stuff like that was nothing but mental jacking off: It might feel good at the time, but in the long run, it wouldn't get you anywhere.

Bobby found an old *Simpsons* episode and left the channel where it was. He turned up the volume just a bit and told himself not to laugh unless he wanted his aching head to explode. He settled back against the so-firm-it-was-almost-hard hospital mattress and tried not to think about how much his head hurt.

The doctor who'd taken care of Bobby in the emergency unit had asked him how he'd managed to hit his head so hard, but he hadn't been able to give the woman a good answer. He remembered sitting on the porch with his twin brother Brad, their sister, and a few of their friends, just hanging out and shooting the shit while they waited for Mom and Dad to get home from work. And then he'd felt as if a pair of strong invisible arms had grabbed him around the middle and heaved him into the air. He'd been so surprised that all he'd been able to do was flail about with his arms and legs as he fell head-first toward the concrete walkway. After that, he didn't remember anything until he woke up in the ER.

Nobody had believed him about the invisible arms, though. Not the doctor, not Mom and Dad (who were back at home now but who'd promised to return first thing in the morning), and certainly not his brother and sister, who'd accused him of having "scrambled eggs for brains" now. Who knows? Maybe they were right. He *had* hit his head pretty damn hard. The doctor had said he was lucky to be alive, that he might have a concussion, and that it might be days or weeks before the full extent of the brain damage he'd suffered would make itself known. Even so, he could still remember what it had felt like when those unseen arms had enveloped him and began to lift . . .

"Hello, Bobby."

Startled, he turned toward the voice and moaned as jagged bolts of pain shot through his head and neck.

"Mrs. Colton?"

She stood next to his bed, smiling at him. Which was weird, not only because visiting hours were over, but because he hadn't heard her come in. And why would she be coming to see him anyway? She didn't like him, or anyone else in his family. And why was she still dressed in her gardening clothes, gloves and all?

79

"How are you feeling?" Her voice was pleasant, almost too much so, as if she thought she were in her classroom, and he were still one of her little pupils. He had been once, but that had been years ago. He'd hated having her as a teacher then, and he still hated her today. She was a nosy, judgmental, bitter old bitch. But despite all that, he was touched that she'd come to see him. Maybe the rotten hag wasn't so bad after all.

"My head hurts." He managed a smile. "No big surprise there, huh? But I'm due for some more pain medication soon, so I should be all right before too long."

"You took quite a nasty fall, Bobby. But not quite nasty enough, it seems."

Bobby frowned. What the hell did she mean by that?

"I'm not the sort of person who likes leaving a job half finished, Bobby. Especially when it comes to pulling weeds."

Her smile took on a hard edge, and there was a strange glow in her eyes that made Bobby uncomfortable. "I don't know what you're talking about."

"Of course you don't. That's because you're an idiot, Bobby. Just like the rest of your family. All your kind know how to do is smoke, drink, fuck, take drugs, and turn the world into more of a sewer than it already is."

Bobby was starting to get scared. He'd known Mrs. Colton could be mean, but he'd never thought she was crazy—until now, that is. "Look, I don't what your problem with me is, but my head's really pounding, and I could use some rest. So I'd appreciate it if you would leave. Now."

"I'll be going in just a moment, Bobby. Don't worry about that. But as I said before, I have a job to finish first."

She stepped closer to Bobby's bed and put her gloved hands on the rail. He tried to scoot away from her, but he had nowhere to go.

"Have you heard the expression a mind is a terrible thing to waste?"

"Yeah, I guess."

"Well, it's also a wonderful thing to *taste*." She smiled, revealing a mouth full of razor-sharp teeth more suited to the mouth of some carnivorous beast than that of a sixtyish elementary school teacher.

Bobby Markley opened his own mouth to scream, but before he could make a sound, Mrs. Colton's jaws unhinged like those of a snake preparing to feed. She lunged for him and bit through his mummy bandage, her nightmarish teeth penetrating his skull and plunging into the soft, sweet meat inside.

One good thing: At least Bobby wouldn't have to worry about his headache anymore.

Miles away, Emma sighed contentedly in her sleep and snuggled further under the covers. She had a smile on her face and a thin trickle of blood running from the corner of her mouth.

Chapter Six

"I assure you, sir, 111 *is* a non-smoking room."

The man standing before the front desk narrowed his eyes, as if he thought Claire were trying to put one over on him.

"Don't tell me it's a non-smoking room. I'm very sensitive to the presence of tobacco products, and that room *reeks* of cigarette smoke. The walls are even yellow from nicotine residue!"

Claire decided it wouldn't do her any good to point out that the hotel's rooms had off-white wallpaper. This idiot wasn't in the mood to listen. She forced herself to smile and hoped it didn't look too much like a grimace.

"I'll be happy to put you in another room if you'd like. Just let me see what else we have that's available."

"You bet your ass you'll find me another room—and no jerking me around this time, either!"

Mr. Natural—as Claire had come to think of him—was almost cadaverously thin and pale (a

Tim Waggoner

vegetarian, she guessed). This was the second time he'd requested in less-than-polite terms to be moved to another room, and Claire knew that no matter where she put him, it wouldn't be good enough.

As she turned to the computer screen behind the front desk, she caught a glimpse of someone else walking into the lobby. She swore inwardly. Tuesday nights were usually pretty slow, so her boss only scheduled one person to work the front desk from nine P.M. to six A.M. But after the night she'd had so far—starting with Bobby Markley's accident, beginning her shift with a woman who refused to believe her credit card wasn't valid when she tried to check in, and moving on to Mr. Natural here—she could use some help, even one of the bubble-headed teenagers with the big boobs that her boss loved to hire.

As she began tapping keys, the new guest walked up to the front desk. Without taking her gaze off the screen, she said, "I'll be with you in just a moment, sir."

"Take your time. I'm in no hurry."

Her hands froze on the keyboard. She knew that voice, and though she hadn't heard it outside of home videos for the last seventeen years, somehow it came as no great surprise that she should hear it now.

She looked up and there, standing slightly behind Mr. Natural and off to the side, was Jerry, her long-lost husband. He looked exactly as she remembered him, as if the last seventeen years

84

hadn't touched him in the slightest. Six feet tall, broad-shouldered, the merest beginning of a paunch, brown hair, strong chin, thin lips that didn't look like they'd be much good for kissing, but which Jerry knew how to use to maximum advantage. He wore a blue windbreaker over a brown plaid shirt and jeans: his usual autumn outfit. It seemed his taste in clothing hadn't changed in seventeen years, either.

Jerry smiled and gave her a wink, and suddenly she felt flushed, as if she'd been hit by an instant fever. It took everything she had to force herself to turn back to the computer screen and finish finding another vacant non-smoking room for Mr. Natural.

"How about 313?" she asked him. "It has a lovely view of the river." And before he could say anything, she added, "And yes, it is a non-smoking room. It always has been."

Mr. Natural grunted as if his daily allotment of fiber was backing up on him. "It had better be, or I'm going to have a few words with your manager."

At this time of night, her boss was probably sitting in front of a TV in his underwear, beer in one hand, remote control in the other. But she doubted Mr. Natural would care to hear that. So she took his current plastic key-card and reset it to open 313.

She managed a smile as she handed back the key. "I hope this solves your problem, Mr. Saltzman."

He hrumpfed, snatched the key out of her hand, bent down to pick up a backpack, and without so much as a thank-you, stomped off.

Frowning, Jerry watched him go. "Doesn't he have any luggage?"

"Just that backpack," Claire answered.

"What do you suppose he has in there?"

"I've been in the hotel business for too many years. I know better than to ask questions like that."

They both laughed, and the oddity of having such an ordinary conversation with her missing husband hit Claire then, and she felt ridiculous. But she also felt confused. How was a person supposed to react when her husband returned after having disappeared without a word nearly two decades ago? What was she supposed to say? Should she curse him a blue streak for abandoning Damara and her? Or should she come around from behind the counter, throw her arms around him and kiss him while tears fell from her eyes like rain? In the end, she did neither of these things.

"How are you doing, Jerry?" She was surprised at how easily the words came out and how even her tone was.

Her smiled sadly. "Not so bad, I guess. Though I've been awfully lonely without you and Damara these last few years."

Claire opened her mouth to speak, but he held up his hands to stop her.

"I can guess what you're thinking: *he's* been lonely? What about *us?* And you'd be right, of course. I know I don't deserve it, but I hope you'll give me a chance to explain why I did what I did."

So many conflicting emotions were surging through Claire that she half expected her head to explode from the pressure of trying to contain them all. Fury, joy, relief, curiosity, love, hatred . . . She wanted to tell Jerry that he could fuck off and die, that indeed he'd been gone long enough for her to have declared him legally dead if she'd had a mind to.

But he looked at her with a combination of love and contrition, almost like a puppy that had been caught crapping on the new carpet and was hoping his cute face and big moist eyes were going to get him out of trouble. Jerry Ruschmann had been a good husband and father for the most part, and he'd had few occasions to use this puppy-dog expression on Claire. But whenever he had used it, it had always worked.

So though Claire hated herself for saying it, she said, "I guess it won't do any harm just to talk."

Jerry grinned, displaying a mouthful of white, even teeth. Though his teeth hadn't been terrible when he'd cut out, his parents hadn't been big on dentists, and as an adult, his teeth had become yellowed and slightly crooked. But now they were perfect, like something out of a tooth-whitening commercial. She wondered where he'd gotten the money to get his dental work done. She decided that it was a foolish detail, especially when they had so many other important things to talk over, and she resolved to put the thought of Jerry's new teeth out of her mind. Still, she had to admit that he had a much nicer smile now.

"We could sit here in the lobby and talk," she said. "The kitchen's closed this time of night, but there's a coffeemaker in the back office. I can brew up a pot if you like."

His smile widened, and his teeth seemed to become even wider. "Coffee sounds good, but the lobby's a little . . . public, isn't it? Especially for the kinds of things we need to talk about. You know . . . personal . . . intimate . . ."

She didn't remember Jerry being quite so well-spoken. She decided she liked it. His blue eyes (when did he get blue eyes, they'd always been hazel . . . maybe he was wearing tinted contacts, but his vision was fine, or at least it had been) seemed to grow larger until they merged into a single field of deep blue that encompassed the whole world. Claire found herself getting lost in that blue—it had always been her favorite color—and she realized that she not only agreed with Jerry, she was willing to do whatever he asked. After all, wasn't this what she'd been hoping, praying, wishing, dreaming for all these long years? For him to come back to her?

"I could always check us into a room," she said, heart pounding. "But I can't leave the front desk. I'm the only one on duty tonight."

Though it was impossible, his smile widened even more and the deep blue of his eyes grew darker, until it was almost black. "Isn't there someone you could call to come in to take your place? You could always tell them you're sick or something."

"Uh, well, I guess I could try Debbie. She's a single mother with four kids, and she can always use the extra money."

"There you go, then. This way we'll be able to have a proper reunion, won't we?" Jerry's white teeth seemed to glitter now, the sparkles like stars set against the endless black depths of his eyes.

Claire smiled. "That sounds wonderful."

She quickly reserved a room on the hotel's computer system and activated two key-cards—one for him, one for her.

"Why don't you go on to the room and wait for me?" she said. "It'll take a little while before Deb can get here to take over."

She held out a key-card for Jerry to take. As he did so, his fingers brushed hers, and the contact almost made her gasp. She hadn't exactly been celibate for the last seventeen years, but it had been a while since she'd felt a man's touch. A long while. And no one had ever touched her like Jerry had.

"It's 3041, just around the east side of the building. There's hardly anyone booked over there tonight, so it'll be nice and quiet."

"Sounds perfect. Try to hurry. We've been apart too long as it is." He held her gaze a moment before turning and walking out of the lobby.

She watched him go until she couldn't see him anymore. Then she grabbed the phone and almost frantically pushed the buttons for Debbie's number. It never occurred to her to question why she was so eager to do what Jerry asked of her, any more than it occurred to her to wonder how he'd known to come here to find her. She hadn't been working here seventeen years ago, and if he'd stopped at home first and spoken with Damara, she'd have called to tell Claire.

When a dream comes true, you don't question it, lest you risk making it vanish with a pop like a child's soap bubble floating on the air. No, you don't question a dream come true . . .

. . . even when you should.

"So I said to her, 'If you think you're all that and a bag of low-carb chips, then *you* try to sell the damn place.' And do you know what she said then?"

Kenneth didn't really want to know, but he said, "What?" anyway.

Nancy—who went by the *nom de screen* NOT-E-DD—grinned. "She said, 'Just forget it. But if you *do* sell that house, I'll give you my commission on my next two sales *and* I'll eat you out!'" She burst out laughing.

Kenneth was taken aback by his companion's sudden display of crudity, but he knew he shouldn't be. Though he'd only spent twenty minutes or so with her, this was far from the only—or indeed the crudest—such comment she'd made.

Kenneth had driven past Spinners numerous times over the years, but he'd never been inside. Now that he had, he knew he hadn't been missing anything. The place was decorated with too much dull chrome and cheap neon to suit him, and the music blaring from speakers throughout the place was awful, mostly eighties pop with a sprinkling of barely tolerable seventies rock. The bar had a small mirrored dance floor in one corner, complete with a disco ball spinning overhead, but no one was dancing tonight. The place might be jumping on the weekend, but right now in was nearly deserted, save for a bartender, a single server, and a handful of customers sitting at the bar or at tables, alone, in pairs, or small groups, drinking quietly. Perhaps if the music hadn't been so damn loud, they'd be talking to one another. As it was, Kenneth and Nancy had to shout to be heard, and while she didn't seem to mind, Kenneth was already starting to get a hoarse voice.

Nancy took a sip of her scotch and water, and very little water at that. "I sold that house yesterday. I haven't seen Connie since, but I can't wait to see the look on her face when I tell her it's time to pay up!" She laughed again, loud and brittle. A drunk's laugh.

Kenneth wondered if Nancy was kidding or if she really did intend to collect on the bet—*all* of it. He imagined her calling Connie into the restroom of the real estate office where they worked, closing and locking the door, then saying, *On your knees, bitch!* His cock, which had been erect since the moment he'd walked into the bar now twitched, and Kenneth thought he was going to spooge in his pants right then. But he didn't. It was almost as if the old boy had not only roared back to life but was better than ever. He'd never been able to maintain an erection this long before, and though he was no one-minute man, he'd never had this sort of control before. He wondered if his prostate operation had something to do with it, if it had somehow improved things downstairs instead of messing them up like the doctors said.

Whatever the reason, it was a damn good thing his meat was in tip-top condition, because NOT-E-DD didn't look like the pictures she'd sent him. They hadn't been fakes; Nancy clearly was the same woman. But those photos had been taken several years—and several dozen pounds—ago. She wasn't a complete dick-drooper now, but she'd passed beyond what the Adult ConnXtions site euphemistically referred to as having "a little extra padding." She was squeezed into a pair of jeans that were too small for her; so much so that Kenneth feared the straining seams might burst any minute and cover the bar with scraps of denim. Her blouse complemented her figure more than her pants did, but that was primarily because she'd left the top few buttons undone to better display her impressive overabundance of cleavage. Kenneth understood that her breasts were so large in part because the rest of her was so large, but he didn't care. Big tits were big tits as far as he was concerned.

Normally, Kenneth might have been disappointed, even angry, at Nancy's deception, but tonight he was so horny that she'd still look good to him even if she were missing all her teeth and one or more extremities. All he cared about was that she have a nice wet garage where he could park his dick for a little while.

Nancy downed what was left of her scotch in a single gulp.

God, but that gal can drink, Kenneth thought. That was fine with him. The more panty-peeler she swallowed, the better.

Nancy's cheeks flushed red, and she fanned herself with her hand. "Is it just me, or is it just me?" Then she giggled. "I mean, is it me or it is just hot?" She giggled again. "Sorry. Guess I shouldn't have drank that one so fast." She swirled her glass and watched the ice cubes slide around inside. "I'm glad you took a chance and e-mailed me, Kenneth. It's been a while since I did anything this impulsive." She continued looking at the ice cubes as she spoke, as if, like tea leaves, they might have some important message to impart. "Hell, it's been too long since I did anything, and with any*one,* for that matter." She looked up at Kenneth and gave him an embarrassed smile. "Listen to me getting all maudlin. We're here to have fun, right?" Before Kenneth could respond, she set her glass on the table and stood.

"How about you and me go outside and get some fresh air, sugar?" She held out her hand to him.

Kenneth stood and took her hand. "That's a fine idea, darlin'. Mighty fine." He tossed some cash onto the table to pay for their drinks; then both of them grinned as they headed hand in hand for the exit.

* * *

They started walking toward Kenneth's van, but Nancy pulled him in another direction, and he let her lead him around the side of the bar to the rear of the building. She continued to lead him to a nook between the Dumpster and the back wall, and Kenneth had the sense that this wasn't the first time she'd met a gentleman friend at Spinners, nor was it the first time she brought one of her new friends back here. The thought excited him even more.

It doesn't matter how many men you've brought back here for a quickie, Kenneth thought. *You've had the rest, so get ready, baby, 'cause tonight you're gonna have the best!*

Giggling, Nancy turned Kenneth around and pushed his back against the wall. Normally he was the aggressor when it came to sex, but he found Nancy's assertiveness to be a most welcome change of pace from Emma's frigid refusals.

She leaned forward, mashing her gigantic tits against his chest and pressing her lips in the general vicinity of his mouth. Man, was she wasted! But that was fine with him; after all, liquor was the best lubricant there was. Their lips found each other, then their tongues, and for several minutes they coated each other's faces with saliva. When Kenneth could no longer resist, he grabbed double handfuls of her boobs and began kneading them as if he were a baker and they were two large mounds of dough. He expected her to protest, say he was being too rough, that she really didn't like having her breasts fondled, let alone squeezed this hard. Emma didn't like him to touch her breasts at all, and her nipples—which she claimed were "too sensitive"—were strictly off limits. But not only didn't Nancy mind Kenneth giving her boobs a solid workout, she actually seemed to be enjoying it, moaning and wiggling as he squeezed the soft meat and teased the hard nipples through the fabric of her clothes.

He reached into her shirt, intending to unsnap her bra so he could feel her bare tits with his hands. Touching them through fabric was okay, but touching the actual flesh was a thousand times better. Besides, that way he'd have the chance to suck on those rock-hard nipples of hers. He'd never had a woman with tits this big before, and he wondered if her nipples would be extra-large as well. They sure as hell felt like it, but he wanted to see—and taste—for himself.

But before he could go to work on her bra, she gently took hold of his wrist and pulled his hand out of her blouse.

Kenneth scowled. "You some kinda tease?" he demanded.

Still smiling, she shook her head. "No, there's just something I want to do first."

She got down on her knees, almost falling over as she did, but Kenneth put a hand on the woman's shoulder to steady her. Nancy began to undo his belt, and when it was open, she slowly drew down his pants zipper. She then tugged his pants down around his knees, revealing the huge bulge in the front of his underwear.

"My god," she breathed as she lightly ran her fingers over his package. "Did you put a brick in your shorts? 'Cause that's what it damn well feels like."

Kenneth grinned. "Why don't you take a look and see for yourself?"

"Exactly what I had in mind." She gripped the band of his underwear with both hands and pulled his shorts down.

Free of its cloth restraint, his cock bobbed in the cool night air, skin stretched shiny tight, head so engorged with blood that even in the fluorescent glow emitted by the parking lot lights, it seemed a dark crimson-purple. His dick jerked in time with his pulse, and though Kenneth wasn't sure, it almost looked like the veins in his cock were expanding and contracting as blood gushed through the vessels.

Nancy examined Kenneth's penis with wide eyes, as if she'd never seen one before. And she reached out and slowly—as if his cock were some sort of wild animal she was afraid to touch but couldn't keep her hands off—she began to gently stroke her fingers across the taut skin.

Kenneth moaned as waves of intense pleasure rippled outward from his dick, the sensations far more intense that anything he had ever felt before.

Nancy gripped his shaft and began pumping his penis as she gently licked the head, tonguing the slit, nibbling the spongy-hard flesh. Then she took the head completely into her mouth and it was as if Kenneth had stuck his cock into a jarful of warm honey. He gasped and pressed back against the wall harder to brace himself.

"If you keep doing what you doing, it won't be too much longer before I cum," he said hoarsely.

His words excited her even further, and she began to pump his cock more vigorously, sucking the tip as if she were attempting to inhale it. Within mere moments, Kenneth felt the tingling heat of impending orgasm in his balls, and he knew that he was about to shoot his load into Nancy's mouth.

"I'm gonna cum, baby," he gasped. "Cum like a shotgun . . ."

She made an *mmmmmm* sound and increased the speed with which she worked his cock.

"Oh, yeah . . ." Kenneth gritted his teeth and tried to hold off as long as he could. But he was able to forestall the inevitable only a few more seconds when a wave of pleasure rolled forth from deep inside him and rippled along the length of his monster of a cock.

"I'm cumming, baby, I'm cumming!" Kenneth grunted like an animal as the first gout of sperm blasted out of his cock.

Nancy's eyes flew open wide and her hand clenched tight on his dick. With a sickening hollow-wet sound, like a pumpkin being slammed onto concrete, her head exploded in a shower of blood, brains, and semen, splattering Kenneth with gobs of meat and bits of bone. Her body shuddered and jerked, but her hand continued to squeeze his cock in her death spasms, gripping the shaft so tight it felt as if she might tear it off. Nancy's head was gone, and a fountain of blood jetted up from the ragged stump of her neck. His cock continued to spew gooey white as his orgasm subsided, his sperm splattering onto her neck stump and mixing with the bubbling dark blood.

I'm gonna cum, baby . . . cum like a shotgun . . .

Nancy's body soon grew still and swayed for a moment, her hand giving his dick a last reflexive squeeze before letting go. Her headless corpse fell onto its side, landing in a wet mass of spilled blood, torn tissue, shattered bone, and broken teeth.

My god, she's . . . she's . . . The word *dead,* even the concept of *dead* refused to form in his mind. There was no way this could be happening, no way such a thing was possible outside a nightmare.

His cock was slowly beginning to go limp, but semen continued dribbling out. He watched the milky strands stretch down toward Nancy's neckhole and then land, turning pink as they mingled with her blood. He imagined thousands, millions of sperm swimming around Nancy's blood cells, perhaps even mistaking them for ova and latching on to them. Shitfire, he realized. He was fucking her on a microscopic level!

His horror and revulsion faded, and along with them went the memory of ever having experienced such emotions in the first place.

A couple last spurts of cum dribbled onto her body, and then Kenneth's cock began to deflate. He stared at the headless corpse of the woman he'd first known as NOT-E-DD as his penis continued to empty itself. After a bit his mouth stretched into a wide grin.

"God-*damn!* Now *that* was an orgasm!"

Chapter Seven

Tristan lay in bed—the same bed he'd slept in from childhood until he'd left for college—tossing and turning as he desperately sought a comfortable position. The bed was a single, and he slept on a double in his apartment in California. He felt cramped trying to sleep in this smaller bed, and he couldn't escape feeling that he was going to roll over in his sleep, fall onto the wooden floor, and probably break his arm or something. It didn't help that the mattress was old and saggy. If he didn't fall out of bed in the middle of the night, he might slowly sink further and further down into the mattress until he was trapped and couldn't pull himself out. Not very likely, probably, but the thought didn't do much to help him get to sleep.

It also didn't help that his mother had used his old room as yet another storage area for her junk. The floor was covered with lopsided stacks of cardboard boxes that nearly reached all the way to the ceiling. The boxes were covered with dust, and breathing the air made his eyes water and sinuses ache. Plus, he couldn't keep from wondering if one or more of the unsteady box towers would fall over onto him during the night. Some of the boxes were light, but some were quite heavy. With his luck, a box full of anvils, or maybe cannonballs, would land on his head, crushing his skull and reducing its contents to spongy gray jelly. He hadn't helped the stability of the stacks by moving some boxes around so he could get from the door to the bed. It could have been worse, though. His sister's old room was so packed full of junk that he hadn't been able to get inside yet. He was starting to wonder whether he was going to have to buy some dynamite and blast in there in order to be able to clear enough space to move.

During his last visit home for the funeral, he'd slept on the living room couch—he hadn't been able to bring himself to sleep in his mother's bed then, and he still couldn't—and he'd tried to do so again tonight. It was really more of a loveseat than a couch, and there was no room for him to stretch out his feet, but he didn't care much. The cushions were firm without being rock-hard, and if he did roll out during the night, he'd land on soft carpet. Best of all, there were no unstable mountains of junk ready to collapse onto the couch. But tonight the stench from the kitchen—or more precisely, from the homemade dump in the basement—had filtered into the living room, coating everything with its greasy stink. He'd tried to tough it out on the couch, but the foul odor finally got to him, and he retreated to his old bedroom. The smell was in here too, but not so strong as to be intolerable. If he didn't do something soon about the ungodly mess in the basement, he feared the stink would settle into the house, penetrating the plaster walls and wooden floors. And once an odor that bad had seeped into a house's structure, he knew there was no way to get rid of it, short of burning the place down.

First things first, he cautioned himself. He had to get all that glop in the basement out and dispose of it before even joking about burning down the house. But even then he figured the smell would linger, forcing him to wash the walls and floor with bleach. Arson was sounding like a more viable option all the time.

He decided to do his best to put the house out of his mind for the rest of the night and instead focus on something far more pleasant: Damara. Seeing her had brought back so many memories, but the most vivid had occurred right here in this very room, this very bed. They'd both been sixteen years old. . . .

"Are you sure your mom's not going to come home and catch us?"

Tristan wasn't sure of any such thing, but he said, "Don't worry. She won't be back for hours." In truth, he had no idea where she was. She hadn't told him where she was going, and she hadn't left a note. Her car was gone from the driveway, and his sister wasn't around, so he figured that maybe the two of them had gone shopping, but he really didn't have a clue. Wherever his mom was, she wasn't here right now, and that was all that mattered to a horny teenage boy who'd finally coaxed the girl across the street—the girl who had been both his best friend and one true love since they'd been kids—into his bedroom.

They knelt on his saggy mattress, facing each other. The bed was made, comforter drawn neatly up over the sheet. Tristan hoped that whatever they did here this afternoon—and he hoped it would be a lot—they'd be able to do it without pulling back the comforter and getting under the sheets. He had wet dreams almost every night these days, but his mother would only do laundry once a week, regardless of how often it needed to be done. He still had two more days until the next laundry cycle began, and he didn't want Damara to see the dried cum stains on his sheets.

"Well . . . if you're *sure* . . ." Damara smiled at him, but it was a smile he'd never seen on her before. One filled with promise and secret knowledge, as if she knew exactly what he was thinking, and it amused her to play along. One of his friends in band, Ron Santarini, a pear-shaped kid who'd had even less experience with girls than Tristan, had once passed along this tidbit of masculine wisdom: *When it comes to sex, women are the ones really in charge. They decide where, when, and if they're going to do it. All us guys can do is hope they choose US to do it with.*

At the time, Tristan had thought Ron was

merely rationalizing his nonexistent luck with girls, but now, after seeing that knowing smile on Damara's face, he wasn't so sure.

Damara leaned forward, closing her eyes, and Tristan did the same, only he kept his eyes open. They'd kissed lots of times before, but Tristan loved looking at Damara's face when they did. Hell, he loved looking at her face no matter what they were doing.

They kissed for several minutes, starting off slow and then with increasing passion. It had been raining all day, and the sound of water hitting the roof and pattering on his bedroom windows enhanced the romantic atmosphere. Their tongues met and explored each other, and their hands touched faces, shoulders, legs, backs . . . Tristan ached to touch Damara's breasts, but he was too afraid to do so without her explicit permission. He didn't want to upset her and risk scaring her off. Besides, he'd never touched a girl's breasts before, and he wasn't quite sure how to do it. He didn't want to squeeze too hard and maybe hurt her or, almost as bad, come off looking like a complete idiot in her eyes. He didn't think he could bear that.

But as one of his hands moved across her shoulder blade, he realized that all he could feel beneath her sweater was skin. She wasn't wearing a bra.

Evidently knowing what he'd just figured out, Damara pulled away and giggled. Tristan felt his cheeks flush, but then Damara gazed at him with such understanding and love that any embarrassment he felt melted away.

105

"Go ahead. I don't mind." She paused, as if considering whether to go on, then smiled shyly. "I want you to."

Tristan's penis had already been straining painfully against his jeans, but now it got so hard that he had to fight to keep from grimacing. The last thing he wanted was for Damara to think he was making a face because of what she'd said. He tried to think of a delicate way to tell her that he needed to shift his position to get more comfortable.

"I . . . uh, could we maybe . . . idunno, lie down or something?"

Again that knowing smile, and Tristan wondered if all women were born with the power to read men's minds and just kept it a secret among the members of their gender.

Damara nodded and lay back on the mattress, pulling Tristan down with her. They kissed for a few more minutes before Tristan worked up the courage to gently slip his hand under her sweater. He felt the taut, warm flesh of her stomach, then the slight depression of her belly button. He moved his hand farther, Damara taking in a small gasping breath as he did. He felt her ribs, smaller and more delicate than his own, and then the tips of his fingers encountered the swell of her left breast.

Tristan's own breath caught in his throat, and he felt suddenly warm, as if the room temperature had shot up twenty degrees in the last few seconds. He was lying half on Damara as he kissed her and brushed the bottom of her breast with his fingers.

His penis was pressed against her leg, and he felt a warm tingling in his balls. He knew if he wasn't careful, he was going to cum in his pants. As good as that might feel, it would be embarrassing as hell if Damara found out, and he shifted his position so he wasn't pressing against her leg so hard.

Slowly, savoring each inch of flesh gained, Tristan moved his hand along the curve of Damara's breast until his questing fingers encountered a hard nub. Damara gasped more loudly this time and, encouraged by her reaction, Tristan took her erect nipple between his thumb and forefinger and began gently massaging it. Damara moaned and undulated slowly, as if waves of pleasures were coursing through her body. Like any teenage boy, Tristan constantly thought about sex, but those thoughts always focused on the pleasures *his* body might experience. But now that he was doing this with Damara, he realized that sex was far more than merely feeling good. It was also about making someone you loved feel good too. And maybe that was the most important thing about sex—maybe that was why some people referred to it as making love, while others just called it fucking.

He had no doubt which one he and Damara were doing.

He continued massaging her nipple, going a bit faster, applying a bit more pressure, when he caught a glimpse of movement out of the corner of his eye. At first he ignored it, too caught up in Damara to care about anything else. But then he saw another, and another, and as difficult as it was, he took his attention off Damara, drew his lips away from her, and looked.

The room was a swirling mass of color—bright reds, striking blues, warm yellows, vibrant oranges, soothing greens . . . At first they were nothing *but* patches of color, darting and dipping as they circled around and above the bed. But as Tristan watched, the colors began to solidify and take on form, becoming sharper and more distinct, as if he were looking at them through a slowly focusing lens. They were butterflies, dozens of them, soaring silently through the air on wings of bright primary colors. Tristan was awed by their beauty. He'd never seen butterflies like this, with colors so intense they almost glowed.

He withdrew his hand from beneath Damara's shirt, prompting her to open her eyes.

"Is something . . ." She broke off, eyes widening as she saw the mass of butterflies that filled the room.

"Aren't they beautiful?" Tristan said in a hushed voice. He was afraid that if he spoke louder he'd break this wonderful enchantment. He looked at Damara's face to gauge her reaction and was surprised to see she stared at the butterflies with horror.

"No . . . please, not here . . . not *now!*"

The despair in her voice nearly broke his heart.

"What's wrong, Dee? They're just butterflies. I don't know where they came from or how they got into the house, but they aren't hurting anything. It's almost like . . ." He wanted to say that it was almost like they had been drawn by the love Damara and he shared, had come to celebrate it . . . perhaps had in a sense even been *created* by it. But the words sounded too much like something out of a bad romance novel, and he couldn't bring himself to say them aloud.

"I've got to go, Tristan. I'm . . . I'm sorry!" She leaped off the bed before he could stop her and, holding her hands up to shield her face, she ran through the swirling cloud of butterflies parting to make way for her.

He heard the front door open and then shut before he was halfway down the hall. By the time he reached the door and opened it again, Damara was in her yard, sprinting through the rain toward her own front door. Tristan stepped onto the porch, intending to go after her, but he saw his mom's Sunbird coming down the street, headlights on, wipers swishing back and forth over the windshield. She honked and waved as she approached the driveway, and Tristan saw his sister was sitting in the front passenger seat.

His hesitation had given Damara more than enough time to get inside and shut her door. There was no way he could hear from across the street, especially not with the rain and the sound of the Sunbird's tires rolling over wet asphalt, but he imagined that Damara had locked the door as soon as she'd closed it. Without bothering to return his mom's wave, he went back inside and trudged miserably down the hallway to his room, trying to figure out what the hell had just happened. He felt somehow as if he might've been responsible, at least in part, for Damara's reaction to the butterflies, though he couldn't say why. It was just a feeling he had.

Speaking of the butterflies, he wondered how he was going to get rid of them. He could open the windows in his room, but with the way it was raining, he doubted they would fly outside. He might be forced to try and catch them, though he didn't have anything he might use as a butterfly net. But when he stepped back into his bedroom, he discovered that his musings had been academic. The butterflies were gone.

Tristan sighed in the dark. He never had found out where those butterflies had come from or where they'd gone. He'd tried talking to Damara about them a couple of times, but she'd been unresponsive, and soon after they'd stopped talking altogether, aside from exchanging a few *how ya doin*'s at school. Before long, they didn't even do that much.

Tristan had thought about that rainy afternoon many times over the last twelve years, trying to understand what had gone wrong between Damara and him. They had been so close to something special—and not just the sex, though he imagined that would've been wonderful, too. He'd always had the feeling that they'd been on the verge of forging a connection beyond friendship, beyond boyfriend-girlfriend, beyond even lovers. A soul-to-soul connection that would've bonded them together forever. But something had happened to ruin it, and he wished to God he knew what it was.

He let out a bitter laugh. There he was, sounding like a poorly written romance novel again. *Soul-to-soul connection . . .* Still, that's how he'd felt at the time, with the intensity of emotion that only a teenager was capable of. Still, he'd been encouraged by tonight. It seemed that a spark of what Damara and he had almost had still existed, and he hoped that given a little time, that spark might grow into a flame.

He thought of Damara and brilliant-hued butterflies, and as he did, sleep finally came to him.

While he slept, patches of color appeared in the darkness above him, colors that merged to form the outline of a woman—a woman with multifaceted eyes, like those of an insect. She regarded Tristan's sleeping form for a time and then, as if coming to a decision, she unfurled her rainbow-colored wings and crawled on top of him.

Damara lay on the couch, staring at the TV without really watching it. She had the sound turned down so low that it was nothing but a soft murmur. She was absolutely exhausted, so tired that she could barely hold her head up, but she wasn't sleepy. She felt drained of energy, as if she were coming down with something. Since she didn't go out, she rarely got sick unless her mother caught something and passed it on to her. But now she felt as if she might be starting a nasty bout of flu.

Tim Waggoner

She glanced at the digital clock on the cable box and saw it was 1:54 in the morning. Dawn was still a long way off.

A very long way.

Chapter Eight

Damara knew she should try to sleep, but the idea of crawling into bed and tossing and turning in the darkness didn't appeal to her. With nothing else to do, she'd think, and when she thought too much, she started imagining, and when she started imagining, bad things happened. But she knew a way she could get to sleep fast, and without having any dreams.

She got up from the couch and headed for the bathroom—*not* the one near her bedroom, but the one next to Mother's. She turned on the light, then stepped to the sink and opened the door to the medicine cabinet. On the top shelf was a row of prescription bottles, all with labels bearing Damara's name. Pills for allergy, migraine, depression, anxiety, and what she had come seeking relief from tonight: insomnia. She took the bottle off the shelf, opened it, shook out a single pill onto her palm, and then, thinking better of it, shook out another. She set the bottle on the counter, pulled a

113

Dixie cup out of the dispenser and filled it with water. But as she lifted the pills toward her mouth, she hesitated. She knew from experience that two pills would knock her out within minutes and keep her unconscious for close to twelve hours. Twelve hours of peace, twelve hours of not having to worry that her imagination might be slipping out of her control . . . so why was she hesitating? She wasn't sure, but she thought maybe it had something to do with Tristan.

Taking the sleeping pills would be the easiest way to escape her fears, at least for a while. But that was the problem—it would be *too* easy. She'd been taking the easy way out for the last ten years. Taking a pill whenever she couldn't sleep, was worried or depressed. Staying inside the house, only going out for doctor and dentist appointments. But Tristan wasn't taking the easy way out of his problem. He'd come back home all the way from California to get his mom's house ready to sell. Though the task was sure to be emotionally difficult, he wasn't leaving the job to someone else. He was here, and he was going to do it himself. Damara admired that in him, and she was ashamed of herself for wanting a chemical escape so badly.

She looked at the pills cupped in her hand, then replaced them in their bottle, put the cap back on, put the bottle back in the medicine cabinet, poured out the water, crumpled the Dixie cup, and threw it into the wastebasket beneath the sink. When she was done, she smiled, proud of herself for not taking the easy route. But her feeling of pride soon vanished as she realized she was still faced with the same problem as before: how to get sleepy.

Well, she was already in the bathroom. Why not take a shower? A warm, soothing shower would be just the thing to relax her, and with any luck, once she was relaxed, sleep wouldn't be long in coming. Decision made, she disrobed, dropping her clothes to the tiled floor, then got a big fluffy towel and washcloth from the linen closet. She flipped on the ceiling fan to keep the bathroom from becoming too steamy, then walked over to the shower and reached inside to turn on the water. But she didn't turn the knob right away. Instead, she looked down at the drain in the center of the shower floor.

She thought of how she'd been forced to use the other bathroom earlier this evening, and of the sounds she'd heard coming from the tub drain . . . and then later from the drain in the kitchen sink. She didn't think she could stand in the shower, naked and vulnerable, while those sounds issued from the drain between her bare wet feet.

Don't think about it, she scolded herself. *Thinking about it might make it happen!*

She concentrated on the idea of a polar bear trapped in a blizzard, but try as she might, she couldn't picture a completely white expanse of nothingness. The harder she tried, the more the image eluded her. All she could think about was the wet gurgley sounds of movement, the *skritch-*

skritch of claws on metal, the lonely plaintive voice of a little boy calling, *Mara? Maaaaaaaaraaaaa!*

She almost turned and fled the bathroom before her imagination could become reality, but then she thought of how brave Tristan was being, coming home to confront his past and make peace with it before selling it off to the highest bidder. She wanted to be brave like him, to be brave *for* him.

The image of the polar bear still refused to come. Instead, she saw Tristan's face, his eyes, his smile, heard the kindness and humor in his voice. Her fear began to subside, and though it didn't recede altogether, it became more manageable. She took a deep breath and then turned on the water. She kept her fingers in the spray as she carefully adjusted the water temperature. Her mom liked hot showers—the hotter, the better—and she insisted the water heater be kept on a high setting. Damara always had to be careful not to scald herself when she used the shower. When she had the temperature just right, warm but not too hot, she stepped into the shower and slid the glass door shut.

She stood with her back to the water and closed her eyes as the warmth trickled over her shoulders, breasts, stomach, back, butt, and legs. She kept her breathing even and relaxed, and without any conscious effort on her part, her mind achieved a state of calm, if not total equilibrium. She turned slowly around until the spray was hitting her chest. The sensation felt good on her nipples, almost ticklish, and they became erect. She lightly brushed her hands over her breasts, shivered with

pleasure, then dipped her head beneath the spray
to wet her hair. She rubbed water over her face,
then turned her back to the spray once more and
reached for the soap. She gripped it too tightly and
it squirted out of her hands. It hit the shower floor
with a loud *clack!* and slid around in a half circle
before coming to a stop.

Right next to the drain.

She looked down at the bar of soap, water
streaming down from the sides of her face. Maybe
she should just forget about the soap. After all,
she'd come in here to relax, not necessarily to get
clean. Besides, her mom had a bottle of body wash
on the shower rack alongside their shampoos and
conditioners. She could just use that and worry
about picking up the soap later. She stared down
at the soap again—it was only an inch or less from
the drain—and felt disgusted with herself. This
was ridiculous! All she had to do was bend down
and pick up the soap. It wasn't like she would be
any closer to the drain by doing so. Her feet were
already only a few inches away from it. True, her
face would be closer, but that was more a matter
of psychological distance than physical, wasn't it?
If her face was closer, she might hear something
coming from inside the drain, might even catch a
glimpse of something below the grating. But if
anything was there, it would be there whether she
bent to retrieve the soap or not.

Somehow, that last thought failed to be of much
comfort.

Tristan would pick up the soap, she thought.

The girl she had once been, the Damara who had been both brave and foolish enough to sneak into the Riverfork amusement park in the middle of the night would've picked up the soap.

"Shit," she muttered, and bent down.

Her fingers brushed the soap, and it slid away from her grasp. She tried again, water pounding on her back, pouring off her like rain, pattering onto the shower floor around her. Slowly . . . slowly . . . This time she managed to catch hold of the soap. Grinning with triumph, she started to straighten up. And that's when she heard it.

"Mmmmmm . . ."

Though the water temperature hadn't changed, Damara suddenly felt cold, as if she were standing beneath the frigid flow of an arctic spring.

God, no!

"aaaaaaaraaa?"

She wanted to stand, wanted to throw open the shower door and run, wanted to smash the soap against the drain and shove it in, plug the drain up, seal off the sound along with whatever—or whoever—was making it. But she remained hunched over, water streaming off her as if she were some strange manner of fountain statuary. She couldn't move; all she could do was stare at the drain and listen.

"Maaraaa? Are you up there?" The voice was muted, distant, and thick, as if whoever it was, were speaking underwater.

Whoever it was . . . Damara knew she was being dishonest with herself. She knew damn well

118

who was speaking. It was Jason, her little brother. Her long-*lost* little brother.

"Jason?" she whispered. "Is that you?"

At first there was no reply, and the only sounds Damara heard were water spraying out of the shower nozzle, pounding against the skin on her back, and splashing onto the floor. She began to hope that there hadn't been any voice, that it had been nothing but an auditory illusion created by the shower noise and her own anxieties.

But then she heard it again.

"Mara . . . let me out . . . " The voice was louder, closer, and accompanied by the sound of claws scrabbling on metal, as if something were climbing up the drain pipe toward her—something large.

Damara knew that nothing larger than a mouse could fit through the narrow pipe, and with the shower water pouring down, a small animal or insect wouldn't be able to make its way upward against the flow. But then, a small animal or insect wouldn't be speaking with Jason's voice, would it?

"You're open, Mara. Wide open . . . "

She had no idea what the voice was talking about, but the words nevertheless chilled her.

The *scuttle-scratch* of claws was louder now, and though the shower was still running, Damara could no longer hear water falling. All she could hear was the sound of sharp nails on metal. She couldn't take any more of this. She reached around to turn off the water, but before she could do so, the voice spoke again.

"You have to stop, Mara . . . stop now. If you don't stop, we'll stop it for you."

The round metal cover flew off as a green clawed hand covered with spikes thrust upward. It didn't matter that the opening was too narrow for a normal hand and forearm to pass through, let alone one that sprouted wicked-looking black barbs. And it didn't matter that nothing larger than a goldfish could fit inside the pipe. Jack Sharp could reach up through the drain because Jason had once imagined he could, simple as that.

Damara no longer cared about turning off the water. She wanted to get out of the shower and away from Jack Sharp. She reached for the shower door, intending to throw it open and stumble out to safety. But she only managed to slide the door a few inches before the spiny green hand took a swipe at her legs. Damara screamed as ebon needles raked her skin, lay open her flesh, scraped against bone . . . Blood poured from the wounds, ran over her feet, mixed with the shower water, circled red around the drain. The bulk of the monstrous arm blocked the drain, though, and crimson-tinged water began to rise.

Jason's words came back to her then. *If you don't, we'll stop it for you . . .* Maybe it wasn't only Jack Sharp she was facing. Maybe somehow the spine-covered thing was Jason, too. Perhaps they'd merged into a single entity, one that wanted revenge on a sister who, once upon a time, had failed to protect her little brother.

Damara pressed her back against the tiled shower wall and spread her feet out until they touched the corners of the stall. Jack Sharp kept reaching around, fingers clawing the air as they sought to catch hold of her once more. But the creature's elbow was below the level of the drain, so it couldn't bend its arm, greatly restricting its range of motion. Damara was safe for the moment, but she was trapped. As long as the arm stretched upward, there was no way she could pass by it without getting shredded further—which was bad for several reasons. Chief among them being that her leg wound was bleeding like a sonofabitch, and if she didn't get out of the shower and stop the bleeding, she'd pass out soon. And once she was unconscious, she'd collapse limply to the shower floor, and then Jack Sharp could slice and dice her at his leisure.

Her leg throbbed, and the warm water pouring over her wound made it hurt even worse. She felt like crying, like screaming, but she forced herself to maintain control. If she lost it, she was as good as dead.

Maybe that wouldn't be so bad, she thought. If she were gone, then her imagination would cease to exist along with her. And once her imagination was shut down, the people around her—the people she cared about—would be safe.

The hand stopped reaching for her and swayed back and forth as if it were some manner of serpent that traveled through household plumbing.

Tim Waggoner

"Don't be so sure, Mara. If a mother gives birth to a child, does that child cease to exist when she does? Or does it continue to have a life of its own?"

She wasn't certain if the hand had given up its attack or was merely pausing a moment. Whichever it was, Damara knew she couldn't afford to keep bleeding like this. With her gaze fixed firmly on Jack Sharp's hand, she bent down and pressed her own hand tight against the gashes on her foreleg. The pressure made her wound feel as if she'd dipped it in kerosene and set it aflame. She ground her teeth so hard, she wouldn't have been surprised if shards of enamel shot out of her mouth, but she managed to refrain from screaming and avoided falling into unconsciousness.

"Why are you doing this?" she said in a voice made quavery from equal amounts pain and fear.

"Because you can't go, Mara . . . you can't!"

Blood was dribbling between her fingers, and she began to feel weak and lightheaded. She figured the blood loss was starting to affect her and shock was beginning to set in. She had to do something, and do it fast.

A thought occurred to her: If she had imagined Jack Sharp—or at least helped Jason to imagine him—maybe she could *un*imagine him. She did her best to concentrate past her pain, to think through the thick layer of cotton wrapped around her brain. She pictured the arm growing smaller, shrinking, then spinning around and around as it was sucked down the drain, dwindling away to nothingness as it went.

But the arm stayed the same size and remained where it was.

"You can't wish us away, Mara. You're wide open. Others have tapped into your mind and are drawing on your power. You've grown weak—in more ways than one. So . . . time to play! Red rover, red rover, send Mara right over!"

The hand wiggled its fingers, making a "come here" gesture.

Damara's field of vision had narrowed, and now it seemed as if she were looking at the spiny hand from the other end of a long, dark tunnel. She understood what Jack Sharp . . . Jason . . . *they* wanted. If the shower door had been open, then maybe she could've tried to execute some sort of half-assed jump over the hand. But the door wasn't open, not more than a couple inches anyway, and if she attempted to jump over the hand, she risked smashing into the door and breaking the glass. She'd likely end up cutting herself to ribbons faster than Jack Sharp could. She had to think of another way out of here, and quickly, before she bled to death.

She thought of grabbing the bottles of shampoo and conditioners and pouring them all over the hand. Maybe the chemicals would filter down to wherever the creature's eyes and mouth were. She had no idea if the chemicals in the products would have any effect on Jack Sharp, but she decided to try. She took her hand away from her wound, rinsed the blood off in the shower spray, then reached up and gripped a bottle of shampoo. She flipped open the lid and was about to squeeze shampoo onto Jack Sharp's hand when she remembered that the arm blocked the drain, so the chemicals wouldn't be washed down the pipe. With a hand shaking from a combination of terror and blood loss, she put the shampoo back on the shower caddy.

Think! she told herself. *Use your mind; it's the only thing left you have to fight with!*

Despite how long the shower had been running, the water was still warm. As high as her mom kept the water heater set, Damara never ran out of . . . An idea occurred to her then, and she smiled grimly. *Thanks, Mom.*

She adjusted the angle of the shower nozzle so the spray struck the spiny hand dead on. She then turned the cold water off and cranked the hot water as high as it would go, pressing her body against the side of the stall to keep herself from getting burned. Within seconds, steam rose from the water, filling the shower with moist white haze. Jack Sharp's hand began to thrash back and forth, and his/its/their scream was one of heartache, loneliness, and pain. Damara felt so sorry for the creature that might or might not be her little brother, and she started to turn the hot water off. But before she could, the arm withdrew, disappearing down the drain. Damara turned off the water, opened the shower door, and hurried through. She stepped onto the bath mat, leaving a bloody footprint on the blue fabric. From behind her, she heard Jack Sharp's wails becoming more and more faint as he headed back to wherever it was he'd come from.

But she didn't have time to worry about that. She had a wound to tend to. She grabbed the towel she'd left hanging over the shower door handle and pressed it hard against her lower left leg. She took in a hiss of breath; damn, that hurt! She kept the towel pressed to her wound for a few minutes, letting the fabric sop up the blood. Then she pulled the towel away and took her first good look at her injury. There were three deep furrows—made by Jack Sharp's claws, no doubt—and several smaller scratches caused by his spines. As she watched, they immediately began to fill with blood once more.

"Shit!" she swore. Of course this would have to happen when Mom was at work. And though Damara had taken driver's ed in high school, her license had long ago lapsed, and it had been years since she'd driven a car. Not that she had a car of her own, and not that she could drive it bleeding like this. She needed help.

She took the towel—which already had a crimson patch where blood had soaked through—and quickly tied it around her wounded leg. Then she hobbled out of the bathroom in search of a phone.

Chapter Nine

Damara smiled with relief when Tristan walked into the emergency room lobby carrying a brown grocery sack. He was dressed in a blue windbreaker, a rumpled white shirt and equally rumpled jeans, and tennis shoes. His hair was mussed, and his eyes were only half open. He stopped, looked around, and saw her sitting in a wheelchair over by a TV set mounted on the wall. She waved and he hurried over to her.

"My God, are you all right?" As he spoke he stared at the gauze-wrapped leg poking out from her bathrobe. It had been the only clothing she'd had the presence of mind to grab after calling 911, and there were dried bloodstains on the hem. She didn't even have on a pair of panties, since there'd been no way to slip them over her bleeding leg without getting them soaked in blood.

"I don't mean to shock you, Tristan, but it doesn't talk. My leg, I mean."

He lifted his gaze to meet hers and grinned in

embarrassment. "Sorry. Over the years, I've taught enough students with disabilities to know better than to talk to you without looking in your eyes. So? How are you?"

"Twenty-eight stitches altogether. I lost some blood, as you might well imagine, so they gave me a pint or so to top me off. "She reached into her robe pocket and brought out a plastic prescription bottle. "And they gave me some great pills." She shook the bottle for emphasis. "They don't take away all the pain, but they dope me up enough so I don't give a damn about it."

Tristan smiled. "Ah, the wonders of modern science!"

It was 5:20 in the morning, and aside from a nurse at the front desk and a man with blond hair and a goatee who'd come in a few minutes ago claiming to suffer from appendicitis, the lobby was deserted. The poor man—who wore a trench coat over a pair of pajamas—sat hunched over, grimacing in pain as he worked to fill out a sheaf of forms on a clipboard. The décor was bland and impersonal: white tiled floor, white walls, white ceiling . . . chairs, couches, and side tables all brown, all square and rectangular. Everything illuminated in the harsh blue-white of fluorescent lights overhead. The lobby had all the charm and comfort of a morgue, Damara thought. As if whoever had designed it hadn't bothered to consider the people who'd be using it. The walls could be painted puke green and the floor bare dirt. What did it matter? The patients would all be in too much discomfort to care what the hell their surroundings looked like anyway, right?

Damara nodded toward the sack Tristan carried. "I assume those are some of your mother's things."

"Yep. Some underwear, a turtleneck, a sweater, and a pair of sweatpants. I was afraid her regular pants would be too big for you. At least with the sweats, you can tighten the drawstring."

He held out the sack and she took it and set it on her lap. Tristan's mother hadn't been obese, but she'd been heavier than Damara, and her pants probably wouldn't have fit. At least, she *had* been heavier—until the cancer had started eating her alive.

"Thanks, Tristan."

He looked genuinely puzzled, which was so like him, Damara thought. It would never occur to him that he'd done anything special by coming to help her.

"For what?"

"For coming here to get me, especially at five-thirty in the morning. And for letting me borrow your mother's clothes."

He gave her an uncomfortable smile. He'd never been very good at accepting someone's gratitude, Damara recalled.

He sat down in a chair next to her. "Hey, what are friends for, and other assorted clichés. Besides, I was up anyway. I had trouble sleeping . . . had the strangest dreams." He shook his head as if to clear it. "I'm just surprised that the doctors are going to let you leave so soon. From the way you described your cuts over the phone, I figured they'd at least keep you for a day or so."

"It's the age of managed care. They don't keep you unless you're dying, and even then they'd probably put a bandage on you and send you on your way." The truth was the doctor who'd stitched her up *had* wanted to keep her—mostly because of the amount of blood she'd lost—but Damara had insisted on leaving, and since her injuries were no longer life-threatening, the doctor had relented, though he hadn't been happy about it. But she saw no need to tell Tristan all that.

"How *did* you cut yourself, anyway?" Tristan asked. "You said something on the phone about an accident in the shower, but I didn't quite understand what you were saying."

Damara wanted to tell Tristan the truth, but she knew this wasn't the time and place. Besides, she feared that he'd think she was crazy if she told him what had really happened.

"Like I said, I was taking a shower and I grabbed hold of a bar of soap to wash myself. I started with my left leg, and as I ran the soap across my skin, I felt a stinging sensation. At first I figured that I probably had a little cut that I didn't know about and some soap got in it and made it sting. But I felt the same sharp stinging when I started washing again. Then I saw the blood. I looked at the soap and saw that a razor blade was stuck in it. Mom keeps her razor on the same shelf where we keep the soap, and I guess one of the blades came loose and one of us put the soap down on it after our last shower."

That had actually happened to her a few years ago, except that she'd started soaping her arm and she'd realized something was wrong after the first sting, so she hadn't cut herself very badly. She hoped Tristan would believe her story. The doctor had looked skeptical when she'd told him, but he hadn't questioned her further.

Tristan winced. "That must've hurt like hell. You're lucky you didn't get cut even worse."

Damara saw Jack Sharp's spine-covered hand reaching for her.

"Yeah, I sure am."

They were silent for a few moments, and then Tristan asked, "Have you managed to get hold of your mom yet?"

"I called the hotel again, but I got the same woman I spoke with before. I'd hoped the manager would've shown up by now, but I guess it's still too early. The woman told me the same thing as before: that Mom called her around midnight, told her she was sick, and asked if she could come in to relieve her. The woman agreed, and when she got to the hotel, Mom was gone, leaving only a note behind for the woman that said, 'Thanks, owe you one!' Mom didn't even take the time to sign it."

"I assume you tried calling your house again?" Tristan asked.

Damara nodded. "Twice. I got the machine both times."

"And you don't have any idea at all where she might be?"

"None. It's not like her to take off work, even when she's sick. She has to be at death's door to even *think* about staying home, and even then she'd probably go in for a couple hours. And if she were sick, she'd come straight home."

"Maybe she didn't think she could make it all the way home and went to a friend's place instead," Tristan offered.

"I doubt it. None of her friends work third shift, at least none that I know about. She wouldn't want to bother them that late at night."

"Don't worry. I'm sure there's some logical explanation for where she went."

Damara let out a bark of a laugh. "That's the sort of thing people say when they don't want to admit they haven't got a goddamned clue."

Tristan smiled. "I like you when you're on pain medication. It makes you feisty."

"Feisty? Isn't that a word you used to describe an old woman?"

"How about sassy then?"

Damara pretended to think about it a moment. "On second thought, I think I'll stick with feisty." She grew serious then. "I've got some bad news. After I called you, I asked the nurse at the desk if she could check on Bobby Markley for me. She looked him up in their computer system." She paused to take a breath before going on. "He's dead, Tristan. He died sometime before midnight."

"How? I mean, I know he had a bad head injury,

132

but from what you told me at your place, he was moving when the paramedics took him away."

Damara sniffed back tears. "The same paramedics came to get me, you know. They said there must be a curse on our neighborhood or something." As soon as she said the words, she wished she hadn't. There *was* a curse on Pandora Drive—and the curse was her. "The nurse either couldn't tell me how Bobby died or she wouldn't. Either way, I didn't find out anything else about him. I guess his head injury was the cause."

Tristan shook his head. "God, that sucks. Bobby was a kid, and to die like that, from a simple fall . . . Hell, we used to fall all the time when we were kids, remember? We never got any head injuries, didn't even suffer so much as a single broken bone. And Bobby trips on his front steps and dies a few hours later. Luck of the draw, I guess."

Damara wasn't certain luck had anything to do with it, but she wasn't ready to tell Tristan that—not just yet.

The man with appendicitis must have finished completing his forms, for he stood up—still hunched over—and hobbled toward the nurse's desk. The woman was typing on her computer and didn't look up at he approached.

"I hate to ask you for another favor, Tristan, but if you wouldn't mind . . ."

"Sure, Mara. Anything you need."

She felt a rush of love for Tristan then, because she knew he wasn't just saying that; he meant it.

"Would you mind driving me to the hotel where

Mom works? I'd feel better if I could take a look around myself. Maybe Mom left some indication where she was going, and the woman who filled in for her missed it."

She was afraid that Tristan would tell her that she was clutching at straws, but he smiled and said, "Sure. It'll keep me from having to get started cleaning my mom's place. But are you sure you're up to it? You must be exhausted, not to mention groggy from your medication. And is it really a smart idea for you to be walking right now?"

"I'll manage. The doctor said I could walk as long as I took it easy. And I don't plan on sprinting anytime soon."

"But the wheelchair?"

"Hospital policy. They wouldn't let me walk to the lobby on my own. Probably afraid I'd trip and sue the hospital. I figured I'd sit in it until it was time to go. Just let me wheel on over to the women's restroom and change, then we can—"

Damara was interrupted as the man with appendicitis—who now stood over at the nurse's desk—let out a cry of pain.

"God*damn,* that hurts!" He sounded like he was scared and in agony. Damara didn't blame him a bit.

He pressed his hands to his abdomen. "Feels . . . urg! . . . like the fucking thing . . . is trying to get out!"

As soon as he spoke, Damara stood up, ignoring the stabbing pain in her injured leg.

"No!" she shouted, but it was too late.

The man screamed as his abdomen exploded in a shower of blood and loops of intestine. As he fell to the floor—which was no longer as white as it had been a few seconds ago—a small narrow piece of inflamed meat plapped onto the blood-smeared tile and wriggled away from its previous home as fast as it could go, leaving a crimson trail in its wake like some manner of demonic snail.

HEADLESS BODY FOUND BEHIND LOCAL BAR

Kenneth felt an electric thrill shoot through his cock as he read the headline. Zephyr wasn't a large enough town to have a daily paper—Dayton and Cincinnati were the closest cities with dailies—but the weekly came out every Wednesday. Kenneth was surprised, but pleasantly so, to see the story about Nancy. He'd thought their little tête-à-tête had occurred too late to make this week's edition.

He picked up his coffee mug from the dining table and took a sip before quickly skimming the article to make sure his name wasn't mentioned. He didn't see how it could be, but it didn't hurt to be careful. Several customers in the bar had reported seeing Nancy leave with a "middle-aged man," but there was no further description. Kenneth was sure the cops assumed that man was the killer, but if they didn't have any more details to go on, they'd never figure out he was that man. He was as safe as a baby floating in its mother's womb. He went back to the beginning of the article and read it more slowly this time, lingering over certain phrases, such as "head completely destroyed as if by a shotgun blast" and "an unidentified substance was found at the scene." He knew damn well what that substance was, didn't he? High-octane Kenny love-juice!

He closed his eyes as he recalled the incredible sensations of the orgasm that had brought about Nancy's demise. What did they say, fuck off and die? That certainly fit Nancy—she'd gotten him off and then she'd died, face, skull, and brains disintegrated in the greatest cum-blast in the history of the human race. He started to get hard again just thinking about it. His penis pushed against his underwear and bulged against the fabric of his robe.

Deep inside him, somewhere in the darkness of his soul, a part of Kenneth that was still sane cried out in despair over what he'd done to Nancy/NOT-E-DD. But the rest of him didn't listen. It was too busy reliving that glorious moment when the pressure had built up inside him and his cock swelled to the bursting point in Nancy's mouth. And then, when he could no longer hold back—

"Are you reading that filth?"

Kenneth's eyes snapped open and he scowled, irritated at having been torn away from such a pleasant memory. He glanced over his shoulder at Emma, saw she was dressed for school in a white blouse and a denim skirt. She had one earring in and was in the process of putting in the other.

His scowl melted away and became a sly smile. The paper lay open on the table before him. "If you're referring to this—" he tapped the article about Nancy's death with his index finger—"then yes, I was. Did you read it?"

Emma made a face as if hot bile splashed the back of her throat. "It's lurid and disgusting! Not fit for a cheap tabloid, let alone the town paper. *And* they put it on the front page where anyone—including children—might see the headline."

Kenneth's smile widened, and he felt his cock grow harder. He wasn't certain, but he thought he could hear a slight tearing sound, as if the fabric of his underwear were starting to rip.

"So you did read it."

Emma hrumpfed and, second earring in place, headed back to the bathroom to finish putting her makeup on. Kenneth watched her go, admiring her trim form. A lot of women put on weight as they aged, but not his Emma. She was exactly the same dress size she'd been on their wedding day. He thought about sneaking into the bathroom and opening his robe to reveal the erection straining at his underwear just to see how Emma would react. Would the sight of his newly reborn monster cock ignite the dormant embers of desire in her? Or would she recoil in horror? Kenneth couldn't decide which reaction would turn him on more. Either way, he could yank that denim skirt of hers down and give her a taste of what Nancy had gotten last night.

He took a last sip of coffee and started to stand—already wondering what would happen to Emma's body when he came in her—but then he caught movement out of the corner of his eye. He turned to look out the window and saw Anne Marcino and Autumn walking down their front steps, Anne carrying a cardboard box full of papers, and Autumn wearing her backpack. Her hair was done in pigtails today, and somehow they made her look at once older and younger. Kenneth found the look unbearably sexy and his cock gave an excited twitch in his underwear.

Easy, boy, Kenneth thought, and he had to resist the urge to reach down and pat his quivering erection as if it were some sort of anxious pet that needed reassurance. He got up from the table and walked to the front window. It was a chilly morning, and both Anne and Autumn wore jackets. He was disappointed, especially about Anne. He preferred warmer weather, when women wore less clothing and he could get a better look at their shape. Still, Anne was wearing a skirt, and though the hemline wasn't as high as he would've liked, it still gave him a good look at her legs. From this distance, he couldn't tell whether she was wearing hose or not. He chose to think of her legs bare, and maybe she wasn't wearing any panties, either.

Are you going commando today, Anne? He'd sure love to find out. He imagined standing next to her, talking to her about something, maybe what had happened to that obnoxious Markley kid last night. He imagined slowly reaching his hand under her skirt, exploring with his fingers, eager to discover whether he would touch soft cloth or warm wet flesh. . . .

When they reached the bottom of the steps,

Anne kissed Autumn on the forehead and headed for her car, which was parked in the driveway. She loaded the box of papers into the trunk while Autumn sat down on the bottom step to await the school bus, the same way she did every morning.

"Kenneth Arthur Colton! You should be ashamed of yourself!"

Kenneth frowned as he turned to face his wife. "What are you talking about?"

Emma pointed at his crotch. "I'm talking about *that!*"

Kenneth looked down and saw that his penis—his very naked, very *erect* penis—was sticking out from his robe. That was weird. He hadn't pulled his underwear down and let his cock free. So how had it . . . He saw a tiny piece of white cloth sticking out of the slit of his penis. The organ twitched and the scrap of cloth was sucked inside. Kenneth realized what had happened. His dick, eager to be free of the confinement of his underwear, had made an exit for itself.

He looked back up at Emma. The expression on her face hadn't changed, so he doubted she'd noticed his cock slurp up the bit of cloth.

"Ashamed? Take a good long look at it, Emma. This isn't just a dick anymore. It's a monster cock! Hell, it's the goddamned *king* of cocks!"

As if responding to his words, Kenneth's penis swelled even more, the skin turned dark purple, and violet-blue veins stood out, pulsing gently as blood flowed through them.

Emma's upper lip curled in disgust, and she

looked away from his erection, past his shoulder, and out the window. When she saw what—or rather *who*—he'd been looking at, she let out a snort that was almost, but not quite a laugh. "The reason you should be ashamed is because you got . . . *that way* from ogling Anne Marcino and her daughter!"

Kenneth felt a sudden urge to cover himself, as if he were a kid who'd just been caught masturbating by his mother. But then a voice whispered in his mind, one that was both his and not his. And though it seemed to originate in his head, he knew it came from somewhere farther south.

Don't let her intimidate you, Kenny! You don't have to take shit from her—you don't have to take it from anyone—not with what you got swinging between your legs!

Kenneth took a step toward Emma, his cock so hard it barely jiggled as he moved. "So what if I did? Anne's a real piece, and it's not like you do anything to get me stiff."

He took another step toward Emma, and she started to retreat before him, but at the last instant she held her ground.

"Anne's got great tits, great legs, a great ass, blowjob lips . . . Do you think she'd be able to take this monster of mine in her mouth without gagging? I bet she could. I'm sure she's had lots of practice."

He took another step forward, and now the smaller, shiny head of his cock was only inches from Emma's belly. She continued to avert her gaze, but she did take a step back this time. She'd never given ground to Kenneth before, not like this, not so completely, so *fearfully*. He liked it, like it *a lot*.

"As for Autumn, I bet she'd choke if she tried to swallow so much Kenny-kielbasa. That is, if she didn't just faint dead away as soon as she saw the King coming at her. Course, if I put it in any of her other holes, I'd probably end up splitting the poor thing right down the middle."

Another step forward for Kenneth, another step backward for Emma.

"What do you think, darling?" he said. "*Could* Autumn take it? Could *you?*"

He took a last step toward Emma, but this time she didn't back away, and the head of his cock bumped into her stomach. Kenneth winced. Her blouse was cold as ice, as if she'd kept her clothes in a deep-freeze all night instead of the closet. Without meaning to but unable to stop himself, Kenneth took a step back. The tip of his penis ached from the cold, and though his dick remained erect, it wasn't quite so hard now.

Emma's face was no longer pale, her eyes no longer filled with uncertainty. Though he was certain it had to be a trick of the light, her skin appeared to take on a greenish cast, and her eyes smoldered with barely restrained fury.

"Don't push me, Kenneth." Her voice was low and dangerous. "You might think you're a big man now just because your *thing* is working again, but I'm not exactly Little Miss Helpless. The neighborhood's starting to become overgrown with weeds, and the worst two are growing right across the street from us. It's high time I did something about them, don't you think?" Then she reached toward his cock, made a pair of scissors with her fingers, and slid them around his shaft. "And if you don't watch out, I might just prune this too while I'm at it. Snip-snip!"

Then she smiled, withdrew her hand, turned, and walked away, leaving Kenneth just standing there. By the time she'd gotten her purse and her school bag and left through the back door, his penis was as limp as a strand of spaghetti. A moment later he heard the engine of Emma's Geo start, and he turned back to the window.

Anne was already in her car and backing out of her driveway. She waved to Autumn as she backed onto the street, then honked and waved to Emma as she drove off. Emma didn't honk, and though Kenneth couldn't see her from this angle, he doubted she waved, either. Emma pulled out of the driveway then. Autumn waved at her, but Emma didn't so much as look in the girl's direction as she headed down the street, driving faster than usual.

Glad that his wife was finally gone, Kenneth reached between the folds of his robe and into his underwear, intending to get himself hard again so he could masturbate while he watched little pigtailed Autumn wait for the bus. But his monster cock refused to return, and his dick remained a tiny lump of cold, shapeless meat. Kenneth reached farther down, grabbed hold of his testicles and squeezed them in frustration.

Goddamn that Emma . . . goddamn her straight to frigid-bitch hell!

Emma watched Autumn grow smaller in her rearview mirror as she drove down the street. She gripped the steering wheel, her knuckles turning white. "You little tease," she muttered. "Nothing but a whore-in-training. Cunt. Slut."

Emma might not have been particularly fond of sex—it had been something of a relief when Kenneth's equipment had refused to function after his prostate operation, actually—but that didn't mean she tolerated her husband's roving eye. Kenneth was *her* man, no one else's, and whether she chose to make use of it or not, his penis was hers, too. Her goddamned *property,* to do with as she saw fit. And no one was going to take it away from her. Not that tramp Anne . . .

. . . and certainly not her little cooz of a daughter.

Emma continued driving toward school, and as she did, she began to make plans.

Inside Tristan's house, up in the attic that was crammed almost ceiling to floor with cardboard boxes full of the forgotten detritus of a family's life, she rested. It was warm up here, and far from feeling uncomfortable in the cramped attic, she felt snug, safe, secure. She hung upside down, clinging to the exposed ceiling beams with all of her limbs, her delicate wings folded against her

143

back, brown hair hanging down and brushing the top of a box. But though she rested, she did not sleep.

She was tired after the night she had spent with the man. They had done many things together—many *good* things—but sleeping had not been among them. This morning, *she* had called the man. The Other. And he went to her, though where exactly he had gone, she did not know. She did know one thing, however. It was the Other the man truly loved, not her. During all the good things that they had done together in the dark, it had been the Other he was thinking of the entire time. She understood that she was a substitute for the Other, and that if it came down to a choice, the man would choose the Other over her. This knowledge made her sad and angry.

Her multi-faceted eyes detected movement and locked on to a small spider crawling across one of the beams not far from her face. She opened her mouth, unrolled her tongue, and extended it quick as a whip toward the spider. A split-second later, she was chewing, then swallowing, and thinking about how much she'd like to do the same thing to the Other.

Chapter Ten

Tristan got breakfast sandwiches and coffee for them at a drive-thru, and they ate as he drove to the Econo Inn over in Waldron where Damara's mother worked. As if by unspoken agreement, neither of them said anything about the man whose appendix had burst out of his body then made a run for it. The man had died from shock and blood loss, but there was no sign of the renegade organ. Damara had heard one of the doctors who had rushed to the ER lobby too late to help the man say that the appendix had ruptured so violently that it had for all intents and purposes disintegrated into blood and shredded bits of meat. But Damara knew better; she figured the appendix had succeeded in escaping.

Damara wondered if she shouldn't have called 911, shouldn't have come to the hospital, should've stayed home instead and let herself bleed to death. If she had, the man with the appendix would still be alive. She hadn't killed him on purpose, of course, but her ability, power, talent, curse, whatever the hell it was, had provided the impetus for bringing his morbid fantasy to life.

She glanced at Tristan. He had one hand on the steering wheel and held his coffee in the other. Every moment she spent in his presence put him in further danger. She should have him take her home right now where she could be alone and not be a threat to anyone. She almost asked him to do just that, but then she thought of her mother. Something was wrong with Claire. It wasn't like her to just disappear. Damara was determined to find and help her mother, but to do so, she needed Tristan's help. She would just have to hope that he would keep a lid on his imagination as long as they were together.

The sun had risen over the horizon by the time they reached Waldron, and a short time after that, they pulled into the parking lot of the Econo Inn. Tristan parked at the curb in front of the lobby so Damara wouldn't have far to walk, and she was grateful for this thoughtfulness. Despite the pain medication, her leg throbbed and she felt muzzy-headed both from the pills and lack of sleep. She wasn't confident that she could take more than two steps without losing her balance and falling.

Damara opened the door and started to get out, but Tristan told her to wait. He hurried around to her side and held out a hand. She took it and he gently helped her climb out of her seat and limp over the curb onto the front walk. Tristan then closed her door, locked the car with his key-chain remote, then extended an elbow for her to take.

"I see living in California has made you quite the gentleman." She put her hand in the crook of his arm and let him steady her.

"Not really. I just *seem* like a gentleman compared to all the self-centered jerks out on the coast."

Tristan grinned and Damara laughed, and together they walked into the hotel lobby.

A short, heavy woman in her fifties with hair dyed so black it was glossy sat behind the front desk. Damara hadn't met her before, but she recognized her from her mother's description. This had to be Arlene, the woman who took over the desk when Mother's shift ended. Damara wanted to hurry to the desk, but her injured leg wouldn't let her. The best she could manage was an unsteady hobble, and even then she could only do that because Tristan had hold of her elbow.

A sign propped on the counter said Enjoy Our Continental Breakfast. Next to the sign was an old coffeemaker with a pot full of foul-smelling black liquid and beside that a tray covered with stale donuts and crumbly muffins. Damara wondered on just what continent people considered this crap breakfast.

Arlene looked up at they approached, and Damara saw that she'd troweled her makeup on as thick as paste this morning. Her eye shadow was parrot-green, her lipstick a strange bluish gray that

147

made Damara think of oyster flesh, and her foundation was so heavy, it made her face as tight and unmoving as a mannequin's. Damara had always thought her mother had been exaggerating when she talked about Arlene's makeup. Now Damara knew that, if anything, Claire had been understating the truth.

"Can I help you folks?"

Damara was taken aback by the woman's voice. It was soft, gentle, mellow, with just the right hint of sexiness underneath. With a voice like that, Arlene could've been a radio announcer, a voice-over actor, a phone sex operator . . .

Damara was suddenly aware of how plain her own voice was as she spoke. "I'm Damara Ruschmann, Claire's daughter."

Arlene's eyes widened, creating tiny cracks in her green eye shadow. She smiled, revealing teeth so white they gleamed. Damara wondered if they were capped or false. They couldn't have been natural, not with a shine like that.

"Yeah, yeah . . . Claire's talked about you before. Sometimes I get here early and we shoot the shit before the manager gets here. He always strolls in late—and today's no exception." Arlene laughed, and despite her lovely voice, the sound was harsh and grating, like a donkey's bray. "Is Claire doin' all right?'

"I'm not sure."

Arlene frowned. "The girl who was here when I came in said your ma took off sick last night. I thought you lived with her."

"I do."

Arlene's frowned deepened, causing a seismic shift in her foundation. "Then you should know how she's doin', right? You woulda been there when she got home . . ." Arlene's voice trailed off and she looked at Tristan as if only just noticing him. Her frown smoothed away and her oyster-colored lips stretched into a grin. "Or maybe you *weren't* home last night." She chuckled. "And your ma's always sayin' how she's afraid you're gonna end up an old maid!"

Damara was becoming increasingly uncomfortable with the turn the conversation was taking. She knew her mother worried about her, but she hadn't realized that she'd shared those worries with anyone else.

"I *was* home last night," Damara said, unable to resist adding, "and I was alone." She glanced at Tristan. He looked like he was trying very hard not to smile.

I'm glad one of us is amused, she thought.

"The reason we're here, Arlene, is because Mom didn't come home last night. She didn't even call to tell me she was sick. I only found out when I called and spoke with the woman who took over for her."

Arlene's frown returned, so deep this time that it threatened to shatter her foundation like flesh-colored glass. Damara wondered what would be left behind if that happened. A faceless skull? Or maybe just a great vapid void.

A tiny fissure appeared on Arlene's forehead and a small dark-red bead of blood welled forth.

Sudden terror jolted Damara, and she squeezed her eyes shut and thought about polar bears and snowstorms. When she opened her eyes a moment later, she was relieved to see both the blood and the fissure were gone.

Arlene had been too busy talking to notice Damara closing her eyes, but Tristan had. He gave Damara a questioning look, but she responded with a quick shake of the head, as if to say, Not now—later.

". . . weird. I mean, it's not like Claire to do something like that. She's real responsible, you know? She would've made manager by now if she'd wanted to. But to just take off like that, say she's sick and then not go home . . ." Arlene gave a little gasp and touched her hand to her mouth. "You don't think something's *happened* to her, do you?"

There was a host of implications in the way Arlene stressed *happened,* all of them bad.

"I don't know," Damara said. "I hope not."

"I hate to say it, hon, but did you call the police? God forbid your ma's been in an accident or anything, but if she has . . ." Arlene broke off and stared past Damara.

Puzzled, Damara turned in the direction Arlene was looking and saw a woman walk into the lobby. She wore an over-sized flannel shirt untucked and jeans that didn't quite fit her. Her hair was mussed and her feet were bare. It took Damara several seconds to realize that she was looking at her mother. Despite Claire's atypical appearance—she always prided herself on looking her best, especially at work—Damara felt relieved. Whatever was going on, at least she now knew that Mom was safe.

Arlene was the first to speak to her mother.

"Hey, Claire, where the hell have you been? Your girl's been worried sick about you!"

Claire didn't answer right away, didn't even look in Arlene's direction, and Damara wondered if her mother had even heard the other woman. Claire walked up to the counter, grabbed two styrofoam cups from the stack next to the pot and began filling them with the tarry substance that was intended to pass for coffee. Claire had a lazy, sleepy smile on her face, and her eyes had a faraway look to them, as if they were focused on something only she could see.

Damara was almost afraid to say anything to her mother. She remembered an old bit of folk wisdom about how you weren't supposed to wake someone who was sleep-walking. That's what Claire looked like to her—someone who was walking in her sleep, or maybe caught in a trance.

But she stepped past Tristan and hobbled over to her mother. Claire had already finished pouring one cup of coffee and was just starting on the second.

"Mom? Are you . . . are you all right?" She almost added, *It's me—Damara,* but doing so would have been like acknowledging that something was seriously wrong with her mother, and Damara wasn't prepared to do that yet.

Claire responded without looking at her. "Hmmm? Oh, I'm fine, honey. Better than fine. In fact, I'm pretty goddamned great."

Damara was shocked. It wasn't as if her mother didn't swear from time to time, but it was completely out of character for her to do so this casually.

"Where have you been all night? When you didn't come home, I called here and was told you'd left because you were sick. What happened? *Are* you sick?" Damara felt as if she were babbling, but she couldn't help herself. All her worries of the last few hours were pouring out of her, and there was nothing she could do to stop them.

Claire finished pouring the second cup of coffee. She put the pot back on the coffeemaker's burner, then picked up two white plastic lids to put on top of the steaming cups. She still didn't look at Damara as she answered.

"It's a long story, sweetheart. I'll explain it to you later, I promise. But I have to get back now. You understand." Then, without so much as a glance at Damara, Tristan, or Arlene, she put the lids on the cups and headed back the way she'd came. Damara could only watch in stunned confusion as her mother walked off down one of the hotel corridors.

For a moment, no one spoke, but then Arlene said, "Don't *that* beat all to shit!"

Damara could only agree with the woman.

"She's got to be checked into a room here," Tristan said. "I mean, given the way she was dressed."

"Maybe," Arlene said. "If she felt sick enough, she might've decided to use an empty room to rest in. We're not supposed to, of course, but it wouldn't be the first time." She turned to the computer at her workstation, moved the mouse around, clicked a few times, pressed a few keys before finally saying, "Yep, and she registered under her own name. Room 3041. Maybe she's got the flu or something." She lowered her voice. "Could be the change of life, too. My sister had her brain scrambled something fierce for a couple years—memory problems, mood swings—until her doctor finally got her on the right medicine. If that's what it is, you tell Claire to get her butt to her doctor and ask about getting some of those pills for herself."

"We will," Damara said, just to shut the woman up. "Thanks." She turned to Tristan, and as if he read her mind, he nodded, and together they headed for the corridor Claire had gone down.

It took them a little while to get there because of Damara's leg—and her pain meds were wearing off so her injury was beginning to throb—but after traversing a hallway and taking an elevator up two floors, eventually they found themselves standing in front of room 3041. Damara was breathing heavily, as if she'd just run a foot race, but now that they were here, she wasn't sure what to do.

"Something wrong?" Tristan asked.

"I'm not sure whether I should knock. It's kind of like an invasion of privacy, isn't it? After all, Mom's an adult. If she wants to check into a hotel room, what business is it of mine? Besides, she said she'd tell me about it later."

"It's your decision. But you got worried in the first place because this isn't normal behavior for

Claire. She took off sick at the start of her shift, then didn't call you before she checked into this room . . . and you have to admit, she *was* acting weird in the lobby. Whatever the reason she's in there, I'm sure she'll understand why you were concerned and wanted to make sure she was all right."

Damara thought about it for a moment, then smiled and nodded. Tristan was right.

She raised her hand and, trembling only slightly, knocked softly three times. When that got no response, she knocked three more times and said, "Mother? It's Damara. Are—are you okay in there?"

At first, nothing happened, and Damara started to fear that Arlene had given them the wrong room number, or maybe Claire hadn't gone back to her room, or worst of all, maybe she *was* inside but unable to come to the door because she really was sick.

Damara knocked again, more frantically this time. "Mother, open the door! Please!"

She was on the verge of tears when she heard the sound of someone in the room walking toward the door. Locks disengaged and the door swung open, but the person standing in the doorway wasn't Claire Ruschmann. It was a man wearing only a pairs of jeans—the same pair that Claire had on only a short time ago, only they fit him better. He scowled at Damara and Tristan and barked, "What the hell do you want? Do you know how early it is?"

Damara couldn't answer. She could only stare open-mouthed at the man. It was her father. But this wasn't Jerry Ruschmann the way he would be today: a man in his fifties. This was Jerry Ruschmann as he'd been on the night he'd vanished in the park. A man just ending his thirties, still relatively young and in his prime.

So many emotions ran through Damara at the sight of him that she stood frozen, unable to breathe, let alone move. Joy upon seeing her father for the first time in seventeen years, resulting in an almost overwhelming urge to rush forward and wrap her arms around him, to touch him, hold him, confirm that he was solid, that he was *real*. Fear, because *she* was the reason he had gone to Riverfork that night, had gone into Alacrity's Spectatorium, and never came out. Did he blame her for what had happened, worse, did he *hate* her? Confusion, for how could he look *exactly* the same, as if the last seventeen years had passed for everyone else on the planet except for him? And denial, because she knew deep down that this wasn't *really* her father, that whatever he was, he was here because somehow she'd created him.

Tristan looked at the man standing in the doorway for a long moment before turning to Damara. "This can't be who I think it is . . . can it?"

From within the hotel room came the sound of a woman's voice. Claire's voice.

"Jerry, honey? Whoever it is, tell them to go away and come back to bed!"

The man in the doorway, who looked as if he'd

stepped out of an old photograph of Jerry Ruschmann, turned and called back over his shoulder. "Okay, babe. Just a minute." He turned back to face Damara and Tristan. "You heard the lady. You get ten seconds to tell me what you want before I close the door in your faces." He smiled to take some of the harshness out of his words. "Sorry to be such a hard-ass, but this is kind of a reunion for us. We haven't seen each other in a long, long time."

"But you're not going to leave me again, are you, Jerry?"

Once more Jerry turned to call back over his shoulder. "That's right, babe, I'm not going anywhere. You and me, we're going to be together forever!" Again, he turned back around to face them. "Five seconds left, better make it quick."

Damara gazed deeply into the eyes of the man who was the exact copy of her father as he had been almost two decades ago, and for a moment she found herself hoping that somehow it really was him, her father come back to her.

"Daddy, it's me . . . Damara. Don't you recognize me?"

Jerry—or rather his doppelganger—narrowed his eyes as he examined Damara closely. Finally, he scowled. "Look, I don't know what kind of joke this is, but my daughter is eleven years old. And your ten seconds are up." He shut the door and engaged the locks.

Damara listened for a moment, heard footsteps moving away from the door, heard the sound of someone jumping onto a bed, heard a woman who sounded far younger than her mother giggle. She knew the man who'd shut the door in her face wasn't her father, only an image of him, and yet his rejection of her hurt just as bad as if he were the real Jerry Ruschmann. She sniffed back tears and wiped at her eyes. She didn't want to break down here, in the hall with Tristan standing right next to her.

"Mara, what's going on here?"

She looked into Tristan's eyes, saw confusion and fear there, but most of all concern. Concern for her.

She forced a smile. "How about you buy me a cup of coffee—somewhere other than the front lobby, that is—and I'll try to explain."

Tristan looked at the door to 3041 for a moment then back to her.

"Okay. But it's too bad there aren't any bars open this early in the morning."

Damara knew just how he felt.

Inside 3041, Claire—now lying naked on the bed—wrapped her arms around her husband's bare back and hugged him to her. When she'd first disrobed in front of him hours ago, she'd felt terribly self-conscious about how much her body had changed in the last seventeen years—none of it for the better. But Jerry had made it clear that he didn't care, that it was *she* he loved, not her body, and then he'd spent the next several hours proving it.

She pressed her face into the corner of his neck,

breathed in the sweet smell of him—a smell she hadn't forgotten in all these years—and gently pressed her mouth to the vein in his neck and felt his pulse flutter on her lips.

"Did you mean it?" she whispered. "When you said you'd never leave me again?"

" 'Course I did. We'll be together—"

"—forever," she finished. She released him from her embrace and reached down to take his hand. Then fingers intertwined, clasped tight, and their flesh began to merge.

Together.

Forever.

Chapter Eleven

"I didn't know there was a Starbucks in Waldron."

Tristan laughed. "Mara, there's a Starbucks *everywhere*. They pop up overnight like mushrooms after a long rain. I wouldn't be surprised if there was one on the moon by now."

She smiled. Tristan's jokes had grown more sophisticated over the years, but he still retained his sense of humor.

"I don't get out much." Damara took a sip of what Tristan called "candy coffee," a Caramel Frappuccino. It was sweet and smooth, not bitter at all. It was good, but in a way Damara regretted her choice. She could use the taste of something bitter and bracing right now.

Though it was midmorning on a Wednesday, the place was packed. There were a few business types in suits tapping away on laptops or talking into cell phones, but the customers mostly consisted of young men and women in their late teens and early twenties. Students from the community college nearby, Damara guessed, though only a few of them looked to be studying. The rest were chatting and laughing, enjoying one another, enjoying being young, enjoying life. She envied the hell out of them.

Music filtered out of speakers in the ceiling, a woman singing a slow, earnest ballad accompanied only by an acoustic guitar. Damara had no idea who the performer was, but figured she was bound to be someone trendy. She and Tristan sat near the back of the coffee shop, Tristan across from her at the small round table they'd chosen. The chairs were tiny and cramped, and Damara kept shifting her weight in futile attempts to get comfortable. She felt out of place here—too old even though she was only twenty-eight, and underdressed in the sweat pants Tristan had brought to the hospital for her, though some of the college students were dressed even grubbier. Part of her discomfort came from not being used to crowds, but a larger part was due to what they had come here for: so she could tell Tristan the truth about what was happening, at least as far as she understood it.

Despite everything that had happened in the last day or so, Damara couldn't help feeling a certain amount of excitement at being here as well, at being *anywhere*, as long as she was out of her house. She started to remark on this to Tristan, but stopped herself. A place like this was bound to be nothing special to him. He taught at a community college in California and probably went to Starbucks a lot like this one all the time.

Tristan took a sip of his drink—plain old black coffee.

"I'm surprised you didn't get something more adventurous than coffee," Damara said, teasing him. "I thought you had a better imagination than that."

Tristan smiled. "Maybe my imagination is starting to atrophy with age. Besides, of the two us, you were always the more imaginative."

Damara nearly dropped her Frappuccino as he said this, but she managed to put it down on the table with a trembling hand.

"That's what I wanted to talk to you about, Tristan. Sort of." She'd never discussed this openly with anyone in her entire life—not even her mother—and now that she was prepared to tell Tristan, *had* to tell him, she had no idea how to go about doing so.

"I don't understand." No impatience, no frustration, just a statement of fact.

"I'm not sure I do, either. Not completely, anyway." She started to reach for her drink again, but her hand was shaking even worse now, and she was afraid she might spill her "candy coffee," so she put her hands in her lap to hide their trembling from Tristan.

"Do you remember when my little brother . . . disappeared? And how a couple years later, my father left and never came back?"

Tristan put his coffee down on the table. "You're kidding, right? How could I forget? Those were the worst few years of your life. I still don't know how you made it through all that."

She smiled. "I made it because of my mother, and because you were my best friend."

Tristan shrugged. "I'm not sure I did all that much."

"You were there when I needed you, and you cared for me," Damara said. "I'd say that's plenty."

Tristan smiled back at her. "Well, if I helped, I'm glad. So yeah, I remember about your brother and your dad. What about them?"

Damara took a deep breath and then said it.

"What happened to them was my fault." And then, as if a floodgate had been opened, the words came tumbling out of Damara's mouth, one after the other, and before she knew it, she'd told Tristan everything. When she finished, he didn't respond right away. He cradled his coffee cup in his hands, gently rubbing it, rotating it back and forth as he frowned in thought.

After a bit he looked straight at her and said, "What are you telling me, Mara? That you have the power to bring people's dreams to life?"

"Their fantasies and fears. I don't do it on purpose, though. It just kind of happens."

"I see." More rotating of the coffee cup, as if he were using it to stall for time to think. "How about *your* fantasies? Can you bring those to life as well?"

"I try real hard not to," Damara said. "But the more I struggle to keep a lid on my own thoughts, the more my ability? Gift? Curse? The more *it* begins to leak out and affect the people around me."

Tristan actually took a sip of his coffee this time

instead of just playing with it. Damara didn't try to drink any of hers; she feared she'd spill it the way her hands still trembled. What was Tristan thinking? That she was crazy? That she was a monster? Both?

"So you're telling me that you're some kind of supernatural version of Typhoid Mary, a carrier of this whatever-it-is without being a victim yourself."

"That's one way to put it, I guess," Damara said. "So here's where you tell me I'm insane and suggest in a calm, quiet voice—to avoid upsetting me—that I should consider *seeing someone.*"

Tristan looked pained, as if he'd been caught thinking that very thing, but he said, "Give me some credit, Mara." Then in a softer voice he added, "I remember the butterflies."

Damara felt a sudden urge to take his hand, but to do so she would've had to reach across the table, and she couldn't bring herself to do it, not then, not there.

"So the guy in the emergency room . . . your father . . . the hand in the shower . . ."

"Were the result of this weird power I have," Damara confirmed. "And though I'm not quite sure how or why, I'm afraid I somehow caused Bobby Markley's accident, too."

Tristan didn't say anything more for a time, just sipped his coffee and stared past her at the people around them. He had a troubled look on his face, and she had the impression that he was remembering something.

"What is it?" she asked. "Has something strange

happened to you, too?" She prayed it hadn't. She didn't think she could live with herself if whatever was wrong with her had spilled over and affected Tristan.

"Hmm? Oh no, not really. I had a . . . strange dream last night. *All* last night, actually. But it was just a dream. A real dream, I mean. It had to be."

But he continued gazing past her, and Damara doubted his words. She believed it likely that he *thought* he was telling her the truth, at least the truth as he wanted it to be. But she decided not to press the point right now. Whatever had happened, he was obviously unharmed, and he'd tell her about it whenever he was ready.

Bullshit, Damara told herself. *You're just afraid to find out what it is, and maybe also find out that Tristan hates you for making it happen.*

"That's the reason I couldn't allow our . . . friendship to continue," Damara said. "I didn't want to put you in any danger. It was getting harder and harder for me to maintain control over my power, and I knew it would affect you sooner or later." When next she spoke, it was in a whisper. "I'd already lost Jason and Dad. I didn't want to lose you, too."

Tristan finally met her gaze then, and she saw that his eyes held no anger, no fear. Just pity and understanding.

"That's why you don't go out, isn't it? You don't have arthritis. That's just a cover story. The real reason is that you don't want to risk being exposed to other people's thoughts, to their dreams."

She nodded. "If I hadn't been injured, I wouldn't have left the house. And if I'd stayed home, the man in the emergency room wouldn't have lost his appendix the way he did. I probably shouldn't be here right now, but after seeing Mom and . . . *him*—" she couldn't bring herself to say *my father*—"I didn't want to go home. Didn't want to be alone." She gave Tristan a small, sad smile. "Pretty selfish of me, huh?"

"No, not selfish. Just human. So how long have you had this . . . I don't know what to call it. Talent?"

"All my life," Damara said. Her hands were almost completely steady now that she had told Tristan everything, so she took another drink of her Frappuccino. "I have no idea where it came from, or why it seems to be flaring up so strongly right now, like some supernatural version of a herpes outbreak. As far as I know, no one in my family has ever had a similar ability. I suppose I'm just a freak of nature."

Tristan reached across the table and took both of her hands in his. She almost pulled away, afraid of his touch, of how much she wanted it, of what might happen to him if she allowed it, but she didn't stop him and she was glad.

"You may be a lot of things, Damara Ruschmann, but a freak isn't one of them." He squeezed her hands and she gave him a grateful smile.

And that's when the screaming started.

There were two women sitting at the table next

to them, one thin with short red hair and a sprinkling of freckles on her nose, the other stout, with
frizzy blond hair and a tiny nose ring in her left
nostril. They both wore clothing that looked as if it
had come from Goodwill and heavy men's work-
boots. The frizzy-haired blonde was screaming,
her hands balled into fists and pressed against her
cheeks as if she were trying to hold her screams in
and failing miserably.

Across the table from her, Freckle-Nose was
shaking and jerking as if in the throes of a seizure.
Her left eye was swelling like a white balloon shot
through with bright red capillaries, while her right
eye subsided into her face, the flesh closing over it
like pale pink water. Her nose receded until it was
gone, leaving only a single ragged opening that
dripped mucus and whistled as she breathed. Her
jaw jutted forward and shifted to the left with a series of cracking and popping sounds. Her teeth
crowded together and twisted until they stuck out
in all directions. Drool spilled from the corner of
her mouth as terror and agony shone out of her
bulbous left eye.

And still her hideous transformation wasn't finished.

Her shoulders drew together, merged, rounded,
became a hump. Her right arm withered, the fingers on the hand becoming misshapen stumps.
Her breasts—which had been small before—grew
large and pendulous, and she sprouted several
more. A small puckered orifice opened on her

throat, and a new eye looked out at the world, blinking moistly.

Damara gripped Tristan's hands as tight as she could.

"You've got to stop it, Tristan!" She had to shout to be heard over Frizzy-Hair's screams and the red-headed woman's keening wail as her metamorphosis continued.

But Tristan couldn't take his gaze off the malformed thing the woman had become. His eyes were wide with disbelief, his face pale with horror.

Damara dug her nails into his hands as hard as she could. "You're thinking about freaks, Tristan, and you have to stop, stop *now!*"

His gaze shifted to her, but from the confusion in his eyes, she knew he didn't understand.

"Think of a snowfield," Damara said, "a white cloud, a blank canvas, an empty piece of paper . . . *anything*, just as long as it's *nothing!*"

The red-haired woman's legs lengthened, became boneless as octopus tentacles. Her boots slipped off what once had been feet, and her rear changed shape, flattened until she could no longer remain seated. She slumped sideways in the chair, then fell to the floor with a sickening soft smack. The horrid lumpy mass she'd become bounced and quivered, as if she had no bones remaining in her body at all.

Tristan kept shaking his head back and forth, trying to deny what was taking place in front of him. The frizzy-haired blonde jumped up from her

table and took a couple steps away from the
mound of clothing and flesh her friend had become, as if she feared that whatever had caused
the nightmarish transformation was contagious.
Frizzy-Hair still had her fists pressed to her
cheeks, but she no longer screamed. Now all that
came out of her mouth was a soft mewling sound.

The red-headed woman lifted a boneless hand,
fingers waving like the fronds of a strange under-
sea plant, and she reached toward her companion,
a thick gurgling noise bubbling up from somewhere deep within her reconfigured anatomy. It
was difficult to tell, but Damara thought it
sounded like she was trying to say *Help me . . .*
Then with a wet sound like a dozen balloons filled
with shaving cream exploded, the woman's bowels
let go, and reddish-black shit streamed through
the fabric of her jeans, the force of the expulsion
enough to make the thick liquid penetrate the
cloth's tight weave. As the shit splattered onto the
hardwood floor, a vicious stench erupted in the air.
Rank, nauseating, foul, stomach-churning . . . it
was the stink of waste and rot and death.

Up until this moment, the coffee shop customers had all been staring at the red-headed
woman, transfixed by her metamorphosis. But the
stink broke their group trance, and people leaped
up from their tables, some screaming, some sobbing, some holding hands to their mouths to keep
from vomiting, others shotgunning undigested
blasts of lattes and biscotti onto themselves, the

table, the floors, and each other as they stumbled, clawed, and fought like animals to reach the exit.

Damara felt hot bile sear the back of her throat, but she struggled to keep from puking, for the frizzy-haired blonde still stood mewling, but now tiny fleshy pseudopods were beginning to grow out of her forehead.

"Tristan!"

He didn't look at her, so she stood and attempted to pull him to his feet. But he was deadweight in his chair and she couldn't budge him. She slapped him across the face, hard, and when he didn't react, she slapped him once more, even harder. His eyes darted back and forth several times, almost as if he were a machine resetting itself. Then his gaze locked onto Damara and he said, "I didn't mean . . ."

But Damara didn't wait for the rest. She grabbed his arm and yanked him out of his chair. This time he helped, and she got him up and moving toward the exit. Her injured leg throbbed like a sonofabitch as they went, but she ignored the pain and kept hold of Tristan's hand the whole way to make sure he made it.

Just before they passed through the exit, Damara glanced back over her shoulder. When she saw the tendril-covered monstrosity that the blonde was in the process of becoming, she wished to Christ she hadn't.

Chapter Twelve

Autumn sat by herself on the school bus. Sometimes she sat with Missy McIntyre and Lindsey Shelhaus, but both were chatterboxes and talked nonstop from the moment they got on the bus until the moment they got off. And while sometimes they could be fun, Autumn wasn't in a chatty mood today. Besides, it wasn't like she was best friends with them or anything, and Autumn wanted to be alone so she could think.

This morning while she and her mom had been getting ready, the phone rang. Her mom answered it. Autumn was in the bathroom brushing her teeth, so she couldn't see her mom or overhear her side of the conversation. When Autumn finished, she spit, rinsed, wiped her mouth on the hand towel hanging next to the sink, and left the bathroom. She found her mother standing in the kitchen, leaning back against the counter with a cold cup of coffee in her hand. She gazed straight ahead and Autumn noticed that her hands were shaking. Not a lot, but enough to worry her.

"Is everything okay?" she asked.

Her mom turned abruptly to look at her, her eyes widening as if she didn't recognize Autumn at first. But then she smiled—though the smile looked fake to Autumn—and said, "Everything's all right, honey. Why do you ask?"

Autumn shrugged. "I don't know." It was a standard answer she gave whenever she didn't want to say anything more about an uncomfortable subject. It always worked with her mother, and today was no exception. Her mom just nodded, as if in agreement with something Autumn hadn't said, then took a sip of her cold coffee. Autumn knew it was cold because her mom always made coffee first thing in the morning, even before she got Autumn up, and once it was done, she turned the coffeemaker off. By now the coffee was surely cold, and since her mom *loathed* cold coffee, she always heated it in the microwave before drinking it. But Autumn hadn't heard the hum of the microwave working, hadn't heard the ding of the bell that indicated its job was done. So that meant her mother *was* drinking cold coffee, something Autumn had never ever known her to do—and she didn't say anything about it, didn't complain, didn't make a face. She just drank it as she once more stared straight ahead, as if she didn't even taste the coffee, or if she did taste it, she didn't care that it was cold.

Autumn grabbed a strawberry fruit bar from the

cupboard, then poured herself a glass of apple-cranberry juice. She took a bite of the bar and chewed.

"Who was on the phone?" Autumn asked, voice muffled by cakey-strawberry gunk.

"What?" Her mom's gaze darted to her, then just as quickly darted away. A hummingbird gaze. "No one. Just a sales call."

Autumn knew she was lying. Her mother couldn't look someone in the eye when she did. The last time she remembered a phone call having this sort of effect on her mom was a few months ago, when Dad had called to tell her he was dating someone else, even though the divorce wasn't final yet. Autumn's mom had acted similarly then—hands shaking, gaze distant, putting Autumn off whenever she asked if something was wrong. So Autumn figured the call had probably been bad news. She just wondered *how* bad.

The bus pulled into the parking lot of Klyburn Elementary, and the driver stopped at the curb in front of the side entrance. She opened the door, and Autumn stood up at the same time the other kids did, and filed off with the rest of them, still thinking about her mom and that phone call. Weighed down by her heavy backpack full of books, Autumn trudged down the hall toward Mrs. Hamilton's classroom, surrounded by a laughing, joking, gossiping, teasing mass of children. She paid no attention to them and ignored those who called her name, inviting her over to talk to them or just greeting her as she passed. The hallway walls were covered with posters, pictures, and construction-paper displays taped up by various teachers. One was titled Study Buddies and showed photographs of students working together on math problems. Another was Voyages of Discovery, and showed maps drawn by students that traced the journeys of great explorers like Columbus, Marco Polo, Leif Erikson, Lewis and Clark, Amerigo Vespucci, and Ernest Shackleton. But regardless of their academic focus—which was sometimes vague at best—the displays projected the same gung-ho, cheerful, our school is great and our students are *awesome* attitude. Autumn knew that the displays were another way the teachers tried to reach kids and get them excited about learning. Even though they were obvious and all too often cheesy, it usually made her feel good to see them. But not today.

She figured she was being stupid worrying so much about her mom and that phone call, but she couldn't make herself stop. Since her dad had moved out, all Anne and Autumn had left were each other. Well, Autumn had Damara too, but while she was great, she didn't replace Autumn's dad. Autumn felt protective of her mother. She'd been hurt so much when dad left, even more than Autumn had, she thought. Autumn figured her mother had been hurt enough for a while—a *long* while—and she just didn't want her to get hurt anymore.

Autumn was so caught up in her worries that

she didn't notice when she walked by Mrs. Colton's classroom.

"Good morning, Autumn."

The words were friendly enough, but there was a coldness in her tone that made Autumn stop, the instinctive reaction of a child hearing an adult authority figure calling her name as if she were in trouble.

She tried her best to smile as she turned to face Mrs. Colton, who stood in the open doorway of her classroom. It was bad enough having a teacher living across the street from you, but both Autumn's mom and Damara said that Mrs. Colton was "nosy" and a "busybody," and so Autumn was always doubly on guard whenever she spoke to the woman. Plus, there was that creepy husband of hers . . . Autumn hated the way he looked at her sometimes.

The walls on each side of Mrs. Colton's door were bare. No cheesy, encouraging displays for her. Her door was bereft of decoration as well, with only a small laminated white sign that said MRS. COLTON in stark black letters. There were two signs, actually—one on the outside of the door, one on the inside, as if she didn't want students forgetting who she was, like *that* could ever happen. No one wanted to get Mrs. Colton for a teacher, and Autumn was grateful that she'd been lucky enough to escape being assigned to her classroom.

She peeked past Mrs. Colton and looked into her room. The desks were arranged in precise, orderly rows, and her students were already sitting at them, staring at the chalkboard, not talking to one another, not even looking at one another. Just sitting quiet and still, waiting for class to begin. Poor kids, Autumn thought. They looked miserable. Still, she was glad she wasn't one of them.

Mrs. Colton's classroom had one pleasant touch, however. There were plants everywhere: on shelves, on counters, hanging from the ceiling, sitting on her desk—green and leafy, lush and healthy. Autumn remembered something Damara had once said to her about Mrs. Colton's love of gardening.

I'll never understand how a woman like her can bring such beauty into the world.

That was something Autumn didn't get either, but then grown-ups were funny. They seemed one way on the surface, but they could be a whole different person inside. Even Damara was like that a little. Sometimes Autumn had the feeling that Damara was almost *afraid* to talk to her, as if she knew she shouldn't be doing it but couldn't help herself.

Grown-ups could be so weird.

"I saw you this morning," Mrs. Colton said. Her thin, bloodless lips stretched into a smile, but there was no kindness in the woman's eyes.

Autumn wasn't sure how to respond. Mrs. Colton *always* saw her waiting for the bus. And even though Autumn always waved to her to be polite—just like her mom had taught her—Mrs. Colton hardly ever waved back. Autumn lowered her gaze from Mrs. Colton's face and noticed that she was holding on to a tiny flower planted in moist black soil inside a Styrofoam cup.

"It's a buttercup," Mrs. Colton said. "I have some flowers growing in my classroom, and I took this one and put it into a cup when I got to school this morning. Do you like it?"

It was nothing special, just a flower, but Autumn said, "Yeah, sure," because she didn't want to make Mrs. Colton mad.

"Here." Mrs. Colton thrust the flower toward Autumn, almost as if she intended to hit her with it. "It's yours."

Autumn stared at the flower for a moment. She understood what Mrs. Colton had told her, but she couldn't quite bring herself to believe it. Mrs. Colton had never given her anything before, not even at Christmas time. Autumn's mother usually took some of her chocolate walnut fudge over to the Coltons during the holiday season, but though they always accepted the gift, they'd never reciprocated. Autumn's mom had never seemed too put off by the Coltons' failure to make a return holiday gesture.

You don't give gifts because you expect to get something back, her mom had said last Christmas when Autumn asked why she kept making fudge for the Coltons each year. *You do it because you want to, because it makes you feel good.*

Now, after never giving anything to either Autumn or her mother for years, Mrs. Colton was giving her a flower in a Styrofoam cup.

Tim Waggoner

"Go ahead, take it." Mrs. Colton's voice was strained, as if she were irritated and trying to keep from showing it. "You only have a couple minutes to get to your classroom before the first bell rings."

Mrs. Colton's mention of the first bell got Autumn moving again. She reached out with both hands and took the flower. For one instant, the tips of her fingers brushed Mrs. Colton's and Autumn was surprised to find them ice cold. She also saw they were tinted light green, as if smudged by colored chalk or marker.

Autumn tried to smile but couldn't, so she just said, "Thanks."

Mrs. Colton's lips drew back from her teeth in what Autumn guessed was a smile. It must have been a trick of the light or something, but for an instant, Autumn though Mrs. Colton's teeth were tinted green, just like her fingers.

"You're very welcome, child." Her voice was no longer strained. Now she sounded almost as if she were purring. "But you must make me a solemn promise. This little flower—" she reached out and gently touched her green-tinged fingers to the buttercup—"is quite fragile. It will need a great deal of loving attention from you. It would be best for the next few days if you didn't let it out of your sight. Not for an instant. Until it's grown strong enough. Can you do that, Autumn?"

Autumn looked at the tiny yellow flower. It seemed healthy enough to her, but then she didn't know a lot about plants—certainly not as much as Mrs. Colton did.

178

"Sure, okay."

"Good." Mrs. Colton's lips drew even farther back from her greenish teeth and a strange glint came into her eyes. "*Very* good."

At 10:23 Kenneth pulled his van into the parking lot of an office complex. Most of the spaces were already taken, but he found one in front of a pediatrician's and grabbed it, having to cut off a little old lady in a Caddy to do so. The blue-haired munchkin behind the wheel gave him the finger, then stomped on the gas and roared off.

Kenneth smirked. *First come, first served, bitch.*

He cut the engine and, though it wasn't especially warm out, cracked the windows. After he retired, he'd sold his "certified pre-owned" Lexus because he didn't want to fuck with the payments anymore and bought a used van, just to have a second vehicle to run around in. The van was painted light gold, and the interior was stained with faint splotches of what he took to be juice and chocolate. No doubt the vehicle had been used as a kiddie-mover by the previous owners. But today he planned to put it to a far different use. Before leaving the house, he'd removed the two back rows of passenger seats and stored them in the wooden shed in the backyard where Emma kept her gardening tools. He'd need plenty of room for what he had in mind.

The office complex was a long two-story building that sat in the middle of a sea of black-top. The design was professionally generic—salmon-colored brick, green sheet-metal roof, lots of large rectangular windows. The complex was divided into dozens of smaller units, each housing a different business: doctors, tax preparers, psychologists, orthodontists, opticians, lawyers, and the like. But the business that Kenneth was most interested in was located three offices down from the pediatrician's he'd parked in front of. Browning, Curlow, and Burroughs: Accountants. But not only wasn't Kenneth a customer of theirs, he'd never even been inside their office. He was here because this was where Anne Marcino worked.

Once during the summer, he and Anne had been out mowing their lawns at the same time. He'd gone over—just for a little neighborly chat, of course. Although Anne wearing tight cut-off jeans and a bikini top might've had a little something to do with it. Anne obviously wasn't thrilled to see him coming across the street, but she turned off her mower and gave him a reasonable facsimile of a welcoming smile. They'd talked for maybe fifteen minutes, mostly about neighborhood horseshit like how bad the Japanese beetles were this year and whether or not it would rain soon. But at one point during the conversation, Kenneth had started talking about what it was like being retired, and that got them onto the subject of work in general, and the next thing he knew, Anne was telling him she was an accountant for Browning, Curlow, and Burroughs. Kenneth memorized the name on the spot, and when their conversation died off and Anne returned to mowing, Kenneth hurried inside his house, got out the phone book, looked up Browning, Curlow, and Burroughs, then dog-eared the page. At the time he hadn't been sure why he'd done it. He'd simply been acting on instinct, feeling that maybe the information might come in handy someday.

Like today.

He shifted in his seat so he had a good view of the accountants' front door. He'd really gotten lucky with this spot. Any farther away and he would've had a more difficult time watching the door. Any closer, and there was a chance Anne might look out one of those big rectangular windows at the front of the office and see him. Kenneth caught motion out of the corner of his eye and turned to see a short, chubby brunette with huge, heavy breasts carry an infant wrapped in a baby blanket into the pediatrician's. Kenneth figured her breasts were so full because she was lactating, and he imagined her naked, cupping one of her swollen breasts with both hands, taking aim, and then squeezing a jet of white fluid into his face.

He waited for his reborn cock to harden, but it didn't so much as twitch, and Kenneth ground his teeth in frustration. He wasn't certain what had happened between Emma and him this morning—wasn't certain about a lot of things lately, which was why he tried to avoid thinking about them too much. But whatever had gone on, one thing was clear: Emma had done something to ruin his monster cock. Since their confrontation, he hadn't been able to achieve an erection, couldn't even get it partially hard, no matter what he fantasized. It was like whatever miracle had resurrected his cock had been undone, returning him to limp-dick city.

He thought of the fury in Emma's eyes, her fingers mimicking scissors as she placed them around his cock and said, "Snip-snip!"

Goddamned bitch . . . He'd show her—all he needed was a little extra motivation to achieve lift-off. Motivation that only a hot piece like Anne Marcino could provide. He'd just wait here until lunchtime; then when she came walking out the door . . .

As if the thought was all it took to make it happen, the door to Browning, Curlow, and Burroughs opened and Anne stepped outside. Kenneth glanced at the van's dashboard clock and saw it was only a bit past 10:30. Too early for lunch, so what was she doing outside?

Anne didn't have her coat on, but she was carrying her purse. She reached into it and took out a pack of cigarettes and a lighter. Kenneth was surprised; he hadn't known she smoked. He supposed it was no big deal, but he didn't like the smell—or the taste—of cigarette smoke. Besides, watching her put her purse down on the sidewalk that surrounded the complex and light up reminded him of Nancy, aka NOT-E-DD, aka HEADLESS BODY FOUND BEHIND LOCAL BAR. Not the smoking, since Nancy hadn't smoked, but Anne enjoyed dressing provocatively, as had Nancy, and they both had big tits, though Nancy's were larger. Still, Anne was a thousand times sexier than that fat old cunt. Besides, Kenneth thought with a grin, Anne still had her head.

Anne leaned back against the wall, lifting one foot and pressing it to the brick to support herself. She folded her free arm across her chest and hunched her shoulders as if she were cold. She then took a long drag on her cigarette and exhaled a cloud of white smoke into the crisp autumn air. And that's when Kenneth noticed she was crying.

An idea occurred to him then, and he got out of his van, closed the door, and started walking toward Anne, head down, hands in his coat pockets, as if he too were chilly. As he drew near Anne, she said, "Kenneth?"

He resisted the urge to smile as he stopped and looked up. "Oh, hi, Anne. What are you doing here?"

She wiped the tears from her face, then nodded toward the words printed on the office window. "I work here." Her voice was thick, as if she were going to break out sobbing any moment.

He looked at the accountants' office as if only just noticing it. "Oh, yeah. I'm here to see my dentist. Time for the old six-month check-up and cleaning." Kenneth's dentist had an office on the other side of town and he'd just gone there less than a month ago. But he wasn't about to tell Anne that, no sir.

"Look, is everything okay? I mean, not to be nosy or anything, but I can tell you've been crying."

Anne sniffed, rubbed her nose, then let out an embarrassed laugh. "What was your first clue?"

183

She took another drag on her cigarette and blew the smoke out of the corner of her mouth so it wouldn't go into his face.

"I didn't know you smoked," Kenneth said.

"I don't. That is, I quit a few years ago. I sometimes still buy a pack now and then, whenever . . ." She trailed off as a fresh tear rolled down her cheek.

Kenneth invested his voice with as much sympathy as he could fake. "Whenever what?"

Anne took another drag and again blew the smoke away from him. "Whenever I'm really stressed. Or something bad happens." Though the cigarette was only half-smoked, she dropped it to the ground and crushed it with her high-heeled shoe.

Kenneth watched the movement of her leg muscles as she put out her cigarette, and though his cock remained limp, he felt the first sensations of warmth down below.

Anne knelt to retrieve her purse—Kenneth once more enjoying watching her legs work—then stood and tucked it under her arm. "I don't mean to be rude, Kenneth, but I really should go back inside and get to work."

"How many times have I told you to call me Kenny? And whatever's wrong, it might make you feel better to tell someone. I know we're just neighbors—it's not like we're friends or anything—but I still have some time before my appointment, and I'll be happy to listen if you want to talk."

Anne frowned, not in disapproval but in uncer-

GET UP TO
4 FREE BOOKS!

You can have the best fiction delivered to your door for less than what you'd pay in a bookstore or online—only $4.25 a book! Sign up for our book clubs today, and we'll send you **FREE* BOOKS** just for trying it out...**with no obligation to buy, ever!**

LEISURE HORROR BOOK CLUB

With more award-winning horror authors than any other publisher, it's easy to see why CNN.com says "Leisure Books has been leading the way in paperback horror novels." Your shipments will include authors such as RICHARD LAYMON, DOUGLAS CLEGG, JACK KETCHUM, MARY ANN MITCHELL, and many more.

LEISURE THRILLER BOOK CLUB

If you love fast-paced page-turners, you won't want to miss any of the books in Leisure's thriller line. Filled with gripping tension and edge-of-your-seat excitement, these titles feature everything from psychological suspense to legal thrillers to police procedurals and more!

As a book club member you also receive the following special benefits:
- **30% OFF all orders through our website & telecenter!**
- **Exclusive access to special discounts!**
- **Convenient home delivery and 10 days to return any books you don't want to keep.**

There is no minimum number of books to buy, and you may cancel membership at any time. See back to sign up!

*Please include $2.00 for shipping and handling.

YES! ☐

Sign me up for the Leisure Horror Book Club and send my TWO FREE BOOKS! If I choose to stay in the club, I will pay only $8.50* each month, a savings of $5.48!

YES! ☐

Sign me up for the Leisure Thriller Book Club and send my TWO FREE BOOKS! If I choose to stay in the club, I will pay only $8.50* each month, a savings of $5.48!

NAME: _____

ADDRESS: _____

_____

TELEPHONE: _____

E-MAIL: _____

☐ **I WANT TO PAY BY CREDIT CARD.**

☐ VISA   ☐ MasterCard.   ☐ DISCOVER

ACCOUNT #: _____

EXPIRATION DATE: _____

SIGNATURE: _____

Send this card along with $2.00 shipping & handling for each club you wish to join, to:

Horror/Thriller Book Clubs
20 Academy Street
Norwalk, CT 06850-4032

Or fax (must include credit card information!) to: 610.995.9274. You can also sign up online at www.dorchesterpub.com.

*Plus $2.00 for shipping. Offer open to residents of the U.S. and Canada only. Canadian residents please call 1.800.481.9191 for pricing information.

If under 18, a parent or guardian must sign. Terms, prices and conditions subject to change. Subscription subject to acceptance. Dorchester Publishing reserves the right to reject any order or cancel any subscription.

JOIN NOW!

tainty. Kenneth had a good idea what she was thinking. Since when did the old lech who lived across the street become Mr. Sensitive? But he didn't say anything, just kept looking at her while he waited for her to come to a decision.

"I got a phone call this morning before I left for work. It was my mother-in-law. Well, *ex*-mother-in-law. My ex-husband Jamey, he . . ." She took in a shuddering breath. "He was killed in a car accident last night."

"I'm sorry," Kenneth said, though he wasn't, not in the least. "What terrible news."

"Not so much for me, I guess. Don't get me wrong, I'm not happy Jamey's dead, but . . . well, let's just say I made a bad choice when I married him." Her mouth twisted into a bitter grimace. "The world isn't necessarily going to miss him, you know?"

Kenneth was both surprised and delighted to see this side of Anne. A little nastiness added some dark spice to her personality, he thought. He wondered what Jamey had done to earn her hatred. Had he beaten her? Cheated on her? Worse? He supposed it really didn't matter; whatever he'd done to Anne, it was nowhere near as bad as what Kenneth wanted to do to her. But he knew one thing: Anne had lied when she'd said she wasn't happy that her ex was dead. He'd bet she'd fantasized about it a lot. It was probably a goddamned dream come true for her. No, something else was bothering her.

"It's Autumn," she said. "Jamey hasn't seen her

since last Christmas, and he hasn't called since her birthday—and even then he called collect. But despite everything, Autumn still loves her dad. I just . . . don't know how to tell her that he's dead."

All the bitterness was gone from her voice. All that remained was weariness, and in her eyes he saw the pain as she imagined how her daughter would react to the news that Daddy was dead.

As if a switch had been flipped somewhere inside him, Kenneth's cock swelled painfully in his pants, so hard and fast that he thought it might explode. He took a step toward Anne, and the smile he gave her then contained no sympathy and no mercy. Only hunger.

"Let me hip you to something, Anne. Breaking the bad news to Autumn is the least of your worries right now."

Chapter Thirteen

Tristan and Damara drove in silence along a country road on their way back to Zephyr. Damara kept waiting for Tristan to say something, to tell her he never should've agreed to drive her to the Econo Inn, that he hated her for what she'd made him do, how her monstrous power had somehow picked up on his thoughts and brought them to hideous life, resulting in the deformation—and maybe even death—of two women. She waited for him to yell at her for being both selfish and stupid enough to agree to go to a coffee shop when she'd *known* what would happen.

But he said nothing, just kept his eyes on the road as he drove. He might as well have been alone in the car for all the notice he took of her. Finally, she couldn't stand the silence between them anymore.

"It's never been that bad before," she said. "My power, I mean. I've been able to keep control of it ever since that afternoon we . . . spent together."

Tristan still didn't respond. He gripped the steering wheel more tightly and his brow furrowed, as if he were concentrating. But on what? Not knowing was driving Damara crazy.

"I don't know why things have started happening again. Maybe the power can only be suppressed for so long until it reaches some kind of, of critical mass and just *has* to come out. If I'd had any idea things had gotten to this point . . ." She stopped herself. Not because she didn't know what to say, but because she wasn't certain it was the truth. After the attack by Jack Sharp and that poor man in the emergency room, she'd known that her whatever-it-was had suddenly gotten bad. *Real* bad. But she'd been so worried about her mother that she didn't want to admit to herself what a danger she'd become. She'd lived at home all her life, and Claire Ruschmann wasn't just her mother: She was her best, her *only,* friend. Damara's sole companion in her self-imposed exile from everyone and everything else in the world.

She thought of Autumn—the only exception to her exile—and felt a brief flash of guilt. It didn't last long. Damara had a lifetime of experience at suppressing thoughts and emotions, and with minimal effort, her guilt vanished like morning dew in the glare of a hot summer sun.

"Do you know why I haven't killed myself, Tristan?" She'd hoped the question might shock him into reacting, but he might as well not have heard her for all the reaction he showed.

"It's not like I haven't thought about it. I have—

a lot. I've even come close to doing it a couple times. If I were gone, then maybe this power . . . this *force* I have inside me would be gone too, and then nobody else would be hurt by it. But every time I tried to kill myself, a thought stopped me. What if when I die, instead of taking the power with me, I release it? Would the power find someone else to use . . . someone who might not be able to control it as well as I can, or who might not even *want* to? Or would it be free to go wherever it wants, do whatever it wants? Can you imagine what such unleashed power might do?

"And there's something else. What if I succeed in killing myself and I *do* take the power with me. If there's an afterworld, will the power follow me there? And if so, will it bring to life the fears and fantasies of the dead? I don't have any way of answering these questions, so I stay alive, try to control the power the best I can, and pray I've made the right choice."

She paused to see what, if any, impression her words were having on Tristan. He was frowning a little now, which she thought meant he'd been listening, but she wasn't sure.

"Tristan, please . . . *talk* to me!" She didn't like the childish pleading in her voice, but she hoped it would work all the same.

It did.

"I'm afraid to talk to you," Tristan said, his voice so soft it was barely audible above the sound of the car engine and the wheels rolling over the road surface. "Not so much of you and what you can do. But of what I might say or *think* that'll trigger your power. I . . ." He swallowed, glanced at her briefly, then looked away. "I keep hearing that woman screaming as her friend . . . as she . . ."

Damara reached toward him, intending to touch his arm in a comforting gesture. But before her fingers could make contact, Tristan pulled away, a small cry of terror escaping from his throat. He still had hold of the steering wheel and the car veered to the left.

They slid into the opposite lane, and for a terrible instant Damara feared they would slam into an oncoming car, but the road in front of them was empty. Tristan tried to pull them back into their lane, but he overcorrected and the car slid too far. The passenger-side tires grabbed hold of the shoulder, and the car started juddering as it threatened to go off into the ditch. Finally, Tristan managed to get back onto the road and straighten out the car again. He eased off the accelerator and continued driving more slowly.

"I'm sorry, Damara. I didn't mean to react like that. I guess I'm just jumpy after . . . what happened back in Waldron."

Damara's heart was still pounding from the adrenaline rush of their car nearly running off the road. She nodded her head and folded her arms so her hands wouldn't be anywhere near Tristan.

"Sure, I understand."

A sign flashed by. *Zephyr: 8 mi.*

Damara turned her head to look out the window. She watched the fields and farmhouses go past and hoped Tristan wouldn't notice she was crying.

Not long after that, Tristan pulled into Damara's driveway. But he didn't turn off the engine or unbuckle his seatbelt.

Damara got the hint.

"Thanks for picking me up at the hospital, and for driving me to the hotel to check on Mom. Thanks for the clothes, too. I'll return them after I've run them through the wash." She picked up the plastic bag they'd given her at the hospital to hold her robe, keys, and pain medication, then undid her belt and opened the passenger door. She started to get out, but a jolt of pain shot through her injured leg, and she took in a hissing breath. She didn't turn to look at Tristan, though. She didn't want him to feel obligated to assist her in getting out. Because doing so would mean he had to touch her, and she couldn't bear to watch him shrink away from her again.

So she gritted her teeth, took hold of the doorframe and hauled herself out of the car. Hot fire seared her leg and she wondered if she'd torn her stitches. She didn't care if she had, though; she'd made it out on her own.

Tristan leaned over so he could speak to her through the open passenger door. "Try not to worry about your mom, Mara. I'm sure she'll come to her senses soon."

Damara wasn't, but she smiled and nodded just the same. "Thanks again." She started to close the door.

191

"Look, would you like me to call you later or—"

The sound of the passenger door closing cut off the rest of Tristan's words. She gave a last wave, then turned and started heading toward the front door. It took her a long time to make it across the walkway and up the front steps, but Tristan sat in his car and watched her the entire time. She reached the door, fished her keys out of the plastic bag, opened the door and went inside. Only after she closed and locked the door did she hear Tristan back out of the driveway. She wanted to go to the window and watch, but she didn't let herself. Instead, she hobbled to the kitchen, filled a glass of water at the tap, took another pain pill, drank half the water, then poured out the rest into the sink. She set the glass down and paused, listening for the sound of scratching claws or the whispery echoes of a little boy's voice coming from the drain. But she heard nothing.

She then hobbled into her bedroom and, careful of her wounded leg, crawled beneath the covers and cried.

The first thing Tristan noticed when he walked into the house was the smell—a sour odor like rotten eggs and spoiled meat. He went into the kitchen and swore when he saw the gray sludge oozing from beneath the basement door. The towel he'd crammed into the crack yesterday was completely soaked in the gray muck, and he wasn't sure, but it almost looked as if the goo was beginning to eat away at the towel's fabric. What the hell *was* that stuff?

There was no help for it. He was going to have to call someone, a plumber, the sanitation department . . . hell, maybe the national guard. Whatever the gray shit was, he didn't feel like trying to deal with it himself, not after everything he'd seen today. A man with a rogue appendix . . . a long-lost father and husband who returned after seventeen years looking as if he hadn't aged a day . . . two women who'd suddenly, grotesquely changed because of a chance remark he'd made.

He felt ashamed of himself for how he'd treated Damara. He'd acted as if she were a monster—just like she'd feared he would.

Don't be so hard on yourself. It's not every day that you learn a woman you grew up with—whom you nearly made love to, for godsakes—has the ability to bring nightmares to life. Anyone would've reacted the same way, if not worse.

Maybe so. But he couldn't stop thinking about the hurt in Damara's eyes after he'd pulled away from her touch and nearly ran them off the road.

He looked down at the gray sludge. It extended a foot, maybe a foot and a half from the bottom of the basement door. He wasn't sure, but he thought maybe there was more goo now than when he'd first entered the kitchen a few moments ago. A new thought occurred to him then, and accompanying it came a fluttery-crawly feeling in his stomach. Could Damara somehow be responsible for this muck? It didn't look like anything he'd ever seen or heard of before, and last night he *had* been obsessing over the cluttered state his mother had left the house in. He supposed it was possible—after all, not even Damara seemed to understand the extent of her abilities. But even if she had inadvertently brought this gray sludge into existence, unless she could wish it gone with a simple act of will, and somehow Tristan didn't think it would be that easy, then he still had to deal with the muck on his own.

He started toward the drawer where his mother kept the phone book, but he stopped when he saw Damara standing in the kitchen's open doorway. No, not Damara. Something that looked a lot like her . . . And then it came back to him, all of it. Everything the two of them had done last night, and he knew none of it had been a dream.

"I know you want her, Tristan," she said, her voice so much like Damara's, but with the sound of thrumming cicadas underneath. Her multifaceted eyes twitched continuously, back and forth, up and down, but he knew they were focused on him. "But she can't have you. You're mine."

She unfurled her wings, reached out with all her limbs, and came toward him.

The playground was full of children running and laughing, swinging on swings, sliding down slides, and chasing one another for no particular reason other than the pure joy of pursuit. But one girl didn't join in with the others. She walked slowly across the gravel-covered play area, holding a tiny flower planted in a Styrofoam cup cradled against her chest, as if it were a helpless baby animal that needed protection. She made her way to the edge of the playground, where the gravel ended and the green grass of the soccer field began. She sat down, crossed her legs, then placed the cup on the grass in front of her. She looked at the buttercup, examining its yellow petals and its light green stem as she tried to determine if the flower really was as fragile as Mrs. Colton had said.

Autumn felt creepy about accepting a gift from the woman, and she was considering planting the buttercup right here. She poked the ground with her index finger and found the soil soft. She should be able to dig a large enough hole using the scissors she'd "borrowed" from her teacher's class-room. If the flower was strong enough—and de-spite its small size it looked plenty strong to Autumn—it would survive just fine here at the edge of the playground. Sure, winter would be coming before long, but her mom had told her once that trees and flowers didn't die when winter came. They just went to sleep and then woke up in spring, when it was warm again. With any luck, the buttercup would be back in spring, and maybe it would even have babies, too. In a few years, there could be a lot of buttercups here, maybe enough to cover the whole soccer field. The image appealed to Autumn, and she decided to do it.

She reached into her right sock, where she'd

hidden the scissors, and pulled them out so she could start digging right away. She didn't know how long it would take her to plant the buttercup, but they only got fifteen minutes for morning recess, and she wanted to get the job done as quickly as she could so she'd have some time left to play. She chose a spot where the ground seemed softest and plunged the scissors into the soil.

But before she could pull the scissors out of the ground for another jab, she saw a streak of brown coming toward her across the green of the soccer field. She looked up and couldn't believe what she was seeing. It was a tiny dachshund puppy, and it was bounding toward her, eyes bright and tongue lolling happily from the corner of its mouth. The puppy ran right up to her and, without the slightest hesitation, jumped into her lap. The little thing was panting hard and she could feel its tiny heart pounding where its chest rested against her leg. She left the scissors sticking in the ground and began petting and stroking the dog with both hands.

"Hi, puppy. Where did you come from?" Autumn asked. The dachshund's only response was to start licking her hand. It tickled and Autumn laughed, but she didn't pull her hand away.

Klyburn Elementary was located in the middle of a suburban neighborhood, so Autumn knew the dog could've come from anywhere. It wasn't wearing a collar, but it—she did a quick check—*he* looked in good shape, so she didn't think he was a stray.

"You're a good boy, do you know that? A very good boy!"

The dachshund's tail whipped back and forth in doggy delight, the tip curving around so far that it touched his haunches.

Autumn glanced over her shoulder and was glad to see that none of the other kids seemed to have noticed the dachshund's arrival. An animal on the playground was a big deal and always attracted a crowd of children who wanted to pet, play, or just look at it. But Autumn didn't want to share the dachshund, which she was already beginning to think of as hers.

She'd wanted a puppy for as long as she could remember. Her grandmother on her dad's side of the family had several dachshunds, and before Autumn could even walk, she'd loved visiting Grandma's and playing with the dogs. But the dogs were already old by then, and as Autumn grew older, one by one, they died. When the last one was gone, Grandma sold her house and moved in with Autumn's Aunt Patty, who lived in Indiana. Autumn had been begging her mom for a puppy ever since, but pet allergies ran in her mom's family, so every time Autumn asked, the answer was no.

But here was a puppy sitting in her lap, and not just any puppy, but a *dachshund* puppy, and it was a rich chocolate brown, just like she'd always wanted. She knew she couldn't keep the dog. Even if it didn't already belong to someone, *and* she

197

could figure out a way to keep him from running off when she went back to class, *and* she could manage to sneak him onto the school bus and then into her house, her mom's allergies would flare up, the puppy would be discovered, and that would be the end of that.

Autumn leaned forward and let the puppy lick her nose. Sometimes life could be so unfair!

The dachshund stopped licking and turned its head, raised its ears, and growled.

Autumn felt the hair on the back of her neck stand up. "Is something wrong, boy?" She held on to the dachshund, as if she were afraid he might suddenly run off. "What is it?"

She heard a soft rustling sound and realized it was coming from the direction of the buttercup. She looked at the Styrofoam cup and saw that the tiny plant inside was quivering, its yellow petals widening, lengthening, becoming thicker . . . Green tendrils burst out of the side of the cup, unfurled and began slithering forward like featureless snakes as they continued to grow. The yellow petals became flat, fleshy fronds broad as human hands, and their color changed from a warm, cheerful yellow to a nauseating grayish-green that made Autumn think of diseased phlegm. Styrofoam was ripped apart as the plant grew too large for its cup. Potting soil spilled onto the grass, but the mucus-colored fronds didn't fall over. They remained upright, supported by a thick central stalk covered with tiny black thorns. Clear liquid oozed like sap from the tips of the thorns and dripped heavily to the grass. The root tendrils stretched toward Autumn, curling and uncurling like fingers impatient to grasp hold of what they reached for.

The buttercup's transformation had occurred so swiftly that Autumn had barely realized she was in danger by the time the first of the tendrils brushed her shoe. The dachshund puppy started barking then, not high-pitched yaps but deep warning barks, and then it leaped out of Autumn's lap and attacked the plant-thing.

Autumn's grandma had once told her that while dachshunds looked cute, they had originally been bred as hunting dogs. Their tiny legs and long muscular bodies were designed for going down badger holes and dragging their prey back to the surface. *They're tough little fellas,* her grandma had said. *That's one of the reasons I love them so much, I guess.* Seeing the chocolate-brown puppy tear into the ugly thing that Mrs. Colton's buttercup had become, Autumn knew her grandma had told the truth.

The dachshund's teeth pierced a frond and a thick foul-smelling substance that looked like pus gushed forth. The plant jerked and spasmed as if it were in pain, and the tendrils drew away from Autumn and whipped toward the dachshund. The puppy hacked out a mouthful of pus and bit into another frond just as the tips of the tendrils sank into its flesh. The dog whined in pain, but it didn't stop its attack. If anything, it fought more fiercely, biting, tearing, ripping, clawing until the central part of the plant was a chewed-up, pus-splattered mess. But the plant wasn't dead yet. The tendrils continued burrowing into the dachshund, and as Autumn watched in horror, they began to pulse. Within seconds the green tendrils began to darken, turning red, then purple, then black as they drained the puppy of fluid with awful sucking sounds. The dachshund began to shrink in on itself, its coat drawing tight against its skeleton, eyes drying and wrinkling like raisins, tongue withering to a lump of leather in its mouth, but though it was obviously dying—and dying horribly at that—the dachshund fought on.

Autumn felt something happen inside her. It was as if a door within her mind had suddenly been slammed shut, or heavy curtains drawn across a window to block out the light. She slowly stood up, turned, and began walking away from what was left of the plant and the dog. She didn't think anything as she crossed the playground, didn't feel anything, didn't even really see or hear anything. She just kept walking at a slow, measured pace until she reached the door to the school, opened it, and went inside. A few seconds later, the bell rang.

Recess was over.

Chapter Fourteen

It's Wednesday afternoon on Pandora Drive, and the street is quiet. The kids are in school, their parents still at work. The only activity comes from squirrels scurrying about, rustling through leaves, climbing up and down trees, crawling along phone lines with a balance and ease that no human tightrope walker could ever hope to match. Winter is still weeks away, but the squirrels know it's coming, and their kind hasn't survived for thousands of years by putting off till tomorrow what should've been done yesterday.

But if anyone was present to observe the squirrels at work, he or she might notice the animals move faster than usual, their motions abrupt and nervous. They keep sitting up and looking around, whiskers twitching, moist black eyes scanning the area as if they're on guard. The squirrels know winter is coming, but they know that something else is coming, too. Something bad. And it's coming soon.

Tim Waggoner

* * *

"Nice place you got here, Anne. Thanks for asking me in."

Anne didn't answer, but Kenneth didn't take it personally. He figured it was hard to talk with a sock jammed into your mouth and your lips sealed by duct tape.

She lay on the couch, wrists and ankles bound by tape as well. She was naked, her blouse, skirt, and panties on the floor where Kenneth had tossed them. Well, she wasn't entirely naked. He'd left her high heels and earrings on; he liked the look.

Kenneth sat in a wooden chair he'd brought in from the dining room and placed in front of the couch. He'd moved the coffee table out of the way, not only to make space for the chair but to give him room to work. He wasn't quite sure what he was going to do with Anne yet, but he was confident he'd think of something. Right now he was just enjoying gazing at her naked body and feeling the deliciously painful sensation of his hard monster cock pressing against the constraint of his pants. On the floor at his feet rested a knife he'd brought in from the kitchen.

He was grateful to Anne for providing the . . . inspiration he'd needed to achieve an erection again. Not only had Kenneth gotten hard once more, but he'd found strength and renewed confidence surging through his entire body, making him feel thirty years younger. He'd had no problem at all getting Anne into his van, then subduing and binding her. He'd then driven to her place and car-

202

ried her inside, thrilled to find that she seemed almost weightless to him now. He'd plopped her onto the couch, then hurried outside, got in the van, backed out of Anne's driveway and pulled into his. He didn't know how long his play date with Anne would last, and he didn't want Emma to come home and find his van parked across the street.

When he'd returned to Anne's, he'd found her on the floor, trying to crawl toward the phone. Rather than being angry, he'd laughed in delight, scooped her up, tossed her back onto the couch, and removed her clothes. Now he sat here looking at her, his penis throbbing in time with his pulse.

"I've been watching you for a long time, Anne. Ever since you and Autumn moved in, as a matter of fact. And you knew I was watching, didn't you? That's why you dress the way you do. You *want* me to see, you *like* teasing me . . . don't you?"

Anne's eyes held equal measures of anger and fear, and she shook her head no.

"You can deny it all you want, bitch." He smiled. "That just makes the game all the more fun."

Anne let out a muffled cry of frustration and thrashed back and forth on the couch. The motion made her large breasts jiggle and Kenneth watched them appreciatively. She was such a beautiful woman, quite possible the loveliest he'd ever seen in person. She was slender with hardly any fat on her. Her skin was creamy and smooth, and he'd been pleased to see that she kept her blond pubic hair—so blond he wondered if she dyed it—neatly trimmed. A trim quim. Her belly was taut, her arms and legs toned. She had a few stretch marks, souvenirs of bringing Autumn into the world, but instead of marring her beauty, they were a contrast that accentuated it. Her breasts weren't as large as Nancy's, but they were full, round, and firm, the brown aureolae large as half dollars, the nipples thick and erect. It was those nipples that told him she was enjoying this every bit as much as he was. Otherwise, why would they be standing at attention?

Quit stalling, Kenny, a voice within him—hungry, impatient—urged. *Show her what's on the menu this afternoon.*

Good idea.

Kenneth leaned over and took off his shoes and socks. Then he stood and removed his shirt. He let it fall to the floor, then stood for a moment, giving Anne an opportunity to look him over. He figured he wasn't in bad shape for a guy in his early sixties. His pecs weren't as firm as they had been when he was twenty, but at least they hadn't become droopy man-titties. His chest hair was thick and though it was mostly white, there was still some black in the mix. But this was just the appetizer. Time to hit her with the entrée. He began unbuckling his belt.

His cock was so big and hard by now that he had trouble slipping his pants down over it. Anne's eyes widened when she saw the bulge in his underwear, and he laughed. A second later, his underwear was off and discarded, and his monster cock was free in all its tumescent glory. It was nearly as long as Kenneth's forearm now, and just about as thick. The skin was purple and stretched shiny tight, and the shaft was covered with swollen discolored veins the size of fat earthworms. The head was a round hard knob and a drop of clear fluid glistened at the tip.

Kenneth put his hands on his hips and spread his legs out, assuming what he figured was an impressive stance, kind of like Superman or something. Superschlong.

"So . . . what do you think?"

Her eyes grew so wide that Kenneth thought they might pop right out of their sockets.

He grinned. "I figured you'd like it. Gal like you, I'm sure you've seen plenty of cock in your time, up close and personal, eh? But you've never seen one as fine as this bad boy, am I right?"

Anne didn't respond. She just kept staring at his monster cock, her face a shade paler than it had been a moment ago.

"Got any preferences where I put it first? I guess your mouth is out, but that still leaves two other holes for me to play with. I'd flip a coin, but I don't seem to have any change on me at the moment." He chuckled at his little joke.

Anne shook her head and made high-pitched noises through the duct tape. She squirmed as if she were trying to work her way deeper into the couch and get away from him.

Kenneth smiled. "Don't go getting shy on me now, Anne. No one likes a cock tease, you know."

He stepped toward her, and she let out a muffled scream. As if the sound of her terror was a signal, he knelt down, snatched up the knife, and rushed forward. He quickly sawed through the duct tap binding Anne's ankles, and then before she could try to kick him or get off the couch, he pressed the blade to her flat belly.

"Lie still and spread your legs, or I'll slice a hole in your stomach and fuck that." He gazed into her eyes and waited for her to make her decision. He saw the terror drain away, replaced by resignation. She nodded, relaxed, and opened her legs to him. He was a bit disappointed that she'd given in to him so easily, but his cock wasn't. He could feel the blood coursing through it, could sense its eagerness to have its desires sated. It was feeding time at the zoo. Kenneth slid the knife in between the couch cushions where he could get at it if he needed it. He then pushed Anne's bound wrists up over her head and climbed on top of her. He maneuvered his dick into position and thrust it inside her.

Her cunt was as dry as Sahara sandpaper, and she screamed as his monster cock penetrated her body. To Kenneth, it felt as if he were wearing a condom made of fiberglass insulation and steel wool. It hurt like a motherfucker, but it was a *good* hurt, a *great* hurt, a felt-so-fine-he-had-to-grit-his-teeth-to-keep-from-shooting-his-load hurt.

"You think that's something? Wait until you feel this!"

He slowly withdrew his cock and then slammed it into her again. Once more Anne screamed and every muscle in her body went rigid. Kenneth felt warm wetness envelope his dick, and when he pulled back this time, he saw his swollen shaft was coated with thick, dark blood. He smiled. Anne wasn't dry anymore.

"I think natural lubricants are the best, don't you?" Kenneth laughed and started pumping away in earnest. He closed his eyes as waves of pleasure beyond anything he'd ever known, anything he'd ever conceived possible, rippled along the nerve endings of his cock and into his central nervous system before radiating back out to every cell in his body. As he continued to fuck Anne, he imagined his penis growing longer, wider, harder with each stroke.

Anne was screaming constantly now, and she bucked beneath him as her body was wracked by a series of violent spasms. Kenneth opened his eyes and saw that Anne's head was tilted back and resting on the arm of the couch. The center of the duct tape over her mouth was pulsating.

Bigger, he thought. *Longer . . .*

Anne stopped screaming. She made a chuffing sound and blood sprayed out of her nostrils. The tape tore free from her mouth and the sodden crimson mess that had been a sock was forced out. It hit Anne's left breast with a sickeningly wet *plap* and stuck there.

Kenneth watched as the turgid head of his cock emerged from Anne's mouth, slick with blood and bits of viscera. He could see the light dimming in her eyes, but she wasn't gone yet.

"Hang in there, Anne," Kenneth panted as he continued thrusting, the head of his cock bobbing in and out of Anne's mouth in a nightmarish game of peekaboo. "Stay with me just another few seconds . . ."

A guttural cry burst from deep in his throat as thick jets of semen streamed out of Anne's mouth, shot over the arm of the couch, and splashed onto the floor. Kenneth tensed his groin muscles, flexed his cock, and was rewarded with the raw wet sound of tearing flesh as his gigantic member—now more than four feet long—rose upward from the streaming red ruin that had once been Anne Marcino. Cum continued to jet out the tip of his penis for another few seconds until it finally subsided to a trickle that dripped into the open cavity of Anne's corpse.

Kenneth let out a shuddering breath as he gazed upon the remains of his latest lover. A part of him—now so small and weak that it was almost nonexistent—recoiled from the desecration he'd done to his neighbor. But the rest of him felt only exultation.

"Goddamn! I split that bitch right down the middle!" He laughed and considered what more he might do to Anne. After all, just because she was dead didn't mean that he had to stop having fun. But as much as he wanted to go on playing with her, he didn't want to waste any time. School would be letting out soon, and he wanted to be ready to greet Autumn properly when she got home.

Claire was having the most wonderful dream. Jerry had returned to her, and they'd spent the day making love near the bank of a river, beneath blue skies, white clouds, and a warm summer sun. Now they were lying on their backs, naked, covered with each other's juices, the thick musky scent of their love-making hanging heavy and sweet in the air as they looked up at the clouds and spoke of what shapes they saw in them. It was the best dream Claire had ever had, and she never wanted to wake from it.

But then, as if it came from a great distance away, Claire heard the jangling of a telephone. She tried to ignore it, but the noise continued, growing louder and more insistent. The clouds, the sky, the sun, and the river slowly faded, and Claire opened her eyes and experienced a crushing sense of loss. She was lying on a bed in a hotel room, and the phone on the night stand was ringing. At first she wasn't sure where she was or how she'd gotten here, but then she remembered: It hadn't been a dream, at least not the most important part. Jerry *had* come back to her, and they had spent the night and most of the day making love.

The phone continued to demand her attention, but she let it ring. She tried to turn to look at Jerry but her body felt awkward and stiff, and she couldn't quite manage to do so.

"It's okay, babe. I'm still here."

His voice sounded close to her ear. Reassured, she started to reach for the phone, but her right arm wouldn't move. Weird. Maybe she'd slept on it wrong and it had lost circulation. She decided not to worry about it and picked up the phone receiver with her left hand and placed it to her ear.

"Hello?"

"Claire, this is Gene."

At first the name and the voice didn't mean anything to her, but then she realized who it was. Her boss.

She started to sit up, but her body felt heavy and sluggish on the right side, and it took an extra effort to accomplish this simple task. What the hell had happened to her? Had she had a stroke or something? She wasn't ancient, but she was old enough for that to be a possibility, and strokes did run in her family. She was still too groggy to deal with more than one thing at a time, though, and she decided to concentrate on Gene first.

"Hi, Gene. What's up?" Her voice was thick from sleep.

"You are, I hope. I was going over the registrations in the computer and came across yours. I asked Arlene about it, and she just spilled the beans. I'm not happy that you took off at the start of your shift to spend the night in one of our rooms—though you at least had the good grace to pay for it. I'd like you to come in early for your shift tonight so we can discuss the matter. But right now I'd like to remind you that check-out time is noon, and it's now 1:48. Get up, check out, go home and freshen up, and we'll discuss your future with the Econo Inn—assuming you'd still like to have one—tonight." He hung up without waiting for a reply.

Claire held the receiver for a moment longer before replacing it on the base unit. She was almost fully awake now, and she was pissed. How dare that little prick talk to her like that! She had to admit that checking into a room with Jerry hadn't exactly been the most responsible thing she'd ever done, but Gene hadn't even allowed her to tell her side of it. After all, seeing her husband again for the first time in almost twenty years could make any woman a little crazy.

To hell with it. She'd try to smooth things over with Gene tonight before her shift, and if she couldn't and she ended up getting fired, it would be worth it. The time she and Jerry had spent together had been fantastic, better than it ever had been before he'd left, and it had been pretty goddamned good then.

"C'mon, hon," Jerry said. "We'd better get moving." He scooted over to the edge of the bed—as did Claire—and then stood. Claire did the same.

"You overheard?" she asked as they walked together toward the bathroom.

"Of course I did. I'll be happy to tear that little bastard's head off for you if you want."

They stepped into the bathroom and walked over to the toilet without turning on the lights. Jerry put the lid up and peed, and Claire waited until he'd finished. They both felt better afterward. Jerry then flushed the toilet and the two of them went over to the sink to wash their hands.

"Don't worry about Gene," Claire said. "I can handle him. He's not worth getting worked up about."

They finished washing and dried their hands. They started to leave the bathroom, but Claire happened to glance toward the mirror over the sink, and what she saw made her pause. She turned on the light and stepped back to the mirror and took a good long look at her reflection . . . and Jerry's.

"I told you we'd be together forever, didn't I?"

Kenneth sat naked, covered with blood, his erect monster cock shrunken to a more manageable twelve inches for the time being. He'd positioned the chair so that he could watch the front door from the living room while still keeping Anne's corpse in sight. He'd moved the coffee table next to him, and had placed on its surface all the supplies he'd gathered from his search of the house. The duct tape and kitchen knife were still there, but he'd added a coil of rope, an enema kit he'd found in the bathroom, a sawed-off mop handle, an old-fashioned pearl-handled hair brush that was perfect for spanking, and the *pièce de resistance,* a vibrator and a tube of KY that he'd found in one of Anne's dresser drawers. He was ready; now all he had to do was wait. He glanced at the digital readout on the cable box sitting on top of the television. 2:17. School let out at 2:30. He wouldn't have to wait much longer.

He stroked his cock and tried to decide which of his tools he would use on Autumn first.

Tristan thrashed as he tried to free himself from the sticky white substance he was bound in, but it was no use. The stuff was too strong, and he couldn't get any leverage hanging from the living room ceiling like this. His feet were only a few inches from the floor, but those inches might as well have been miles for all the good they did him. He was almost entirely encased in the cocoon spun by the nightmarish version of Damara his mind had conjured. Only his face was uncovered, and even then there were enough strands attached to his jaw that he could barely move his mouth enough to speak.

Below him, the floor was covered by a thin film of gray that grew thicker and deeper the longer he hung here. Much longer, and it would be up to the level of his feet, and he didn't want to think about what the muck might do to his flesh if he got any on himself.

Nightmare Damara hung upside down from the ceiling in front of him, crouching so that her face was aligned with his, their eyes level with each other. He couldn't stop thinking of all the things they had done together last night, and the images that kept playing in his mind made him feel sick to his stomach. How he ever could have mistaken this . . . this *thing* for Damara was beyond him. It was as if he'd been under some sort of spell, a delusion that had made him believe this creature was the real Damara. He wondered if such delusion was part of Damara's power and decided it must be. Look at Claire—she hadn't seemed to notice anything wrong with the Jerry Ruschmann she'd brought to life, even though he remained the same age he'd been when he'd vanished. Tristan wasn't sure why he was no longer deluded himself. Maybe because Damara had told him the truth and he'd witnessed her power at work on others. Or maybe the dreams and fantasies Damara's power brought into existence could only last so long before they began to break down. Whatever the reason, Tristan now saw the nightmare Damara for what she was, but that knowledge was of little use to him now that he was trapped like a fly in a spider's web.

Nightmare Damara gazed at him with insectine eyes, and Tristan couldn't read any emotion or thought there, could only see tiny images of his face reflected in their multitude of facets. He wasn't surprised to see that he looked scared a hundred times over.

"It's going to happen soon, my love," Nightmare Damara said in her cicada-drone voice.

Tristan tried to respond, but his throat was so dry that his reply came out in a soft rasp. "What's going to happen?"

She reached out to touch his cheek—with one of her human hands, thank Christ—and he tried to draw away, but he was bound too tightly to move. Her fingers felt cold on his skin.

"My chance to finally get you all to myself." She smiled. "Won't that be nice?"

And then she leaned forward to kiss him. He closed his eyes as her cold lips touched his and wondered what was going to happen to him . . . and to the real Damara.

* * *

Autumn sat on the school bus and looked out the window. Rosemary Valiquette was sitting in a seat directly in front of her, and she'd turned around and tried to get Autumn to talk to her, but without success. Autumn hadn't responded to her friend's words, had barely even heard them. All she could think about was the way the dachshund had looked—so shrunken and withered—and how it had been killed saving her from Mrs. Colton's buttercup. Except it *hadn't* been a buttercup, had it? It had been something else, something bad, something nasty and evil, just like Mrs. Colton.

Autumn wondered what she would tell her mother when she got home, or if she should tell her anything at all. Her mother was always good about listening to her, but Autumn wasn't sure she'd believe what happened at the playground today. Maybe she'd tell Damara first. But to talk to Damara, she'd have to go across the street and then she'd be next door to Mrs. Colton's house. And she didn't think she could stand being that close to the woman, not after what her buttercup had become and what it had done to her puppy. Well, she still had a little time to decide. She was one of the last kids to be dropped off by the school bus. Maybe she'd figure something out by then.

The bus continued down the street as it made its roundabout way toward Pandora Drive.

Emma finished getting her classroom ready for the next day, then put on her coat, picked up her canvas bag, turned out the lights, and stepped into the hallway. She closed the door but left it unlocked so the custodian could get inside to clean. She started walking down the hallway and when she came to the office, instead of going inside to check her mailbox and say goodbye to the secretary, she kept going. She wanted to get home and get to work.

She'd seen Autumn at lunchtime, but she'd hadn't seen the buttercup she'd given the little temptress. She wasn't sure what had happened to the flower, but she'd had the sense that it had failed in its purpose. She'd taken some measure of satisfaction upon seeing Autumn sitting subdued at the lunch table, not talking to anyone, not eating, just staring off into the distance as if she'd been traumatized. It appeared that her little present hadn't been completely without impact, though it hadn't performed as well as Emma had hoped. But that was all right. Some weeds were more stubborn than others and took more effort to pull, that's all.

Emma Colton—the whites of her eyes tinted a sour green—stepped outside and headed for the teachers' parking lot.

Claire was about halfway home by the time she began to feel comfortable driving. Coordinating her left hand with Jerry's right was almost natural now and required little thought on either of their parts. Her vision was a little wonky, though. Their eyes were still learning to work together, and sometimes she saw a double image. But she figured if she drove slowly enough and stuck to back roads, they'd be okay.

She felt bad for what she'd put Damara through. When she got home, she'd do her best to explain and hope that her daughter understood. She thought she probably would. Damara was a good kid. Oh, sure, she had her troubles, but who didn't?

Jerry was looking forward to getting home, too. It would be the first time he'd set foot inside his house in seventeen years. He'd been gone a long time, but he was determined to make up for lost time. It might take some work, but he, Claire, and Damara were going to be a family again. The three of them, together.

Forever.

Damara tossed and turned in her sleep, and though each movement sent bolts of pain shooting through her injured leg, she didn't wake up, not completely. She hovered in the dusky twilight between sleep and consciousness, nothingness and awareness, and if the thoughts, feelings, and images that drifted through her mind weren't exactly dreams, they nevertheless seemed as real and as disturbing as any nightmare. Images of blood and death, darkness and hate. The past, the present, and worst of all . . . the future.

Chapter Fifteen

Emma pulled into her driveway, glad to see Kenneth's van was there. Whenever he had one of his little episodes of independence, he had a tendency to hop in his van and take off for the day. She didn't know where he went—a bar, a strip club, or maybe just driving around for hours—and she didn't care. He eventually got over his latest childish rebellion against her and came home, and the balance of power in their relationship was restored—in her favor, of course. It looked like Kenneth had gotten over this morning's . . . disagreement faster than usual. She smiled with satisfaction. Maybe after all these years, the fool was finally learning who ruled their roost.

There was room enough to park beside the van, barely, but Emma chose to park behind it, blocking the vehicle so Kenneth couldn't back out if the urge to leave suddenly came upon him again when she entered the house. She turned off the engine, got out, and went into the house through the back door. The moment she closed the door, however, she realized something was wrong. She heard no TV, no stereo, no sound of Kenneth puttering around. Though he always gave in after they fought, he would make more noise than usual around the house for a day or two, his passive-aggressive way of venting his anger at her. But the house was silent.

"Kenneth?" she called. When she received no answer, she went into the dining room, put her canvas bag, keys, and purse on the table, then removed her coat and slung it over the back of a chair.

"Kenneth, are you here?" She called out louder this time, but she didn't shout. She refused to allow Kenneth to provoke her into yelling.

Still no answer.

She wondered briefly if this silence was a new tactic on Kenneth's part, if he was hiding out somewhere in the house, say the attic or basement, and pretending not to hear her. She considered going through the house and checking each room for him, but then she realized that he wasn't here. There was only one place he could be, only one place he'd been obsessed with the last couple of days. The Marcinos'.

Fury welled up within her, but she prided herself on her emotional control. She clamped down on the anger before it could overwhelm her, but she didn't attempt to banish it. She welcomed the anger, for she knew she could make good use of it—as long as she maintained control.

She started toward the front door.

* * *

Kenneth sat up straight when he heard the door-knob turn, and his cock grew a couple inches longer in anticipation. He stood and grinned, imagining the shock on Autumn's face when she saw the present he had for her—and what that present had done to her poor mommy.

But even as the door began to open, he knew something was wrong. He hadn't heard the sound of the school bus pulling up in front of the house and stopping to let Autumn off. A second later, the door swung open wide and he knew why he hadn't heard the bus.

"I thought I'd find you over here, you lecherous sonofabitch."

Emma's voice was cold and deadly, and the menace in it sent a shiver through his penis. The organ retracted several inches, as if it were a frightened animal backing away from a fearsome predator.

No, he thought. *Don't let her get to you.* He was trying to encourage both himself and his cock, and it seemed to work, for his dick stopped its retreat.

Emma stepped into the foyer—leaving the door open—and her gaze flicked to the couch where Anne's mutilated body lay soaking in its own blood. Emma turned back to Kenneth and sneered. "I wish I could say that I'm surprised, but I'm not." She glanced at the coffee table and the assortment of tools he'd gathered. "So now that you've had your way with Anne, you're planning on indulging in more playtime with Autumn, eh?" She took a step forward and her gaze bore into him. "Too bad that I'm going to have to spoil your fun." She raised her right hand. The fingers were gone; sprouting from her wrist in their place was a pair of garden shears, the blades honed to razor sharpness.

Emma grinned, revealing green-tinged gums. "Like I told you, Kenneth: snip-snip!" The shears opened and closed twice to emphasize her words, the *shhkt-shhkt* sound making Kenneth wince.

Kenneth didn't think to question how his wife's flesh and bone had been transformed into deadly steel, any more than he wondered how his limp dick had become a monster cock. It somehow seemed perfectly natural that these things should be so. Besides, what man would take the time to think when his mad-as-hell wife was about to cut his dick off?

Kenneth lunged for the coffee table, intending to grab the knife there, but his fingers instead closed around the vibrator. Emma came at him, and without time to grab a better weapon, he whirled around and slammed the vibrator against the side of her head, his gigantic cock smacking the outside of her leg as he did. Emma let out a grunt of pain as the vibrator shattered in Kenneth's hand. She stumbled to the side and staggered, but she didn't fall. A broken piece of plastic had cut her, and a thin trickle of blood began to run down the side of her face.

Kenneth hesitated for a split second. In all the years they'd been married, he'd never laid a hand on Emma, no matter how many times he'd wanted to and how many times she'd deserved it. A line had been crossed and now that it had, Kenneth knew there was no going back.

He stepped forward—careful to stay clear of Emma's shears—grabbed her by the shoulders and shoved her toward the couch. She stumbled backwards, arms windmilling as she tried to maintain her balance, but then the back of her legs hit the couch and she fell onto Anne's corpse. Or rather, given its eviscerated state, fell *into* it. Emma screeched in fury and disgust as blood splattered her clothes and organs slid beneath her. Kenneth took the opportunity to snatch the knife off the coffee table. He wasn't going to bother with fucking Emma to death. The crusty old cunt didn't deserve to be done in by something as grand and glorious as his monster cock. He was going to slit her fucking throat and be done with it. He gripped the knife tight and stepped toward the couch.

And that's when he heard Autumn scream.

He froze and turned to look at her. She'd dropped her backpack on the floor and was holding both hands over her mouth as if she were trying to hold back her screams. She needn't have bothered, though; they still came through just fine. Her eyes were wild with terror, and Kenneth almost felt sorry for the poor kid, coming home to find her mother gutted, one of her neighbors stuck ass-first in the body cavity, while another stood naked and covered with mommy's dried blood, holding a knife and sporting a giant erection.

Life could be a real bitch sometimes.

Autumn felt dizzy and darkness flickered at the edges of her vision. She'd never fainted before, but she knew she was about to. She also knew that if she lost consciousness now, she'd never regain it. Several seconds went by while she struggled to keep from passing out. The sound of her screaming became faint and the darkness continued to encroach on her vision, and she feared she was losing the battle.

Mr. Colton grinned at her, his teeth a slash of white in the middle of his blood-smeared face.

"Surprise!" he said in an awful, cheerful voice.

Autumn's vision continued to narrow until it became a tiny pinhole in the darkness. Through the pinhole she saw Mrs. Colton sit up on the couch—beneath her a torn, ragged, red, wet thing that Autumn didn't want to think about. She was holding a pair of shears in her right hand . . . no, the shears *were* her hand . . . and she slashed them at her husband.

She hit him on the left side, just under his armpit, and Mr. Colton cried out in pain as blood gushed from the wound. He staggered forward a step, then back, and gave Mrs. Colton a look of absolute hatred before he slumped to the floor. Mrs. Colton stared down at her naked husband as his awful *thing* began to shrink. She then turned to Autumn, the blades of her shears opening wide. It was the sight of those blades—and the knowledge of what they could do—that gave Autumn the strength to drive the darkness back. She stopped screaming and ran out the door.

Autumn burst onto the porch and leaped down the front steps. She almost cleared them, but her left heel clipped the bottom step and she fell onto her right side. She hit the walkway hard, but she didn't feel any pain. Her body was too busy trying to ensure her survival to worry about such trivial matters as transmitting pain signals through her nervous system. The impact, however, did knock the breath out of her, and Autumn gulped for air as she pulled herself to her feet and began hobbling across the walkway. Her right leg didn't seem to want to work properly now, and she couldn't draw in enough oxygen. She didn't stop to catch her breath, though. She knew if she did, Mrs. Colton would surely catch *her.* She forced herself to keep moving and tried not to think about how her mommy was dead, and probably Mr. Colton, too. Between her leg and her lungs, she began to move more slowly, and she felt the darkness threaten to take her away again.

But then she was in the street and her breath started coming more easily. She picked up speed, and though her leg still felt funny, it wasn't holding her back as much as before. And then she'd made it across the street and into Damara's yard. She glanced at the driveway and was relieved to see Mrs. Ruschmann's car. That meant both Damara and her mother were home. As she headed for the front porch, she experienced an urge to glance behind her and see if Mrs. Colton was coming after her, but she resisted. If the woman was going to get her, Autumn wasn't about to give the old witch any help by slowing down.

She made it to the steps and hurried up to the front door.

"Wake up, honey."

Damara heard her mother's voice, gentle but insistent. Felt her mother take hold of her shoulders and shake her. Not too hard, just enough so that Damara couldn't drift back to sleep. Damara squeezed her eyes shut even tighter. She didn't want to wake up, not now, maybe not ever.

"Don't make me go get an ice cube," her mother said in a tone of mock warning.

Despite herself, Damara chuckled sleepily. They'd played this game ever since Damara had been a little girl. Whenever Claire couldn't get her up, she'd threaten to go into the kitchen, get an ice cube from the freezer, come back, and press it against Damara's stomach. Claire had never really done it, of course. The closest she'd ever come was holding a melting ice cube over Damara's head and allowing a few drops to fall on her. Damara had been so surprised that she'd sprung out of bed, and both Claire and she had laughed and laughed.

It was a good memory, and Damara wanted to stay with it for as long as she could. She knew that if she opened her eyes, she wouldn't like what she saw.

"Come on, sleepy-head!" Claire shook her harder this time. "There's someone here who wants to say hi to you—someone who hasn't been in your room for a long time."

"Wake up, Dee." This voice was masculine, and hearing it made frost gather on Damara's spine.

She didn't want to, would've given anything not to, but she opened her eyes.

At first she didn't understand what she was looking at. It was a face, but it was broader than it should be, the space between the eyes—one blue, one brown—too wide. The nose was lopsided, large on the right, small on the left, and one nostril was higher than the other. The left side had a high cheekbone and sharp chin, while the right side was fuller, with a more rounded chin dotted with dark stubble. The hair was short, straight and black on the left, and shoulder-length brown mixed with gray on the right.

"What's wrong?" Two voices came out of a single mouth, one male, one female. "Don't you recognize your parents?"

Damara could only shake her head, as if she might deny the thing that stood before her into nonexistence with such a simple motion.

"I wanted him to never leave me again," said her mother's voice. "And now he won't." Her half of their shared face smiled. "He *can't.*"

Damara understood that her mother's wish had become a quite literal reality. Jerry Ruschmann could never leave her again because they were inextricably joined, melded together in a perverse incarnation of matrimonial union. Claire on the left, Jerry on the right. They wore Jerry's plaid shirt, jeans, and shoes, though the clothes were too large and baggy on Claire's side.

Damara thought of a film she'd once seen in her freshman biology class in high school. The subject of the film had been genetics, and while she remembered very little of it, one image had stuck with her—a scene at a circus sideshow purporting to show the Amazing Two-Headed Cow. The animal had been scrawny, its coat shaggy and matted, and at first there didn't seem to be anything memorable about it. But then the cow turned its head to reveal that its face was bifurcated. It didn't have two heads, more like two faces. There was only one set of eyes, but two snouts with separate sets of nostrils, mouths, tongues, and teeth. Mucus continually dripped out of all four nostrils and the animal—or animals—kept lapping the gunk up with its tongues.

The film's narrator had explained that the animal was a set of twins that had barely begun the process of separation in the womb before it had been halted for some unknown reason. That's what Damara was looking at now: the Amazing Bi-Faced Parent. If she had eaten anything before going to bed, she'd have thrown it up now.

The Jerry hand reached out to take Damara's. She scooted backward on her bed, trying to draw away from him, but her back pressed against the wall, and there was nowhere to go. Jerry grabbed her hand and held it tight. She'd expected the touch to feel alien somehow, the skin texture obviously artificial, too hard, too smooth, too cold, like a mannequin that was able to imitate life without actually possessing it. But his hand felt perfectly normal: warm, soft, and though its grip was firm, it was also surprisingly gentle.

"I'm sorry about the way I behaved at the hotel earlier," the Jerry voice said. "I didn't realize that you're my little girl all grown up. I'm sorry that I've been gone for so long, Dee. But I'm going to make you a promise, right here and now." The right side of the combined face smiled. "I'm never going to leave you again."

The Jerry hand shifted bonelessly around hers, and Damara had the sudden impression that her hand was being caressed by a fleshy invertebrate of some sort. She looked down and saw that the fingers of the Jerry hand were growing longer, flattening out and widening. They merged into a single sheath of flesh that covered her hand like a second skin. She could feel her own flesh responding, growing softer as it began to blend with the Jerry hand. She understood then what her Mother-Father had in mind. They intended to absorb her—mind, body, and soul—and become a trio instead of a duo, a Mother-Father-Daughter combination that would give the concept of family togetherness a whole new meaning.

Damara tried to pull her hand free, but the left side of the Mother-Father gripped her shoulder with Claire's hand and fought to keep Damara still.

"Please, don't make this harder on yourself," said the Claire voice. "You'll be so much happier once it's all over. We *all* will."

Damara kept pulling, but it seemed the more she resisted, the more securely she was held. It was like a Chinese finger trap. The harder you pulled, the more impossible it was to escape.

Maybe it would be for the best, she thought. If she joined with them, her individual identity would merge with theirs, and Damara Ruschmann would cease to exist. And if that happened maybe her power or gift or curse or whatever it was would cease to exist as well. Maybe she should stop resisting and just give in, let herself be absorbed. . . .

Someone pounded on the front door, shouted Damara's name. It sounded like Autumn, and the girl seemed terrified. Damara didn't know what could be wrong, but she had a bad feeling that the shit had finally hit the fan on Pandora Drive.

She pulled her good leg back and kicked the Mother-Father as hard as she could in the stomach. She aimed for the center of the abdomen, hoping that perhaps they would be more sensitive at the juncture of their separate bodies. The Mother-Father grunted in two voices and doubled over. Damara hopped off the bed, letting out a cry of pain as the foot of her wounded leg hit the floor. With her free hand, she grabbed hold of her forearm just above where the Jerry flesh ended and she gave a hard yank. The Jerry voice shrieked as Damara tore away from him, thin strips of flesh from his hand still clinging to hers.

230

She turned and limped out of the bedroom as fast as she was capable of, shaking her hand to dislodge the bloody shreds of Jerry skin. She hurried into the living room, urged on by Autumn's pounding and yelling, both of which had become increasingly frantic. Damara reached the door and with fingers slick with the Mother-Father's blood, she undid the chain, turned the deadbolt, and opened the door.

Autumn flung herself at Damara, nearly knocking her down. Pale and trembling, the girl grabbed hold of Damara and began sobbing.

"Mom's dead! They killed her! Cut her up! She must've used her scissor-hand, and he had a . . . had a big thing! A *real* big thing!"

Damara couldn't make sense of Autumn's words, and she was about to tell the girl to calm down and speak more slowly, but then she glanced past Autumn and saw Emma Colton coming up the porch steps. The woman's clothes were covered with blood and she was bleeding from a head wound. At first Damara thought she held a pair of gardening shears in her right hand, but a split second later she realized that the shears *were* Emma's hand. She wasn't sure what had happened to Autumn, but she knew one thing: She couldn't let Emma into her house.

Damara disentangled herself from Autumn enough to start to close the door, but before she could get it shut, a pair of voices behind her asked, "What's wrong?"

What isn't? Damara thought, and then Emma was coming at them through the door, hand-shears held high, eyes burning with hatred.

231

Chapter Sixteen

The gray sludge was up to the Tristan's thighs now and rising rapidly. The silken prison Nightmare Damara had encased him in was holding up against the corrosive power of the muck so far, but he thought he could feel pinpricks of pain in his feet and ankles, as if the gunk were beginning to finally dissolve the lower part of the cocoon and eat into his flesh. The stench wafting upward was nearly as thick as the sludge itself. It caked the inside of Tristan's nostrils and coated his throat. Every breath was an effort, and it felt as if no matter what he did, he couldn't draw in enough oxygen.

Nightmare Damara appeared unaffected by the fumes. She still hung upside down from the ceiling, well out of the sludge's reach—for now at least. But instead of remaining next to Tristan, she'd crawled across the living room ceiling and now peered upside down through the front picture window.

233

"Things are starting to happen," she said in her insect-drone voice.

"What . . . things?" Tristan managed to gasp out.

Her head turned all the way around to face him, her inhuman neck supple as an owl's.

"Bad things," she said, then turned back around to peer out the window once more.

Tristan felt the gray sludge ooze past his crotch as it continued rising.

"No shit," he muttered.

"Get away from her!" Emma shouted. "That little bitch is mine!" She jabbed her shears toward Damara's face, but Damara swung the door halfway shut in time to block the attack. The blade-points cut into the door's surface, but instead of pulling them out, Emma shoved and pushed the door open once again.

Damara grabbed Autumn's hand and tugged the child farther into the living room as Emma yanked her shears free of the door and entered the house. Emma smiled and opened and closed her shears.

Shhkt-shhkt!

"I don't have any quibble with you, Damara." Emma's voice was calmer now, but there was still an undercurrent of anger to it. "You're an attractive enough girl, and I'm sure Kenneth lusted after you just like he did all the other sluts in the neighborhood. But I didn't catch him with you. I caught him with Anne . . . or rather, I caught him with

234

what was *left* of her. But one slut wasn't enough for him. He wanted another." She closed her shears and pointed them at Autumn. "He wanted *her*. But I'm going to make sure he can't have her, that no one can have her." She glared at Autumn for a second, causing the girl to cling tighter to Damara. "Give her to me," she said, looking at Damara again, "or I swear I'll gut you where you stand. Not that it would be any great loss, considering how many years you've been mooching off your mother."

Before Damara could reply—not that she had any idea what to say to the crazy old bitch—a pair of voices behind her spoke.

"You can't talk to our daughter that way."

Emma looked past Damara and noticed the Mother-Father for the first time. She frowned.

"What the hell are *you*?" she demanded.

The ragged bloody stump where the Jerry hand had been gently pushed Damara and Autumn aside, and the Mother-Father stepped between Emma Colton and their daughter.

"We've already lost one child," the Mother-Father said in its dual voice. "We're not going to lose another."

Emma opened her mouth, but before she could say anything, the Mother-Father rushed forward and fastened the Claire hand around her throat. Emma's eyes registered momentary surprise, and then she brought her shears around and plunged them into the Claire side of the amalgamation's

235

neck. Two voices screamed as one and a crimson fountain of blood sprayed the air.

"We have to go!" Autumn grabbed Damara's hand and tried to pull her away from the front door and the sight of Emma digging her shears deeper into the Mother-Father's wound. But Damara hesitated. While the Jerry Ruschmann part was only a construct fashioned from Claire's longing, Claire herself was real—and Emma was killing her.

Autumn tugged Damara's arm again.

"Damara, please!" The girl's voice broke this last word, and Damara realized that Claire had bought Autumn and her a few precious moments to escape, and she was wasting them by standing here wrestling with indecision. Damara wished she could at least say goodbye—with a last glance if nothing else—but the Mother-Father was thrashing in agony, blood jetting from its ravaged throat while the Claire hand desperately tried to strangle Emma before she could finish what she'd started with her shears.

Damara turned away from her mother and holding tight to Autumn's hand, started running through the house toward the back door.

Emma twisted her shears in the raw, ragged mess that she'd made of Claire's neck. She didn't have anything against the woman—oh, she'd likely done something to run her husband off and she'd coddled her feeb of a daughter far too long—but

Claire had always been an acceptable neighbor, and as far as Emma knew, Kenneth had never desired her. But Claire stood between her and Autumn, and that Emma couldn't allow.

The woman had a strong grip, though, that was for sure. Her fingers dug into Emma's neck like claws, and she could feel Claire's nails cutting into her skin. Emma could still breathe—Claire wasn't *that* strong—but she was finding it increasingly difficult to do so. Her lungs felt heavy and were starting to ache. Pressure built behind her eyes and pinpoints of light dotted her vision. She kept stabbing, digging, twisting her shears into Claire's neck . . . except it wasn't Claire, not entirely; it was someone else too, someone who looked vaguely familiar, though she couldn't tell who it was.

But no matter how much damage Emma did to her . . . to *their* neck, no matter how much blood gushed from the wound, the thing that Claire had become didn't seem to weaken and the grip on Emma's throat didn't slacken.

Her vision began to go gray, and she could no longer draw in any air. Her arm felt weak, tired, and sluggish, and she could barely raise her shears, let alone plunge them into Claire's flesh with any force. Emma understood that she was in serious danger of dying. She doubted the Claire-thing would survive, either, and she took some satisfaction in that, but it wasn't enough. She wanted Autumn.

There was no conscious thought on Emma's part, but the shears sprouting from her wrist lengthened, grew even sharper until they looked capable of cutting a tree limb in two. As the gray that swam in her vision edged toward black, Emma opened her shears wide and slid them around the Claire-thing's neck. Then she gritted her teeth, and with all the strength she could muster closed the shears.

The flesh and muscle were no problem; they parted like tissue paper. But the neck bone proved to be more stubborn, and Emma really had to bear down. Even so, for a moment, she thought the bone was going to defeat her, but then the blades of her shears met, and the Claire-thing's head popped off in a fountain of blood. The head seemed to hang in the air for a second, its eyes— one brown, one blue—looking at Emma with a combination of surprise and resignation. And then the head fell to the floor, hit with a hollow thump, and bounced several times before coming to a stop.

The hand around Emma's throat continued its pressure for another second or two, as if the body were operating on its own. But then the strength began to drain out of the fingers, and the hand released its grip. The body slumped forward, and Emma had to sidestep quickly to avoid being struck by it. The headless corpse fell half in and half out the open doorway, blood from its neck stump trickling onto the front porch. Emma looked at the Claire-thing's head. Its eyes were still open and staring, but they might as well have been made of glass for all the life in them.

Emma took a moment to catch her breath. Her vision cleared, though her throat hurt and she had a headache now. But these were minor inconveniences; certainly nothing that would slow her down, let alone stop her. She looked around the Ruschmanns' living room, but saw no sign of Damara and Autumn. She remembered them running off as she fought with the Claire-thing and decided she would have to search the house for them. But then she heard voices coming from the street, and she turned and stepped through the doorway, over the headless corpse, and onto the Ruschmanns' front porch.

And when she saw what was taking place in the street, she smiled.

Damara led Autumn out the back door and around the side of the house. Piercing pain shot through Damara's injured leg with every step, but she refused to slow down. She had to get Autumn to safety. She had no plan, other than a vague notion that they needed to get to Tristan. Despite how they'd left things between then when he'd dropped her off, Damara had no doubt that he'd help them now. Though what he might do to protect them against Emma, she didn't know.

They made their way down the driveway and into the street, Damara holding tight to Autumn's hand, the girl whimpering as they ran. Damara felt an urge to comfort Autumn, but she kept silent, not wishing to spend her breath on anything other than getting them to safety.

They were two-thirds of the way across the street when the front picture window of Tristan's house exploded outward. A wave of thick gray muck spilled out of the window and onto the front lawn, while the object that had shattered the glass rose up into the air. It moved so swiftly that at first Damara couldn't tell what it was, her eyes registering the object only as a blur of movement and color. But then the thing stopped in midair and above the lawn and hovered in place, giving Damara her first good look at it. It was human-shaped for the most part, and since it was naked she could see it was obviously female. It had long brown hair and was slender, but that was where its resemblance to humanity ended. It had large insectine eyes, and an extra pair of arms jutting out from the torso. They were the same length as the other arms, but thinner and possessed of additional joints. The fingers were long and segmented and each ended in a hooked barb like an insect's stinger. But the most striking features were the huge, multi-colored wings that held the creature aloft, their colors so bright they almost seemed to glow with their own internal light.

Autumn no longer whimpered in fear. She looked up at the hovering apparition, eyes wide with wonder.

"She's beautiful," Autumn said. She turned to Damara. "She looks like you."

With a start, Damara realized Autumn was right. The creature—at least its human aspect—*did* resemble her, to the point where they could've been twins. She remembered what Tristan had said in the car before dropping her off.

I remember the butterflies.

Conflicting emotions surged through Damara. Love for Tristan, joy upon discovering that she was his dream, disgust over the distorted form that dream had taken, and fear of what this creature might do.

The Insect-Damara said nothing, did nothing other than flap her rainbow-colored wings and gaze down at them with her inhuman eyes. Damara looked away from the creature and glanced at the broken window in Tristan's house. The strange muck was pouring out now in a steady stream. It had already covered most of Tristan's lawn and was beginning to flow toward the street. Damara had no idea what the gray substance was, but it stank like hell, and considering how things had been going this afternoon, she doubted it was harmless.

"So you're here . . . the Other."

The insect woman's voice was identical to Damara's, but with the addition of an angry buzzing drone.

"You don't look all that special. Tristan is a fool to prefer you to me."

From the bitterness in her double's voice, Damara realized that Tristan's construct was not only a nightmarish blend of human and insect, it was also jealous of her.

241

"Get behind me, honey," Damara whispered to Autumn, trying not to sound as scared as she felt. She put a hand on the girl's shoulder and stepped in front of her—

—just as her insectine doppelganger attacked.

Tristan tried to call out after Insect-Damara, but the strands of silk stuck to his jaw and facial muscles made it impossible for him to open his mouth wide enough to get much sound out. He wanted to call Insect-Damara back, to plead with her not to hurt the real Damara, for although he couldn't see through the broken window from where he hung, he had a damn good idea what was happening outside. He wanted to go to Damara's aid, to protect her from the insect-thing his subconscious had created from her power. But the cocoon encasing him was as strong as ever, and he still couldn't get any leverage to try to pull his way free.

To make matters worse, the gray sludge was flowing more rapidly now, as if the destruction of the window had been some sort of trigger. The muck was up to Tristan's waist now, but no longer rising, thanks to Insect-Damara creating an exit for the foul-smelling shit. His legs and trunk burned from where the ooze had eaten through the cocoon, but even if the gray muck completely dissolved the silk covering the lower half of his body, he'd still be attached to the ceiling and unable to break free. And if the gunk continued to eat away at his unprotected flesh, when he was eventually found, he'd be a skeleton from the waist down.

The force of the surging ooze pushed the lower half of his body forward, as if it were eager to take him along with it, but the strands affixing him to the ceiling held tight. The muck was no longer coming only from the basement; cracks had appeared in the living room—and throughout the house, presumably—and streams of the viscous gray substance were running down the walls to join the main tide. It was as if the entire house—the walls, floors, and ceiling—were filled with the gunk, as if Tristan's childhood home had been afflicted with an infection that had built up to the point where it was about to burst like a gigantic boil.

And all he could do was hang here and wait for it to happen.

Kenneth opened his eyes and gasped as agony slammed him back into full consciousness.

"Moth-er-*fuck!*"

Kenneth's left side felt as if it were on fire, and for a moment, he didn't know what was wrong, but then he remembered: Emma had stabbed him with a pair of goddamned garden shears that had grown out of her wrist.

He was lying naked on the floor of the Marcinos' living room and ruining their carpet by bleeding all over it. He grimaced as he pushed himself to a sitting position, then—though he was terrified of what he might find—he checked out his wound,

243

gently probing it with his fingers. He didn't have any medical training, but from what he could tell, it looked worse than it was. His left side was smeared with blood, but the actual wound wasn't very large. It looked like Emma's shears had hit his ribs, which had turned her strike downward. Her shears had sliced through a couple inches of love handle on his side, but hadn't penetrated enough to damage any organs.

"Stupid bitch. She should've stuck around and made sure she finished the job." Then he remembered the threat she had made this morning, how she had held out her index and middle fingers like scissors and placed them around his cock.

Snip-snip.

Panic gripped him, far worse than the fear he'd felt while examining his stab wound. Getting mortally wounded was one thing, but to lose your dick . . .

He spread his legs and looked—he was afraid to reach down with his hand, afraid of what he might or might *not* touch. He let out a relieved sigh when he saw that his penis was still right where it should be. It had returned to its normal length and girth, but Kenneth wasn't concerned about that. He was confident his monster cock would come roaring back to life when he needed it.

He glanced around and saw the kitchen knife lying on the carpet a few feet away. He retrieved it, then rose to his feet, gritting his teeth against the fiery pain in his side.

"You made a big mistake leaving me alive,

Emma," he said, and then clutching the knife, he started toward the open door. His cock was already three-quarters erect when he stepped across the threshold.

Chapter Seventeen

Damara threw Autumn to the ground and dropped down beside her as her doppelganger came at them. Her wings were eerily silent as they beat the air, and Damara felt a breeze waft over them as the insect woman passed by. Damara felt a tug on her shoulder, or rather, the fabric of her shirt. When she glanced over, she saw a hole had been torn in her shirt and the ragged edges were moist with a greenish slime. She thought of the extra pair of limbs her other self had, and how the fingers ended in barbs. It looked like those barbs were more than mere decoration; they were weapons, sharp and containing a poison she felt confident was as deadly as any scorpion's sting.

She sat up, keeping a hand on Autumn to make sure the girl stayed down. She looked around quickly for her insect-double and found her crouching on a tree limb in the Markleys' yard. Without taking her gaze off her other self, Damara leaned her head down close to Autumn.

"She doesn't care about you. It's me she's after. I'm going to try to distract her, and when I do, I want you to run away as fast as you can. Keep going and don't look back." Damara didn't know how well she could move on her injured leg, but she was determined to try.

Autumn looked at her with eyes wide with fear, and Damara gave her what she hoped was a reassuring smile. "It'll be okay. Remember, run as fast as you can."

Damara rose to her feet and began half-running, half-hopping down the street in the direction of the Marcinos' house. She hoped Insect-Damara would launch herself into the air and follow her, leaving Autumn free to flee in the opposite direction. It was a good plan, especially for one formed at the spur of the moment. Unfortunately, Damara had forgotten something.

Emma Colton.

Damara ran straight into the woman and collided with her. The two of them fell to the street, and Damara waited to feel Emma's shears slice into her. But she managed to avoid impaling herself on the other woman's blades. Emma was drenched with blood, a good deal of which was now smeared across the front of Damara's shirt. She had a good idea where the blood had come from, but she tried not to think about it. She was afraid if she did, she'd start crying and never stop.

She rolled off Emma and tried to get to her feet, hoping to put some distance between them so she wouldn't be in range of those shears. But before she could take more than two steps, Emma grabbed hold of her shirt with her normal hand and held tight.

"And just where do you think *you're* going, young lady?" Emma said.

Damara tried to pull free from Emma's grip, but the older woman held on with a strength beyond her years and pulled herself to a standing position.

"I *was* going to spare you," Emma said, her voice nearly a growl. "But now you've pissed me off."

She raised her shears, and as Damara steeled herself to feel the blades cut into her, she hoped Autumn had managed to get away. But before Emma could strike, a shriek pierced the air.

"Mine!"

Damara turned to see a rainbow-hued blur coming toward them. She ducked and her insect-double slammed into Emma Colton. Damara's shirt tore as Emma's hand was yanked away, and she almost fell, but she managed to maintain her footing. Her other self struck Emma with such force that the impact knocked her off her feet. Insect-Damara carried Emma through the air, rising upward as they passed over the Ruschmanns' front yard, her second pair of arms repeatedly stinging the older woman with her finger barbs. Emma screamed in pain and flailed at her attacker with her shears. Then it was the insect-woman's turn to scream as gouts of greenish blood jetted from the wounds Emma inflicted. Insect-Damara wobbled in the air. Then her wings suddenly folded and she plunged toward the ground, carrying Emma with her. They crashed to the grass, slid several feet, then lay still, Insect-Damara atop Emma, her multi-colored wings spread wide and covering them both.

Damara didn't wait to see how badly they were injured. If she were lucky, they'd have killed each other. Her main concern was for Autumn. She turned to see if the girl had managed to escape, aware as she did so of a shallow wave of gray muck splashing across her feet.

"I don't know what this shit is, but it's a real bitch to run in."

Kenneth Colton, naked, holding a knife and sporting an erection that was at least a foot and a half long, stood in the middle of the street up to his ankles in gray sludge. With his free hand, he held on to Autumn's arm. The girl was covered with gray gook, and Damara realized that she must have slipped in the spreading muck while trying to flee, giving Kenneth enough time to capture her.

Kenneth gestured toward Damara's yard with the knife. "Looks like butterfly girl did me a favor by taking out Emma for me. To tell you the truth, I'm a little disappointed. I would've liked to kill her myself. But now there's no one to keep me from having some fun with little miss Autumn here." He gave Autumn's arm a yank and the girl cried out in pain. "Who knows? Maybe when I'm finished with her, I'll give you a try. What do you say, Damara? Want to take a spin on Mr. Colton's Wild Ride?"

As Damara watched, Kenneth's erection swelled several more inches.

The sight of his obscenely long organ—and the thought of what he might do to Autumn with it—nauseated Damara. Here was another victim of her power, but Kenneth wasn't treating his deformity as an affliction. He was acting as if he were having the time of his life.

Damara wished she could tap into her own power and consciously use it. If she could, she could stop Kenneth easily, stop *all* of this, make it go away and repair whatever damage had been done. But she had no more control over her ability than a paint brush did over the picture it was used to create. She might generate the strange energies others drew on, but she could never make use of them herself. However, she did have other attributes to fight with.

"Forget about her, Kenneth," Damara said. "She's just a kid. I'm a woman."

Kenneth lifted an eyebrow, looking both surprised and intrigued.

Damara went on. "If you let Autumn go, I promise that you can do whatever you want to me for as long as you want. And I won't put up a fight." She forced herself to smile. "That is, not unless you want me to."

Kenneth laughed. "You're just trying to save the kid. You don't give a damn about me."

"So what?" Damara countered. "My offer still stands."

Kenneth looked at her for several moments, then down at Autumn. "I don't know," he said at last. "It's a good offer, but I'd hate like hell to give this little sweetmeat up, especially after everything I've gone through to get hold of her." He considered a moment longer before finally shaking his head.

"Sorry, no deal."

He turned to go, yanking Autumn along after him, when Tristan's house burst apart in an eruption of gray sludge. A massive wave of the stuff came rushing toward them so swiftly that all they could do was watch its approach. And then the muck engulfed them and they were swept off their feet. Damara closed her mouth so she wouldn't swallow any of the gray goo, and she thrashed her arms and legs, as if she might somehow swim through the mucus-like substance. But it was too thick, like a combination of mud and molasses, and swimming was impossible. All she could do was relax her body and let the gray wave toss and turn her as it carried her along. Her flesh began to burn where the ooze touched it, and she knew whatever this stuff was, it was corrosive. She clamped her eyes shut to protect them, and the world became a dizzying darkness as the muck bore her where it would.

Suddenly her left shoulder slammed into something hard and she stopped moving. She felt solid ground beneath her—a street curb, she thought, which would explain the pain in her shoulder. She was still submerged in muck, and she struggled to sit up, desperate to take a breath. It took some effort, but she managed to raise herself into a sitting position, and by doing so broke the surface of the sludge. She opened her eyes, but immediately closed them again when they began stinging. She reached up with slime-covered hands and did her best to clear the gook away from her mouth. Then she attempted to draw in a breath. The air tasted sour and rotten, but her lungs didn't care. As far as they were concerned right then, air was air.

She tried to open her eyes again, and while they still burned somewhat, the sensation had lessened to the point where she could bear it. The street and the neighboring yards were covered with gray muck. Damara didn't know what the substance was, but she was certain of one thing: One way or another, she was the cause of it. The gray ooze hung from tree limbs in thick ropy strands, and was smeared on windows as if giant snails had crawled over them, leaving slime trails behind. The Ledford house was little more than a shell now. The front was completely gone, and what remained leaned to the left and looked as if it would collapse any moment. Bits of wood, roofing tiles, plaster, and even furniture were spread out across the street and yards, carried there by the gray tide. Damara prayed that Tristan hadn't been in the house when it had exploded, for if he had—

"Mara?"

The voice was weak, but it was unmistakably Tristan's.

Damara scanned the street, searching for him and saw a large lump about a dozen feet from where she sat. The goo was draining off into the sewer slowly but surely, and she could see the lump was more or less human-shaped. She rose to her feet and slogged through the muck toward the lump, treading carefully to avoid slipping. As she drew near the shape, she could see Tristan's face, though that was all she could see of him. It was as if his body were encased in a shell of solid ooze.

She knelt down next to him and wiped gray slime from his face, and he looked up at her with grateful eyes.

"I'm glad it's you, Mara. The real you, I mean."

His skin was red, as if he'd been sunburned, and Damara realized the discoloration was likely due to the muck's corrosive effect. She gazed down at her hands and saw they were equally as red.

"Can you get me out?" Tristan asked. "I'm covered in some kind of cocoon, I'd guess you'd call it. *She* wrapped me in it."

Damara understood then that Tristan wasn't encased in muck; the gray substance was instead covering the cocoon he was trapped in. She reached for him, intending to help him tear free if she could, when she suddenly remembered Autumn.

"Tristan, I have to find Autumn. She's out here somewhere, and Kenneth . . ."

"I understand. Go. I'll be all right."

Damara didn't know if he would, but she couldn't abandon Autumn, was ashamed that she'd forgotten about the girl, if only momentarily.

"I'll be back as soon as I can." Damara stood and gazed at the muck-covered yards and street, searching for some sign of Autumn. Some of the neighbors stood on their porches or peered out windows, gaping at the mass of gray gunk that had erupted in their street. Damara hoped they'd all have the good sense to stay where they were. She feared the worst wasn't over yet.

"Damara!"

She turned in the direction of Autumn's voice. The goo flood had carried Autumn down the street past her own house, and the girl was just now attempting to stand.

"Stay there!" Damara called. "I'm coming!"

She began slogging through the muck in the street as fast as she dared. The level was still up to her mid-calf, and moving through it was like trying to walk through a sea of glue, especially with her injured leg. Autumn obeyed Damara and remained where she was, trying to wipe the worst of the muck off her body.

"Is he gone?" Autumn asked.

Damara knew she was referring to Kenneth. "I don't know," she said, wishing she could bring herself to tell Autumn a comforting lie. "But as soon as I get you, we'll try to free Tristan and then the three of us—"

Damara felt fingers close around the ankle of her wounded leg. The hand yanked and knives of agony sliced through her nerve endings. She shrieked and fell forward, splashing into the muck face-first. She lay there for a moment, unable to do anything other than hurt. She had the sense that someone stood up next to her, and she slowly rolled over onto her back—crying out in pain as she did so—so she could see who it was.

The giant slime-coated erection bobbing in the air above Damara told her everything she needed to know.

"Looks like you lose, girl." Gray ooze dripped off Kenneth's naked body in large phlegmy chunks and plapped onto the muck in the street. His skin, like Tristan's and hers, was red, but either he didn't notice or didn't care. Or, sick bastard that he was, maybe he enjoyed the burning sensation caused by the ooze. He no longer held the knife, and Damara figured he must have lost it in the gray flood.

"You can't have her, Kenneth!" Damara started to sit up, but then Kenneth kicked her hard in the side with his bare foot, driving the breath out of her lungs. She fell back into the muck and gasped for air, noticing that his cock had swollen several more inches.

Kenneth sneered down at her. "Don't be ridiculous. You can't stop me from doing what I want with my little playmate. No one can."

"Really?"

Both Kenneth and Damara turned at the same time to look at Emma. She stood on the other side of Damara, facing her husband. Like the rest of them, she was covered with gray gunk, but mixed with hers was a greenish substance that Damara knew was her other self's blood. There was so much of it that Damara doubted the insect-woman still lived. But beyond the muck and the blood,

Emma's face and arms were covered with swollen black pustules from where Damara's other self had stung her. The pustules looked nasty as hell, large as golf balls, black, skin tight and shiny. But if they had any adverse effect on Emma, she showed no sign of it. Her right arm still ended in a pair of gardening shears, though for the moment she held them relaxed at her side.

Kenneth raised his hands and took a step back, his bravado gone. "Now Emma, let's talk about this." His penis remained erect, but it was beginning to grow shorter.

Emma smiled and stepped over Damara, the older woman's feet dripping muck onto her chest as she crossed. "Of course we can, Kenneth. After all, we've been married for so many years . . . it would be a shame to throw away everything we have over a simple misunderstanding."

Kenneth kept his hands raised, but he stopped retreating. "Really?" he said, sounding half-skeptical, half-hopeful.

Emma took another step toward him. "Really, Kenneth. I've been thinking, maybe I haven't been the kind of wife I should have, the kind of wife you deserve." Another step closer. "Maybe it's my fault that you've been . . . deprived. And maybe I've been depriving myself as well."

Kenneth narrowed his eyes, as if he were trying to see inside her to determine whether she was telling the truth. Another step, a small one this time, and she was in striking distance. Emma took hold of her husband's penis with her normal hand

257

and squeezed it gently. The organ once more swelled in length at her touch.

She looked into his eyes. "I want your cock, Kenneth."

Her right hand flashed, her shears closed—*shhkt!*—and Kenneth screamed. Blood jetted out from the hole between his legs, and he clapped his hands over the wound as if he might physically hold back the blood.

"You . . . fucking . . . cunt!" he growled, eyes blazing with hatred at Emma.

As blood gushed past her husband's fingers, Emma lifted his amputated penis to her face and examined it. It was no longer a giant, tumescent thing, just a lump of limp flesh no longer than a finger.

"That's the last time *you're* going to give me any trouble," Emma said, and Damara didn't know whether she was addressing Kenneth, his penis, or both.

"Give . . ." Kenneth said, but he didn't get the rest out. Blood still streamed out from between his legs to mix with the muck in the street and turn it from gray to reddish black. He swayed and fell back onto his ass, already weak from loss of blood.

"Give it back?" Emma said. "I don't think so. You've caused enough problems with it already." She looked at the flaccid organ for a moment longer, as if trying to decide what to do with it. Then with a single quick motion, she popped Kenneth's penis into her mouth and began chewing.

"NO!" Kenneth screamed. He reached out toward Emma, tried to stand once more, but he fell back down and slumped over onto his side, his red face turning pale.

Blood trickled past Emma's lips and ran down her chin. She chewed for several more seconds, then swallowed. She looked thoughtful for a moment. "Not bad . . . not bad at all." Then, without another glance at her husband or at Damara, she turned and began walking toward Autumn.

Damara was still having trouble catching her breath. Her side hurt where Kenneth had kicked her, and her injured leg felt like it had been dipped in acid. Nevertheless, she managed to sit up and turned to see Emma approaching Autumn. The girl had been true to her promise, she hadn't moved since Damara had told her to stay put, no doubt held there by shock more than anything else.

When Emma reached Autumn, she looked down at the girl for several long moments, her expression unreadable. When she at last spoke, her voice didn't exactly soften, but it no longer contained an edge of insane fury.

"I suppose it wasn't completely your fault you turned out the way you did. After all, you did come from a broken home, and you lived with a mother who was a world-class slut." She paused, as if thinking. "But she's gone now, isn't she? As is Kenneth, so you can hardly be a temptation to him anymore."

"That's right!" Damara shouted, trying not to sound as desperate as she felt. "So why don't you let her go? Give her a chance to grow up to be better than her mother." Damara hated herself for saying this, for even pretending to agree with Emma's warped view of Anne, but she'd say or do anything to save Autumn.

"I've taught hundreds of children over the years," Emma said, "and though I never had any of my own, I used to hope I could compensate for that lack by making a difference in the lives of my students, but I know better now. Parents are the real influence, while teachers are little more than glorified babysitters. And since most parents are small-minded, selfish, hedonistic oafs, it's no wonder their children turn out the way they do." She looked at Autumn once more. "But you no longer have a parent. And you're young enough that you *might* still be salvageable."

Emma touched her fingers to the bottom of Autumn's chin and lifted her head slightly, as if the child were a piece of merchandise to be examined.

"When a plant suffers from disease, the infected areas can be cut away, and if enough remains— *and* with the right care and attention—a plant that was once in danger of dying can not only continue to live, it can thrive."

Emma removed her hand from Autumn's chin and her thin lips stretched into a smile that was almost warm.

"*You're* that plant, Autumn. I can see that now, and it's my duty to take care of you, to tend to you, to teach you and help you grow up right." Her smile widened and her voice took on a cold edge. "Just like me."

Damara tried once more to get to her feet, and this time she succeeded. Most of the street muck had drained away by now, leaving behind a slimy gray film coating the street. She hurried toward Emma and Autumn as fast as she could, half-limping, half-dragging her wounded leg.

"Let her go, Emma! I have this . . . this power and it affected you, turned you into some kind of avenging witch!" She had almost reached them . . . only a few more feet. "You've killed Kenneth and devoured his penis, for godsakes! Is that the act of a sane woman? If you really care for Autumn, you'll let me take her!"

As she reached them, Autumn looked up at Damara hopefully and held out a hand. Damara smiled and reached out to take it, but just as their fingers made contact, Emma swung the flat of her shears toward Damara's head and struck her hard on the temple. Damara fell to her hands and knees and struggled to hold on to consciousness. She fought to lift her head enough to see Emma and watched as the older woman tugged Autumn after her toward the Ruschmanns' yard.

"Come, child," Emma said. "The sooner we get your education started, the better."

The last thing Damara heard before she passed out was the sound of Autumn crying.

"Wake up, Mara!"

Damara was aware that someone was shaking her gently, and she knew it was important that she wake up—though she wasn't quite sure why—but

261

she couldn't manage to do so. It was as if she lay sleeping at the bottom of an impossibly deep well listening to someone shout down to her from the top. Even if she woke and responded, what good would it do her? She'd still be trapped. Better to go on sleeping.

"C'mon, Mara! Emma's taken Autumn and we have to get her back!"

Autumn. The word conjured conflicting images in her mind: trees filled with orange, brown, red, and yellow leaves—and a smiling young girl with brown hair done up in pigtails. Somehow, these images were both Autumn, but that hardly seemed likely. After all, what did trees and a girl have in common? It was all so confusing, and she decided to just go on sleeping for as long as she could, maybe forever, when she remembered. Autumn, Tristan, her mother, Emma, Kenneth, her other self, the flood of gray ooze . . .

Emma's taken Autumn and we have to get her back!

Damara opened her eyes and sat up. Her head throbbed, and she was so dizzy that she almost fell back down, but Tristan put his arm around her shoulders and steadied her. She looked at him, saw his skin was splotchy, sunburn-red with darker patches that edged toward black. His clothes were slick with ooze, as were hers, but he was free of the cocoon.

"What happened?" She started to rise, wobbled, and Tristan helped her onto her feet.

"I told you, Emma—"

262

"No, I mean to you. You were trapped in a web of some kind or a cocoon. Something like that."

Tristan gestured at the street. While most of the gray goo had drained into the sewer, puddles of it still remained here and there. "Whatever that crap was, it finally ate through enough of the cocoon and I was able to tear free. I just wish I could've gotten out in time to prevent Emma from taking Autumn."

Damara was still groggy from the blow on the head Emma had given her. She looked at Kenneth's naked body lying in the middle of the street, and at first she didn't recognize it. But when she saw the wet ragged hole between his legs, she remembered.

She nodded toward him. "Is he . . . ?"

"Dead? Oh, yeah. Bled out pretty fast from the look of it."

She then turned to her yard and saw the muck-covered wings sprouting from the body of her other self. "And her?"

"She's dead, too. After I got free, I checked to make sure you were alive, and then I checked both her and Kenneth. I didn't want either of them sneaking up and attacking us later in case they were playing possum. After I made sure they were dead, I came back to wake you up." Tristan gazed at the dead insect-woman. "Emma sliced her up good. You can barely tell what she looked like."

There was a wistful, almost sorrowful tone in Tristan's voice, as if he were mourning the loss of a friend or a lover. Damara felt a pang of jealousy, but when she remembered how possessive her double had been, she pushed the emotion aside.

263

She looked up and down the street and saw a number of people standing on their porches and lawns, gawking at Tristan and her. Damara wondered how she would be able to keep her power a secret now, and was surprised to find that she didn't much care. Off in the distance, she heard the wail of a siren, and she knew someone had called the police. Unless she and Tristan wanted to stick around and answer the officers' questions—answers that would more than likely earn the two of them a free trip to the nearest asylum—Damara figured they'd better get moving. Besides, Autumn needed them.

"Where did they go? Emma and Autumn, I mean."

Before Tristan could answer, Damara's eye was caught by movement on her front porch. She turned and saw a scaly green figure covered with spines kneeling next to a decapitated body. In one hand, the creature held a severed head by the hair—hair that was a mixture of brown and black. It was the Mother-Father's head, and the creature that was holding it was the one that had taken away her brother, that might somehow even *be* her brother, at least partially: Jack Sharp.

"Christ, it's another one!" Tristan said. "Is that the thing that got your leg?"

Damara didn't answer, only watched as the spine-covered monster lifted the Mother-Father's headless corpse as if it weighed nothing. The creature straightened, tucked the body under its arm—

spines piercing dead flesh—and carrying the head in its other hand, started down the front steps.

Now that she got a good look at it, Damara could see the monster was a blend of reptile, human, and fish covered with spines straighter, thicker, and sharper than any found in nature. As Jack Sharp descended the steps and began coming down the front walk, Damara feared the thing was going to come for her, too, and she grabbed hold of Tristan and held him tight.

But as the creature walked into the street on clawed, finlike feet, it became clear that it wasn't headed for them. It continued across Pandora Drive, toward the sewer grating on the opposite side of the street. As it reached the grating, it paused and turned to look at Damara. Its eyes were human, and familiar, and they were full of sadness.

Then the creature inserted a fin-foot into the grating and both it and the body of the Mother-Father flowed like water down into the sewer and vanished.

Damara stared at the sewer grating. Her entire family was gone now, all victims of her goddamned power. Despair filled her then, stronger and more oppressive than anything she'd ever felt before. She thought of all the devastation she'd caused—knowingly or not—on Pandora Drive. The deaths of Bobby Markley, Anne Marcino, Kenneth Colton, and her mother . . . the destruction of Tristan's house . . . For so many years she'd managed to maintain control of her power, to keep it at bay, but now, in the course of a single day, it had gotten away from her, and look at all the misery it had caused. Better that she had killed herself years ago and risked releasing the power into the world than lose control and have all *this* happen.

But just as her despair threatened to overwhelm her, she remembered Autumn. She couldn't afford to wallow in self-loathing right now, not as long as Emma had the girl.

She turned to Tristan. "We have to save Autumn."

"I know," Tristan said.

"I'd do it alone if I could."

A sigh, followed by a tired smile. "C'mon, they went this way." As the sound of sirens closed in on Pandora Drive, Tristan took Damara's hand and led her toward her backyard.

Chapter Eighteen

It wasn't as if Emma had a plan, certainly not a conscious one. It was the sound of approaching sirens that first urged her to get off the street—she wasn't afraid of the police, but she didn't feel like wasting time explaining things to them. Her situation was already complicated enough as it was. What she wanted, what she *needed* was a retreat, a refuge, someplace where she could go and begin making plans for Autumn's education without being bothered by the rest of the world. Emma thought the girl could use a little time to adjust to everything that had happened to her as well. After all, Autumn's life had undergone some rather major changes this afternoon, and she doubtless needed a bit of time to get used to them.

So Emma led Autumn through Damara's backyard, over the chainlink fence—which wasn't all that easy to negotiate at Emma's age, especially while holding onto a young girl so she couldn't escape. But Emma had wrangled enough children in thirty years as a teacher, and she managed. The poor girl kept sobbing quietly, tears rolling down her cheeks in unbroken streams. But Emma wasn't unduly concerned. She knew that these were healing tears, cleansing tears, and that they were washing away the taint of Autumn's old life and getting her ready to start fresh, with Emma as both her parent and teacher.

The woods behind the Ruschmanns' house were thick with undergrowth, but though it was fall, it was early enough for most of the vegetation to still be green and supple, so while the brush slowed them down, it didn't stop them. As Emma led Autumn down the gently curving slope of the hillside, holding tight to the girl's hand, the older woman realized where they were heading, and she smiled. She didn't know whether her subconscious had directed her this way or whether it was sheer dumb luck, but it was absolutely perfect. She decided not to say anything to Autumn until they were there; she wanted it to be a surprise.

It took another ten minutes before they reached the bottom of the hill. The woods thinned out here and opened onto a field of waist-high grass. The day was warm and a gentle breeze was blowing from the south, making the grass ripple like green water. The sky was blue and cloudless, and birds sang with a hint of urgency, as if determined to make as much music as they could before winter crept up on them. Though Emma couldn't see the Clearwater River from here, she could hear the gentle whisper-hush of running water and smell its muddy-fishy odor.

Emma gazed at Autumn's face to determine if the child had guessed where they were going, but Autumn continued to cry, her eyes puffy and squeezed shut. Her left pigtail had come undone and her hair had fallen onto her face and, moistened by tears, now stuck to her cheek. Still holding securely on to the girl's hand, Emma reached out, intending to brush the wet hair off the child's face. But when she realized that her right hand remained a pair of oversized garden shears, she stopped before she accidentally plunged the tips of the blades into Autumn's cheek. It wouldn't do to injure the child so soon in their new relationship; that was hardly a way to build trust between teacher and pupil.

Emma looked at her shears and concentrated on making them become fingers once again. After all, it wasn't as if she needed them anymore, now that Kenneth was gone. The thought of her not-so-dearly but most assuredly departed husband made Emma scowl. Had she actually cut off his penis and then *eaten* it? It seemed too bizarre, too nightmarish, and yet that was what had happened, or at least, what she remembered happening. But now that she was standing here at the edge of a grassy field—holding the hand of a girl she'd just kidnapped, for godsakes—it all seemed so unreal.

But she couldn't deny the physical reality of her condition. Her right hand remained shears, no matter how much she willed it to return to normal. And what was more, she could see purple-black bumps the size of golf balls on her wrist and forearm. She glanced at the hand holding on to Autumn and saw it too was covered with dark lumps, as was the arm. Emma assumed that her face and neck were similarly affected, though with only her hand-shears free, she could hardly reach up and touch her flesh to check. At first she wasn't sure where the lumps had come from, but then she remembered the insect-woman attacking, stinging her as they both fell toward the ground. Emma had slain the strange creature that had resembled Damara, but it appeared she hadn't escaped their short battle unscathed. If the stings had injected some kind of toxin into her system, though, she didn't feel it. While the lumps were swollen, they didn't hurt, and she seemed to be suffering no ill effects—no lightheadedness, no trouble breathing, no rapid heartbeat. Perhaps the venom hadn't been very potent, or perhaps whatever change had come over Emma in the last twenty-four hours or so made her resistant. Whatever the case, she decided it wasn't worth worrying about, and chose to think about her stings no longer.

Forget the questions, she told herself. *You're a teacher; it's your job to supply answers.*

And so, along with her stings, Emma forgot about the battle on Pandora Drive, about Tristan and Damara, about the two-faced thing Claire had become . . . Most of all, she forgot about Kenneth and whatever vestigial feelings of guilt or remorse she might or might not have felt for what she'd done to him. The past, like the people who inhabited it, was dead. She needed to turn her thoughts to the future, for Autumn's sake, if nothing else.

She started across the field, tugging Autumn behind her. The girl came along without any struggle, which Emma took as a good sign. Maybe the child was already beginning to accept—and perhaps even look forward to—the new life she was about to embark on.

On the far side of the field was a high wooden fence that stretched for dozens of yards in each direction, coiled barbed wire lining the top as a deterrent to would-be trespassers. At periodic intervals along the fence, weather-worn signs warned THIS PROPERTY CONDEMNED in faded red letters. Despite herself, Emma grinned like a little girl. It had been ages since she'd visited an amusement park. This was going to be fun.

She increased her speed until she and Autumn were nearly running toward Riverfork.

"Jesus H. Motherfucking Christ! What the hell happened here?"

The voice cut through the darkness like a laser, and though he didn't want to listen to it, wanted nothing more than to swim through the black waters of the endless night that surrounded him, he couldn't help it.

"Got me. And did you see that thing on the lawn over there? Some kinda fuckin' freak."

A second voice. And there were other sounds,

too. Shoes scraping on asphalt, car doors opening and closing, tinny voices and electronic tones coming from radios. A word came to him from somewhere outside the darkness: *police*. He wasn't sure what it meant, but it held no surprise. It seemed appropriate somehow. Expected.

"I heard Carter found a woman ripped in half in one of the houses, and there's a mess of blood in the front room of that house over there, but no body. Nothing but bloody footprints on the porch that look like they were made by someone wearing swim fins."

"Yeah, well that's nothing compared to Madame Butterfly. And what about *that* house? Looks like a bomb went off and ripped away the whole goddamned front. And don't forget that kid yesterday—Bobby Markley. He was killed in the hospital last night. Pretty damn gruesome thing, too, from what I heard."

He was beginning to become interested in what these two were talking about, and that made him angry because he didn't *want* to be interested, didn't *want* to start thinking about the things they said, didn't *want* to remember. All he wanted to do was be left alone so that he could surrender himself to the great ebon sea and float forever unaware and unfeeling on its strange dark tides. But these two idiots weren't going to let him.

"What about that gray shit? It's all over the inside of the house and the yard. Have you ever seen—or smelled—anything that nasty before?"

"It's all fucked up, far as I'm concerned, but I

gotta tell you, this guy here is the worst of it for me. Makes my balls shrivel just to look at him."

"I know what you mean. Hell of a way to go, huh? Bleedin' to death after a radical dickectomy."

There was something more with him in the darkness now than the two voices. There was anger. A small red-hot spark that grew as the men continued to speak.

"You s'pose whoever cut it off took it with them?"

"I don't know, but I ain't seen it around yet. Hell, a damn dog might've run up and grabbed it for all we know."

A laugh. "A free hotdog lunch, eh?"

Both of them were laughing now, and the anger swelled into a raging fire and burned away the darkness.

Kenneth opened his eyes and saw two uniformed police officers standing over him. They were laughing like men who didn't want anyone to hear them, mouths closed to keep the sound muffled, snorts of amusement escaping from their nostrils.

Kenneth sat up. "What's so fuckin' funny?" he demanded.

The two cops jumped back as if Kenneth had just pulled a gun and fired at them.

"Holy shit!" one of them said, instinctively reaching for his weapon. He was short, thin, and young, with a sprinkling of acne on his cheeks and a sparse black mustache that looked more like a chocolate milk stain than facial hair.

The second cop—taller, middle-aged, white-haired and fat—put a hand on his partner's arm to stop him from drawing his gun.

"We need a paramedic over here now!" the fat cop shouted. "We got a survivor!" He looked at his partner, whose face had turned chalk-white, and then as if convinced the kid wasn't going to start shooting, let go of his arm.

"Why don't you lie down and take it easy, sir?" the fat cop suggested. "Just rest until the paramedics get here." He started forward and reached out as if he intended to gently push Kenneth back down onto the asphalt, but the cop hesitated, hands trembling as if he couldn't bring himself to make contact with Kenneth's flesh.

"What the hell are you talking about? I feel fine." That wasn't exactly the truth. Kenneth didn't really feel fine; he didn't feel anything at all. His entire body was numb. Not even that, for numb was a sensation of a sort, and Kenneth didn't even feel that. He felt nothing, absolutely nothing at all, as if his nervous system had shut down completely.

"I don't know what happened to you, man," the young cop said, "but whatever you are, you damn well ain't fine!"

Kenneth wasn't sure what the dumb fuck was talking about, but then he looked down and saw the empty space between his legs. At first he couldn't comprehend what he was looking at, and when he finally understood, he refused to believe it. But then he remembered the darkness and the anger he'd felt there, the anger that had brought him back.

He remembered everything.

"She did it. The goddamned bitch."

"Who?" the fat cop asked.

"My cunt of a wife. She cut off my dick and then ate it. Fuckin' frigid cooz! But if she thinks she's going to keep me from getting back what's mine, she's got another goddamned think comin'!"

Kenneth started to rise to his feet. It wasn't easy to move since he had no sensation in his body, but he managed.

"Your wife ate your dick? Jesus!" The young cop looked as if he were about to throw up.

The fat cop didn't look much better. "Sir, you've suffered a very serious injury and lost a lot of blood. To be honest, my partner and I thought you were dead. I don't know how you're even able to move right now. Maybe it's shock or something, but I have to insist that you sit back down and wait for the paramedics."

"I don't have time to wait," Kenneth said. "I have to get it back."

"Get what back?" the fat cop said, although from the quavering tone of his voice, it was clear he had a good idea what Kenneth's answer would be.

"My dick, of course. What else?" He looked around but saw no sign of Emma. Just other cops—some of which were starting to head his way—and nosy neighbors standing around in their yards and in the street in groups of twos, threes, and fours. Women and children mostly, since it was still afternoon. No Autumn, either. Or Damara. He wondered where they had gone, wondered how he might find them . . . and then he felt a gentle pull behind his eyes, as if he had a compass inside his head, and the needle was slowly swiveling to point toward . . .

West. That's where Emma had gone, carrying his chewed-up cock nestled in her stomach. She'd gone westward.

For a moment, Kenneth considered going into his house and putting on some clothes, but then he figured, what the fuck? It wasn't as if he had any private parts to conceal anymore. He turned in the direction of Damara's house and started walking.

"Sir, I mean it!" The fat cop grabbed Kenneth's shoulder. "We can't let you leave, not in the condition you're in!"

Kenneth stopped, paused, and then slowly turned around to face the two officers. "What makes you think you can stop me?"

The fat cop swallowed nervously. "We'll physically restrain you if we have to."

The young cop undid the snap on his holster, as if he intended to force Kenneth to accept medical aid by threatening to kill him.

Kenneth became aware of a sound then, a soft whistling as if air were rushing through a long, narrow space. And for the first time since surfacing from the sea of darkness, he felt something. A strong sensation of coolness, of the movement of air, as if he were drawing in a deep breath. Except this sensation wasn't coming from his mouth or nostrils. It was coming from between his legs. He looked down at his crotch and saw not a wound, but rather an empty space filled with Nothing. He realized then that he hadn't left the darkness behind when he'd awakened, not completely. He'd brought a little of it back with him.

The whistling-rushing sound increased and the two cops staggered forward a step, as if they were being pulled by some unseen force. Sudden wind whipped at their hair and clothes, and they stiffened as they tried to back away from Kenneth, faces grimacing, muscles locked tight and shaking with tremendous effort. And then all at once, the pull became too much to resist, and the cops—one middle-aged and fat, one too young and thin—flew off their feet and vanished into the darkness between Kenneth's legs with a soft *fwoop!* Once they were gone, the wind died down and the air grew still again.

Kenneth looked around and saw that the other officers, perhaps a half dozen in all, stood where they were, unmoving, watching him with wide, frightened eyes.

"Anyone else want to try and stop me?" Kenneth called out.

The officers said nothing, but a couple of them shook their heads.

Kenneth sniffed. "I didn't think so."

He turned and started walking westward toward Damara's house and what lay beyond it.

"Better than a trail of bread crumbs, huh?" Tristan said.

Damara didn't reply. The broken section of

fence spoke for itself. Splintered planks lay on the ground, their wood gouged and scarred by deep furrows caused, no doubt, by Emma's hand shears.

"Why do you suppose she brought Autumn here?" Tristan asked.

Damara shrugged. "The woman's insane; she doesn't need a reason." Her wound throbbed and the bandages that covered it were soaked through with blood. Not that a little more blood mattered considering how much she had on her clothes, along with a slimy residue of the gray muck. She looked—and smelled—like she'd just emerged from a sewer beneath a slaughterhouse. Tristan's clothes weren't in much better condition.

"Let's get moving. There's no telling how dangerous it is in there." He nodded toward a THIS PROPERTY CONDEMNED sign. "We need to get Autumn out before a building collapses on her or something." He didn't say what the *or something* might be. He didn't have to. Before Emma changed her diseased mind and killed the child.

"It might be even more dangerous if I do go in," Damara said.

Tristan frowned. "I don't understand.

Damara didn't answer right away. She looked at the opening Emma had made in the fence but tried not to look past it and into the park itself. "The night I snuck in here . . . the night my father disappeared . . . it was almost like Riverfork started to come to life around me. Like it had only been sleeping for all those years, waiting for something to wake it up again."

"Something like you and your power," Tristan said.

She nodded. "I was able to keep it from happening then. I thought a lot about polar bears in snowstorms." She gave him a wan smile. "When I realized what was happening—and that Dad had come after me—I got out of the park as fast as I could. But not fast enough to save my father."

"Do you know what happened to him?"

"Not exactly. He went into one of the buildings that used to house an attraction. I don't remember which one. He never came out again. That's why I shouldn't go in there, Tristan. My dad disappeared because of me. What if, by trying to save Autumn, I cause the same thing—or worse—to happen to her? Or to you?"

"You didn't see what happened to your father after he went inside the building, right? Not to be morbid, but there's a reason the place was condemned. He might've fallen through rotten floorboards or had a ceiling beam collapse on him. Your power might've had nothing to do with it."

"Yes, it did. I'm sure of it."

"Look, Mara, you told me your power works by making people's fantasies and wishes come true. But a place isn't alive. It doesn't have any thoughts or feelings for your power to feed."

Sudden anger flared in Damara. "Don't tell me what my power can and can't do, Tristan! I've spent my whole life trying to figure it out so I could control it, and keep myself and the people I care about safe. But it's not like the damn thing came with an owner's manual, you know. You're looking for logic and reason where there may not be any. All I know is what happened the last time I went into Riverfork, and considering what my power has done in the last twenty-four hours . . ." She trailed off, reluctant even to contemplate the havoc that might result should she pass through the crude entrance Emma had created.

Tristan said nothing for several moments, but when he at last spoke, his tone was kind and understanding. "Maybe you're right, Mara. Maybe there's no way to completely know what rules—if any—your power operates by. One thing seems clear, though. Once a change begins, it keeps going whether you're present or not. It's like people carry a piece of your power with them. Emma's already in there, and for all we know, Riverfork is responding to *her* thoughts and feelings. Perhaps it's already begun to wake up, and maybe your power is the only thing that can put it to sleep again. Maybe you'll make things worse, maybe you'll make them better. I don't know. The only way to find out is for you to go inside. But let me ask you this: If you don't go in, can you live with yourself if something bad happens to Autumn?"

Damara thought about Tristan's words, but she didn't have to think very long.

"All right. Let's go."

Tristan nodded, though now that he'd talked her into it, she saw uncertainty in his eyes. He stepped toward the opening Emma had made in the fence and squeezed through. Damara took a deep breath then followed. Tristan offered his hand to help her, and she took it, using his strength to support her as she gingerly swung her wounded leg through the opening. Once she was inside, she gave Tristan a grateful smile and let go of his hand, but not before giving it a gentle squeeze. Then the two of them turned and took their first good look at Riverfork.

Chapter Nineteen

Since the amusement park had been closed before either Damara or Tristan was born, neither of them had a clear idea what to expect. Damara had been here once before, of course, but it had been dark then, and since that visit had gone horribly wrong, she'd worked to forget as many of the specific details of the park as she could. In the decades since its closure, Riverfork had achieved near legendary status among the children of Zephyr. It had been, so the stories went, the greatest amusement park ever built, with the largest Ferris wheel, fastest roller coaster, and sweetest cotton candy in the world. Its Tilt-a-Whirl could make a kid with even the strongest stomach puke in less than five seconds, and the game booths on the Midway gave out stuffed animals the size of elephants as prizes—and all the games were easy to win. In short, it was the sort of place that children envision when they try to imagine what heaven is like.

The truth, as it usually is, was somewhat more prosaic.

In front of them stood the main entrance, a stone arch with the word RIVERFORK formed out of carved wooden letters. Below the arch were boarded-up ticket booths and rust-laden turnstiles. Beyond the turnstiles was a brick-covered walkway, though the bricks were a dour gray without so much as a hint of magical yellow. Both a roller coaster and a Ferris wheel loomed above the rest of the park, but neither was so large as to be particularly impressive. Both looked as if they'd been built for children no older than ten—kiddie rides, Damara and Tristan would've called them when they'd been kids themselves—and the attractions looked as if they'd been constructed from cobbled-together leftovers of thousands of cast-off tinkertoy and erector sets. They looked so rickety that Damara was surprised they were still standing after so many years of neglect.

Spreading out from the stone arch were walls that were supposed to look like natural stone barriers—craggy and corrugated, colored varying shades of gray—but they were obviously molded plaster. Chunks were missing from the walls, exposing the crumbly white material beneath.

"How do you suppose Emma and Autumn got in?" Damara asked. "They couldn't have climbed over the wall. That stuff looks like it would crumble away as soon as they touched it."

Tristan looked up and down the length of the wall, though you could only see so far in each direction as close as the wooden fence was. "I don't see any holes in the wall big enough for them to crawl through. Do you suppose they went in the main entrance?"

"Those turnstiles look too rusty to turn. And even if they aren't, they're probably locked."

"Autumn could climb under them without any trouble. As for Emma . . ." Tristan trailed off. "Who knows what she's capable of now?" He stepped up to one of the turnstiles and tried to get it to move, but the best he could do was jiggle it. "You're right. It's locked."

"That's because you haven't paid to get in."

They turned toward the sound of the voice and saw that one of the ticket booths was no longer boarded-up. The ticket window was open, and standing behind the counter was a rather haggard-looking woman in her late thirties. Her shoulder-length hair was unwashed and tangled, and while she was wearing makeup, she'd applied it too heavily. She wore a fuzzy pink bathrobe dotted with various unidentifiable stains, and resting on the counter in front of her—along with a glass tumbler half full of clear liquid that was likely either vodka or gin—were three wooden bowls filled with candy. One held lollipops (the kind with bubblegum in the center), another peanut-butter cups, and the third plain chocolate bars.

"Doesn't cost much, though," the woman said, her speech slightly slurred. "Just an answer." Her red-rimmed eyes narrowed and seemed to glitter. "But it has to be the *right* answer."

"Mara . . ."

Damara put a hand on Tristan's arm to reassure him. "Don't you recognize her?"

Tristan gave her a blank look.

"The time we went trick-or-treating when we were six?"

At first, Tristan just shook his head, but then his eyes widened as the memory came back to him. "Yeah . . . she yelled at us, didn't she?"

Damara nodded. Now that she was an adult, it was no big deal, but at the time it had been quite traumatic. Tristan and Damara had gone trick-or-treating by themselves for the first time. Well, kind of—their moms had waited at the corner of each block, gabbing while they kept an eye on their kids. Damara had been dressed as a gypsy princess, which meant she wore a pair of plastic hoop earrings, a green skirt, and one of her mother's scarves on her head. Tristan had put even less effort into his costume. He wore a T-shirt, jeans, and a blue ski mask.

"I'm a bank robber," he'd explained when Damara had first seen him. "I was going to carry a toy gun, but Mom wouldn't let me."

They'd been out for over an hour, it was dark, and their bags were bulging with candy. Their mothers had tried to get them to call it a night, but they'd begged to remain out for one more block, and both moms had agreed. They were down to the last house, and when they walked onto the porch, they saw the front door was open. Before they could say anything, a woman called from inside.

"Come on in, candy's on the coffee table, take one apiece."

They hesitated, looked at each other, shrugged, then stepped inside.

They saw the woman—mussed hair, pink bathrobe, glass of booze in her hand—sitting on the couch, phone receiver held to her ear. She didn't look at either of them as they entered her home.

The candy was indeed on the coffee table, along with a lopsided stack of *TV Guide*s and a collection of cardboard coasters with logos of various beer companies printed on them. Three wooden bowls, three types of candy: lollipops, peanut-butter cups, chocolate bars. Tristan reached for the lollipops, took one, and popped it into his bag. Then he reached for a peanut-butter cup.

"Hey," Damara whispered. The woman was talking on the phone, though her side of the conversation consisted primarily of *yes*'s, *no*'s, and *mm-hmm*'s, and Damara didn't want to disturb her. "She said *one* apiece."

"I know," Tristan whispered back. "There are three bowls. So we get to take a piece of candy from each one."

Damara was about to tell him he was wrong, but then she realized that the woman's words could be interpreted that way. She looked at the woman, hoping that she might notice their hesitation and clarify her directions. But the woman just kept *mm-hm*ing in between sips of alcohol. Damara looked at the bowls. There seemed to be an even amount of candy in each one. If one had contained less than the others, that would've been a clue that they weren't supposed to take a piece of candy from each bowl. But they were even.

Damara wasn't sure what to do, so she decided to err on the side of caution and take only a single piece of candy. She was reaching for the peanut-butter cups when the woman suddenly dropped the phone, reached across the coffee table with her free hand, and grabbed Damara's wrist.

"What the hell is *wrong* with you?" she shouted. "I said one apiece! Can't you fucking *hear?*"

Damara wanted to cry, wanted to turn and run out the door and down the block to her mother. But instead she found her voice and said, "But I haven't taken any yet."

The woman's bloodshot eyes flew wide and her face turned red with anger. "Are you calling me a liar? Are you? Huh? Huh?" With each *huh* the woman tightened her grip on Damara's wrist. It hurt and Damara tried to pull free, but the woman held her fast.

"Let her go, you old butch!" Tristan shouted, the use of one of his odd euphemisms draining away whatever sort of force his words might've otherwise carried.

The woman looked at Tristan then and frowned. "Butch? What the hell are you talking about? Are you are a retard or something? I don't want any fucking retards in my house!" She gave Damara's wrist a last powerful squeeze before finally letting go. Then woman flopped back down onto the couch and picked up the phone.

"Yeah, I'm still here. What were we saying?" The woman had held tight to her booze the entire time and now she finished it off with a single last gulp, put the empty glass down on the coffee table, and started *mm-hmm*ing again.

Though she hadn't told them to get out, Damara and Tristan were only too happy to do so, but not before Tristan had put his lollipop back in the wooden bowl he'd gotten it from. When they got back to their moms, neither of them said anything about the woman, though Damara wasn't sure why. Maybe because they were afraid their moms would drag them back to the woman's house and confront her. Damara had had more than enough of the woman for one night.

She and Tristan had talked about the crazy woman a few times after that, trying to puzzle out precisely what she'd meant by *Take one apiece,* but they'd never reached a definite conclusion.

And now here the woman was, manning the ticket booth at Riverfork, looking exactly like she had all those years ago. Whose memory had she sprung from, Damara wondered. Hers or Tristan's? Both? She supposed it didn't matter. The woman was here and it appeared they had to get past her if they wanted to enter the amusement park. *And* it seemed they were now faced with the same choice they've been given then.

The woman smiled at them, revealing chocolate-smeared teeth. "All you have to do is take one apiece."

"What is this?" Tristan asked. "The riddle of the Sphinx?"

"I guess so," Damara said, trying not to stare at the woman's teeth. "A version of it, anyway."

"We don't have time for this bullshit," Tristan said. "*Autumn* doesn't have time." He turned to the woman behind the counter. "We need to get in right now. We're trying to rescue a little girl that's been kidnapped. Maybe you saw her, she's about ten, has brown hair and pigtails, and was accompanied by a woman with garden shears in place of her right hand."

The woman in the fuzzy pink robe just looked at Tristan, smiling with her chocolate teeth and not blinking, as if she were a mechanical device and someone had hit her pause button.

"I don't think she hears you, Tristan," Damara said. She looked at the woman. "Do you?"

No response. She continued staring straight ahead, bowls of candy laid out on the counter before her.

"To hell with her then," Tristan said. "We'll just climb over the turnstile."

He approached one of the turnstiles, but it was no longer covered with rust. Its metal had become a gleaming silver, and instead of rounded bars, the turnstile now consisted of a series of long double-edged blades like in an old-fashioned push mower. As Tristan took a step toward the turnstile, the blades began spinning, whirling so fast that they soon become a humming blur. The other turnstiles had undergone a similar transformation, and their blades now began spinning as well.

Tristan stopped and stared at the whirling blades.

"Then again, maybe we can't climb over." He walked away from the turnstile and rejoined Damara at the ticket booth. "I guess we answer the question."

"Looks that way, doesn't it?" Damara gazed at the bowls of candy. "Unfortunately, after all these years I still don't know what the right answer is."

"Even if you did, it might not help now. The real-life answer might be the wrong one here. This woman, her question, the whole situation, are all just imagination and memory brought to life by your power, right? In that case, the right answer might be an *un*-real one. It could be almost anything."

Damara hadn't thought of that, but she knew Tristan was right. The woman had been crazy enough in real life. Who knew what sort of bizarre, twisted logic she might operate by now that she was a creature born of Damara's power?

"Let's start by taking a piece from each bowl and see what happens," Tristan said. He reached toward the lollipop bowl, but Damara grabbed his hand and stopped him.

"What if we don't get a second chance?" she said. "Worse, what if there's a punishment for guessing wrong?" She nodded meaningfully toward the whirling blades that the turnstiles had become.

291

Tristan looked at the blades as well, then lowered his hand. "We can't just stand here for the rest of our lives trying to decide!"

"Of course we can't," Damara said gently, trying to soothe him. Tristan sounded scared, and she didn't blame him. She was plenty scared as well. "We just need to think before we do anything, that's all."

"But like you said, we've had twenty years to think about it. Why do you think we'll be able to come up with the right answer now?"

"Because we have to," Damara said.

Her response brought Tristan up short. He blinked at her in surprise, then forced a smile and nodded.

Damara smiled back. Good, Tristan was ready to work as a team to solve this riddle—assuming it could be solved at all.

Now that you've gotten Tristan calmed down, don't you go giving into despair, she scolded herself. There had to be an answer, if for no other reason than Autumn needed there to be one.

Damara gazed at the three bowls of candy and concentrated on interpreting the woman's words. *All you have to do is take one apiece.*

"The first two choices I can think of are the most obvious ones," Tristan said. "Like I said a minute ago, we each take one piece of candy from each of the bowls, or we each select one type of candy and take only one piece of it."

"But we tried those in real life, didn't we?" Damara said. "Or at least, we'd been in the process of doing so when the woman freaked out. You were going to take three pieces of candy and—despite what the woman thought—I was only going to take one. But from the way she grabbed my arm, it seemed like neither choice was the right one."

"So we should avoid doing either this time?" Tristan said.

"Yes. Maybe. I don't know." Now Damara was beginning to get frustrated.

The woman behind the counter continued staring straight ahead, not blinking, mouth still stretched into a smile, chocolate drying to a hard coating on her teeth as she stood there waiting for them to make up their minds. Damara wondered how long the woman would keep standing like that, waiting for them. Hours? Days? Weeks? Months? Years? Forever? And if so, what would happen to Autumn in the meantime? Damara forced herself to keep thinking.

"We could take a bowl and leave the candy," she suggested. "Or *each* take a bowl." When Tristan gave her a skeptical look, she added. "Well, the woman said to take *one* apiece, but she never said one *what*."

"I suppose she didn't," Tristan admitted. "But it doesn't seem very likely, does it? I mean, why would a bowl gain us entrance into the park?"

"Why would candy?" Damara countered.

"True." Tristan looked suddenly thoughtful. "Remember what I said bout the riddle of the Sphinx a minute ago?"

"Yes, but you were just making a joke . . . weren't you?"

"That's what I thought, but what if the comment was true in a way? Or *became* true the moment I said it, like what happened to those two poor women in the coffee shop this morning."

Had it really been that short of a time since the two women had been twisted, molded, and re-shaped by her power? It seemed so much longer.

"All right," Damara said. "So you mentioned the Sphinx. What about it?"

"For a time in college I considered switching majors to philosophy. I took a few classes in mythology and folklore, and I was really into it for a while. In so many stories heroes are put through various challenges—riddles, sacrifices, contests of strength, speed, and bravery—in order to prove worthy of reaching the place they journey to, or obtaining whatever reward they might seek. The Riddle of the Sphinx was always one of my fa-vorites. Another favorite is from Norse mythology. Odin, the chieftain of the gods, visited the magic well Mimir in search of knowledge regarding the future. The spirit of the well was only too happy to grant Odin's request—for a price. The god had to pluck out one of his eyes and throw it into the well. I forget why, but Odin really needed the in-formation, so he did it."

"You mean he just reached up and . . ." Damara's stomach did a flip and she couldn't fin-ish the sentence.

Tristan nodded. "And afterward Odin wore an

eyepatch over his empty socket until the end of time."

"Please tell me you aren't suggesting we pull out our eyes," Damara said.

"I'm not. We need to get inside. An answer to the woman's question is the payment, but after you pay to get into an amusement park, a movie, or a museum, what are you handed?"

"A ticket," Damara said. "But I still don't see where you're going with this."

"A ticket is a token of passage. It doesn't have to be paper. It can be anything."

"Omigod, you're saying that instead of giving her *our* eyes . . ."

Tristan shrugged. "She did say *take* one apiece, didn't she?"

Damara glanced at the woman, but she was still immobile, face frozen in a chocolatey smile as if she were completely unfazed by listening to two strangers discuss mutilating her. Damara wasn't sure, but she thought the woman's eyes were more prominent than a moment ago, as if they bulged outward, almost daring Tristan and Damara to reach for them. A hint, perhaps?

"We tried to take the candy when we were eight," Tristan said, "and we got yelled at. For whatever reason, it was the wrong thing to do then, and I think it's the wrong thing to do now. And what else does the woman have two of that we can take? Without performing major surgery that is?" His voice was strained as he made this joke, as if he recognized how insane it sounded but couldn't stop himself from saying it. "Besides," he added, "it isn't as if she's real."

Damara gave the woman a sideways glance. "Who's to say what's real?" she said softly. Then, more loudly, "All right then." She couldn't believe this madness was happening, couldn't believe she'd agreed to it. "Are you going to take them out or do you want me to do it?"

Tristan dry-swallowed several times, as if he were trying to keep from vomiting. "We both have to 'Take one apiece,' remember?"

"I was afraid you'd say that."

After a moment's hesitation, they reached out together—Damara for the left eye, Tristan for the right. It was wet, soft, and slippery, but the woman remained motionless while they worked, and a few moments later, Tristan and Damara held the woman's eyeballs in their blood-smeared palms. One apiece.

The woman in the pink bathrobe—which was now speckled with red—suddenly began moving again.

"Please keep your tickets with you at all times," she said in a cheery voice as two streams of crimson ran down from her empty sockets like tears of blood. The whirring turnstiles began to slow, and when they came to a stop, the deadly blades were gone, and they were once more perfectly ordinary. "Enjoy your stay in Riverfork, and make sure to take the time to visit all our attractions. After all, there's lots to *see!*"

Tristan took the grisly white orb from Damara

and tucked both it and his into his shirt pocket. The fabric immediately turned dark with blood. He then grabbed Damara's hand and they hurried through the turnstile, neither of them looking back at the woman behind the ticket counter.

They were in.

Chapter Twenty

"Isn't this fun?"

Autumn heard Emma's words, but they were nothing but sound to the child, completely devoid of meaning, devoid of any sense that sound could carry meaning, or indeed, that there was such a concept of *meaning* at all. She followed wherever Emma went—crawled under the turnstile when Emma had told her to, even helped the older woman climb overtop—but she did these things out of blind, automatic instinct. She was no longer capable of doing otherwise because, for now at least, she could not conceive of acting on her own. In fact, at that precise moment, Autumn wasn't a *she,* wasn't even an *it.* She was just a collection of chemicals and water shaped into a particular form that happened to be following a woman named Emma Colton around an abandoned amusement park. It was better this way, because if Autumn didn't exist, she didn't have to think about the terrible things that she'd seen, the awful things that had happened, the unspeakable way her mother had died . . .

To be or not to be? Autumn knew which was better. It was, as she'd often said to her friends at school after a test she'd done especially well on, a no-brainer.

If Autumn had been more than an ambulatory nervous system at that moment, she would've noticed—and been revolted by—the black lumps covering Emma's skin. She would've had a difficult time taking her eyes off them, and if she stared long enough, she might've noticed the lumps were slowly but steadily growing larger.

Riverfork wasn't, strictly speaking, abandoned anymore. After all, Autumn and Emma were there, but the farther they walked along the gray brick path that wound through the park, the more alive the place became. People—or at least the vague suggestions of them—walked past Autumn and Emma. They were hazy, indistinct forms at first, like creatures shaped from mist. But increasingly they gained more substance and detail, became sharper, as if they were images viewed through a focusing lens. Men and women dressed in clothes and wearing hairstyles from the 1950s walked hand in hand, children skipping along at their sides. The children held balloons or ice cream cones, and some of them carried stuffed animals— purple teddy bears, red alligators—that their dads had won for them. These happy apparitions made no noise as they walked, talked, skipped, and laughed. It was like watching television with the sound muted.

The buildings and rides, which had been sagging ramshackle collections of rotting wood and rust-eaten metal, were slowly becoming good as new, the wood strong and solid, the metal smooth and gleaming. Colors returned to the park—bright and cheerful, almost glimmering in the sunlight. Paint seemed to emerge from within the wood and metal, and the dead dry weeds covering the ground retreated into the earth to be replaced with lush green grass and beautiful blooming flowers more appropriate for the height of summer than early fall. And from somewhere close by came the jaunty rhythm of carousel music.

"It's just as I remember it," Emma said. "Clean, neat, orderly . . . attentive parents, well-behaved children . . . Not a scrap of litter on the ground, no kids whining or screaming, no adults yelling or swearing. Everyone doing exactly what they should."

Autumn wasn't really present, despite her body's proximity to Emma, but if she had been, she might well have noticed how strange, how artificial, how *wrong* the park looked. But she wasn't, so she didn't.

"I've got an idea," Emma said. "How about a Sno-Cone? My treat."

Autumn gave no response, just continued to stare off blankly into space.

Emma grinned. "I thought you'd like that! Let's go."

The older woman started walking down the brick path, making her way through a crowd of happy, smiling ghosts. A moment later, Autumn's body began following.

Damara tried not to look at the moist lumps in Tristan's shirt pocket as they walked through the park. At first they were alone on the brick path, but before long Damara began to sense unseen presences moving around them. If she had been anyone else, she would've dismissed the impression as nothing more than imagination. But she knew better. She waited and watched as the presences gradually took on form and solidity, becoming small family groups straight out of a 1950s sitcom. The happy white people seemed real enough, except they made no sound whatsoever. Not even their footsteps were audible.

Tristan waved his hand in front of the eyes of a passing man dressed in a green sweater and khaki pants who reminded Damara a little of Bing Crosby. The man gave no sign that he noticed Tristan—didn't glance at him, didn't slow down— and Tristan had to pull his hand back to avoid accidentally smacking the man as he walked by.

"What are they?" Tristan asked. "Ghosts of some kind?"

"More like memories," Damara said. "Emma's, I bet. She entered the park before us, so she's the first one to have an impact on the place."

Tristan watched a pair of young girls—twins—

skip by, laughing silently. "Funny, I wouldn't have figured Emma for the nostalgic type."

Damara shrugged. "There's no telling what my power will bring to life. It's not like it can consciously be controlled. It just happens, like the weather. All we can do is react to it."

Tristan gazed at the crowd of silent families that moved around them, his brow furrowed in thought. Though whatever was on his mind, he chose not to share it.

Not only were the people returning to Riverfork, the rides and attractions were coming back as well. Old buildings on the verge of collapse were refurbishing themselves, and rides that had been nothing more than immobile sculptures of rusted junk were reclaiming their former glory. The smell of frying funnel cakes and cotton candy wafted forth from a small square building labeled TASTEE SHACK. Close by a mini roller coaster called Bug Out!—its cars once more round and green instead of dented gray-black—began undulating along its track. The cartoonish bug head at the front of the cars wore a top hot and sported a happy grin, as if delighted by its miraculous restoration.

They continued walking, past attractions that urged them to SEE THE FROZEN BABY WHALE and dared them to TAKE A SPIN ON THE DIZZYING WHIRLABOUT! And then they came to a large building, its outside completely covered by shimmering mirrors.

Damara stopped walking and stared at the letters above the entrance. They were formed from glass tubes that glowed an electric neon green and proclaimed COME SEE WHAT MYSTERIES THE MIRRORS REVEAL INSIDE ALACRITY'S SPECTATORIUM!

Tristan also stopped and asked, "What is it, Mara?"

At first she couldn't find her voice, and it took her several tries before she was able to speak. "I remember now. This is the place where my father disappeared."

Large mirrored doors formed the entrance. They were closed, preventing Damara from seeing inside—not that she wanted to. The longer she looked at the mirrors covering the building, the more they seemed to ripple slowly like liquid silver. She had the impression that if she walked up to Alacrity's Spectatorium and reached out toward the glass, instead of touching a cold smooth surface, the rippling silver would gently yield to her fingers, permitting her entire hand to enter.

Is that what happened to Daddy? she wondered. Had he passed through the liquid silver barrier to whatever lay beyond, become lost and unable to find his way back? Was he still in there now, and if so, would she have the courage to go inside and see?

"Are you sure this is the right place?" Tristan asked. "You said it was dark that night."

Damara wanted to say yes, she was sure, wanted to ask Tristan to accompany her inside, wanted to search for her father and, if she couldn't find him, at least learn what had happened to him. But standing there, looking at the rippling surface of Alacrity's Spectatorium and seeing the reflections of herself and Tristan distorted in its glass, she was suddenly eleven years old again and paralyzed with terror.

Besides, she told herself, *Autumn needs us.* And though it was true, she knew that it was nevertheless an excuse.

"Never mind," she whispered. She took Tristan's arm and pulled him away from the building. He gave her a puzzled look, but he didn't question her any further.

They came to an arrow-shaped sign that said TO THE MIDWAY, and without any better destination in mind, they turned in the direction the sign indicated. As they continued making their way through the now living, breathing park, the people around them began to change. Many still looked like refugees from the fifties, but more and more of them were dressed in contemporary clothing and had modern hairstyles. They weren't all white anymore, either. It wasn't exactly the U.N., but the crowd now contained more African-Americans, Hispanics, and Asians.

"Now what's happening?" Tristan asked.

"I'd guess that you're starting to have an impact on Riverfork now, and you have a more modern, tolerant worldview than Emma."

Tristan smiled. "I'll take that as a compliment."

While the crowd was more diverse, still none of them made any sound.

"It's eerie how quiet they are," Tristan continued. "It's almost as if neither they nor we completely exist in the same world, but only overlap a bit. I wonder if Emma's imagination isn't strong enough to give them sound."

"Maybe. Or maybe she really hates noise and subconsciously isn't letting them make any."

"Good guess, girlie-girl! Wanna try your luck over here?"

They turned in the direction of the voice and saw a sleazy carny type leaning across the counter of a game booth.

"Looks like we found the Midway," Tristan muttered.

The gray brick pathway widened here, and on both sides game booths were lined up, crammed so close together that it was difficult to tell where one ended and another began. You could throw darts at balloons, rings over the necks of milk bottles, ping-pong balls at bowls of goldfish, bean bags (three for a dollar!) at pyramids of pewter vases, footballs through hoops that were almost but not quite too small . . . And your reward, should you possess enough luck and skill to succeed at any of these contests, was to pick from a selection of prizes ranging from cheap plastic rings shaped like black spiders or purple gems on up to generic stuffed animals the size of a large child. The games, along with their challenges and prizes, were so ubiquitous and similar that they didn't even have names. But then, none were really needed to draw customers. The seeming simplicity of their tasks, along with a generous mixture of encouragements and insults from the man—and it almost always was a man—running the game was usually enough. Certainly, there were plenty of people ready to chance their luck today. Most were either the 1950s sitcom clones Emma had conjured, though there were a good amount of the contemporary folk from Tristan's imagination as well. Still, there were a few that Damara couldn't place, and which for some unaccountable reason disturbed her.

In front of a ring-toss game, a normal-looking man in a shirt and tie stood arguing with a lean man dressed in an old-fashioned white suit that looked more appropriate for a revival meeting than an amusement park. Damara wasn't sure, but it looked like the man in the white suit had pools of inky darkness where his eyes should be. A few booths farther down, a man in a black suede jacket was trying to win his girl a prize at a shooting gallery by firing wooden pellets from an air rifle at metal targets shaped like woodland creatures. The girl, who was quite a bit younger than her date, wore tight shorts and a halter top that allowed part of a dragonfly tattoo on her back to be visible.

Of all the game booths, only one had no customers standing in front—the one run by the man who'd called out to them.

"Come on, I haven't got all day, and you two certainly don't. Not if you want to save the little girl, that is."

Damara felt a cold twist in her gut upon hearing the man's words, but she grabbed Tristan's arm and pulled him over to the booth. The man grinned as they approached, displaying yellow-brown teeth. What he still had of them, that is, for he was missing both his two front uppers and two front lowers. The gumline where his teeth had been was red and sore looking. He was bald but wore the rest of his straight greasy black hair long as if to compensate. His black mustache was bristly and badly in need of a trim, and his cheeks and chin were covered with stubble. He wore a faded, cracked leather vest without a shirt, exposing a hairy chest, flabby pecs, and the tight mound of his bulging gut. His left cheek was puffed out, as if swollen, and his jaw worked in a rhythmic, mechanical fashion. He held a rusted coffee can in his left hand, and as Damara and Tristan stepped up to his booth, he turned his head and spit a brown stream of tobacco juice into the can.

Unlike many of the other booths on the Midway, his had nothing to do with any shooting, throwing, puncturing, breaking, or knocking down anything. On the counter before him was a neatly stacked deck of playing cards lying facedown. A cardboard sign with crudely painted letters was tacked to the wall of the booth behind him. It said TRY YOUR LUCK, 21 OR BUST!

"My god," Tristan said. "I remember this guy! We saw him at the county fair, Mara, remember? We were . . . hell, I don't know . . . ten, maybe? It was summer and we were playing one morning, and I told you my mom was going to take me to the fair that afternoon. You ran inside to beg your mother to let you come with me. At first she said no—"

"But I started crying and she finally changed her mind," Damara finished. "How could I forget?"

The man spat another stream of tobacco juice into his can, then grinned again. "Nice to be remembered," he said, his voice rough from too many cigarettes, too much booze, maybe both.

"I wouldn't exactly say *nice*," Tristan said. "We'd wandered away from my mom and sister, and you lured us over to your booth with some simple card tricks . . ."

"Like this?" The man put his personal spittoon down on the counter, picked up the deck of cards, and fanned them out facedown. His hands were pudgy, the fingers stubby, but they handled the cards with a surgeon's deftness. He passed his hand over the cards, seeming not to touch them, but when he was finished, the cards were lying faceup. With a quick motion, he scooped up the cards and, using only one hand mixed and shuffled the cards for several moments. When he was finished, he fanned them out on the counter once more, only this time they were organized by both number and suit.

"Just like that," Damara said. "You told us to call you Wheeler, said it was short for Wheeler-Dealer. Then you showed us a few more tricks, had us pick cards that you always guessed, and then you asked if we'd like to see the trailer where you lived."

"Good thing my mom and sister found us then," Tristan said, "or else we might have been stupid enough to fall for your most dangerous trick, and who knows what might have happened to us?"

The man scooped up the cards again and idly reshuffled them once more. He shrugged. "Can't blame a guy for trying. 'Cept that wasn't me, exactly. I'm your memory of that guy, with a few extras added on." He put the cards facedown on the counter in a neat pile, then picked up his tobacco can and spat into it once more.

"What sort of extras?" Damara asked.

"Both you and Tristan thought that I was some kind of magician instead of just a pedophile who knew a few card tricks. So here, in this place and at this time, I *am* a magician. I know all, see all, and tell all—when I feel like it. I can tell you the thing you want to know the most: where Autumn is. But information like that doesn't come cheap. There's a price." He grinned again, and this time his gums were raw and bleeding.

Damara knew they couldn't fully trust Wheeler, but if there was even a chance he could direct them to Autumn . . .

"What sort of price?" she asked.

The man chuckled. "I just love it when a pretty little fish like you nibbles at the bait. Does my shriveled black soul good."

But before he could answer Damara's question, a shadow fell across the Midway. Everyone looked up to see that dark clouds had drifted overhead and now blocked the sun.

310

"Looks like another player has entered the game," Wheeler said.

Kenneth walked through the opening in the wooden fence and found himself standing in front of a stone arch. A *fake* stone arch at that. Pretty damn cheesy, he thought. And everyone he'd ever talked to about Riverfork—including Emma—had always acted like the park had been such hot shit. What a joke! He wasn't irritated, though; he was actually in a pretty good mood. Since he'd awakened on Pandora Drive and made his way down the hill to Riverfork, the feeling had returned to his body, and he felt whole and healthy again—except for the fact that he was still missing his penis, of course.

"Would you like a ticket, sir?"

Only one of the ticket booths was open, and a woman in a fuzzy pink bathrobe stood behind the counter. Her tits were nice, if not spectacular, and Kenneth's gaze lingered on them for a moment as he tried to imagine what they looked like beneath the cloth. Just because he no longer had a penis didn't mean he couldn't look, right? But when he finally lifted his gaze to look at her face, he saw that the woman had no eyes.

Interesting.

"I was going to say that, as you can see, I don't have any money on me, but you *can't,* can you? See, I mean." He liked the way dark blood coated her sockets and painted her cheeks with crimson trails. He wanted to lick the blood on those cheeks, then thrust his tongue into the sockets one at a time, clean out the blood inside, and see if his tongue would stretch far enough to taste her brain. The more he thought about doing these things, the more her empty sockets came to resemble a pair of vaginas. If only he still had his dick, maybe he could've literally fucked her brains out.

Then the woman, who thanks to Kenneth's imagination really did have vaginas instead of eye sockets now, gave him a chocolate-encrusted smile.

"You don't have to pay money to get inside," she said. "All you have to do is make a choice. But it has to be the *right* choice."

She spread her hands and Kenneth suddenly noticed there were three wooden bowls of candy sitting on the counter in front of her. He couldn't recall seeing them there before, but then he'd been too busy staring at the woman's tits and eye cunts, so maybe he just hadn't seen the candy until now.

"Take one apiece," she said.

Kenneth looked at the bowls and frowned. "What do you mean?"

"Take one apiece," the woman repeated, her tone and inflection exactly the same, as if her voice were a recording.

"You mean you want me to take a piece of candy from each bowl? Or do you want me to take only one piece total?"

"Take one apiece," the woman said for a third time.

Kenneth glared at her. "Screw this. I'm going in

and you can just fuckin' bill me." He started for
the turnstile, but suddenly it became a set of rotary
blades that looked sharp as hell. They began spinning, slowly at first, but they quickly picked up
speed until they were a humming blur.

He turned back to the woman. She was still
smiling, but her eye pussies were now larger, the
labia swollen, the soft inner flesh glistening, and
she had pubic hair in place of eyebrows.

"Take one apiece," she said once more, and
though it was subtle, Kenneth thought he detected
a bit of irritation in her voice this time.

"Sorry, I'm not big on games,"

Kenneth stepped back, spread his legs wide, and
let the darkness between them pull in both the
woman and her goddamned bowls of candy. When
she was gone, the turnstile blades stopped spinning and returned to their previously harmless
configuration.

"That's more like it," Kenneth muttered, and he
walked through the turnstile and entered Riverfork. As his bare feet first touched the gray stone
of the main pathway, the sky began to grow dark.

Chapter Twenty-one

Emma paid the smiling glassy-eyed vendor of the Tastee Shack for the Sno-Cones, then turned to Autumn and held out the girl's to her. Autumn didn't reach out to take it, and Emma had to switch her own Sno-Cone to her other hand and hold on to both while she raised Autumn's arm and gently pried open her fingers. When she let go, Autumn kept her hand in that position, and Emma quickly put a Sno-Cone into it and folded Autumn's fingers over the paper cone. Emma half expected the girl to drop her Sno-Cone the moment she let go of her hand, but that didn't happen. Autumn made no move to bring the Sno-Cone to her mouth—as near as Emma could tell the girl wasn't even aware that she was holding it—but she didn't let go. Emma smiled. It was a start.

"I didn't know what flavors you liked, so I gambled and got you strawberry. If you don't like it, I'll trade you. I've got lime."

Autumn said nothing, which didn't especially

surprise Emma. Well, if the girl wasn't going to speak up, she'd just have to stick with strawberry and like it, wouldn't she? Emma started to lift her Sno-Cone—crushed ice drizzled with thick green syrup that looked like antifreeze—and was about to take her first taste when a shadow fell over them. She looked up and saw that what had moments ago been an empty blue sky was now filled with dark clouds. They were bruise-colored, purple-black, and looked heavy with rain. Emma scowled. She didn't like the idea of her first outing as Autumn's new parent being spoiled by bad weather. She supposed they'd have to make the best of it. Besides, this was Ohio, where you never knew what the weather might be like from moment to moment. There was always a chance that the clouds would blow over before they released any precipitation.

"Better get to work on that Sno-Cone, Autumn," Emma said. "Looks like it might start raining soon."

Autumn still gave no sign that she'd heard Emma, so the older woman decided not to worry about her for the moment. It had been years—and far too many of them, at that—since she'd had a Sno-Cone, and Emma was really looking forward to this. She raised the Sno-Cone to her mouth once more and was about to take a taste, when she noticed that the syrup was no longer lime-green. And then she realized it was no longer syrup, either. The ice in her Sno-Cone was now covered with thick red blood.

"Lovely," she muttered. She threw her Sno-Cone to the ground, not bothering to dispose of it properly, even though there was a trash receptacle less than five yards from where they stood. She turned to Autumn, intending to take the girl's Sno-Cone and throw it away, but Autumn held the paper cone tight in her grip. So tight that some of the ice had been squeezed out and had fallen to the ground. While the substance that now covered the ice was still red, Emma knew that it was no longer strawberry syrup.

Autumn stared at her bloody Sno-Cone, eyes slowly widening, hand trembling. Her mouth worked, but nothing came out. Then her hand sprang open and the Sno-Cone dropped to the ground where it splattered crimson-coated ice all over the walkway's gray brick. Autumn's mouth flew open and a shrill scream escaped her lips. With a sudden burst of movement, Autumn turned and fled, arms and legs pumping at a pace that would've done an Olympic athlete proud. Emma made a grab for the girl, but she was too late. Her hand closed only on empty air.

Emma considered chasing after Autumn, but she decided against it. Though she tried to keep in shape, she knew she was too old to win a footrace against a terrified little girl. This was a race she could only win by following Autumn and waiting for the girl to tire herself out. And when that moment came, Emma would reclaim her.

She noted the direction Autumn had run off in, then looked upward. The discolored clouds had merged to form a blanket of darkness over River-fork. The clouds hung heavy now, pendulous and gravid with rain. She could think of only one person who could turn her paradise into a hell: Kenneth. Somehow, even mutilated as she'd left him, the sonofabitch had survived and was coming after her. She could sense it. Her stomach gurgled then, and she gave it an affectionate pat.

Don't worry, she thought. *You'll soon be fed. And next time we'll cut off more than just his dick. A lot more.*

But first things first; she had to get her new daughter back.

Emma started walking in the direction Autumn had taken, her stomach growling softly with every step.

Autumn ran without thought of direction. She had no idea where she was or how she'd gotten here, but somehow she knew this was a bad place, *very* bad, and she had to get away.

The blood . . . the ice had been covered with blood. . . .

Her shoes pounded on hard brick, and she ran past groups of people—mothers, fathers, grand-parents, kids . . . But she didn't call out to them, didn't plead for someone to stop and help her. She wasn't sure why, but she knew there was something wrong with these people. None of them seemed to notice that there was a terrified young girl running in their midst. None of them said anything to her or so much as even flicked a glance in her direction. She was used to adults being too wrapped up in their own concerns to notice anything much past the end of their own nose, but the other kids not looking at her—not even to make fun of her—well, that was just downright creepy. And then there was the sound, or rather the lack of it. Despite the presence of all these people, the only noise Autumn heard was the *slap-slap-slap* of her shoes as she ran.

The longer she ran, the more she began to become aware of her surroundings, and despite the fear that still impelled her, she found herself slowing, slowing and then finally stopping. She stood and stared, unable to believe what she was seeing.

In front of her, a large caterpillar trundled along a set of metal rails, cars rattling as they negotiated the gentle hills and curves of the track. The caterpillar's face was cheerfully cartoonish, almost grotesquely so, and as it rolled around the track one more time, she had the impression that the thing was actually looking at her with its painted-on eyes. As the top-hatted head passed by her, she thought she saw it wink, but then it was moving on, and she wasn't sure.

She turned in a slow circle, saw a machine that allowed you to TEST YOUR STRENGTH (IF YOU'RE MAN ENOUGH)! opposite the caterpillar ride, which according to its sign was called BUG-OUT!, exclamation point included. Not far away, she saw a slowly rotating Ferris wheel and a bit beyond that, an old-fashioned roller coaster, its cars juddering up the first hill, riders holding their arms high above their heads to show that they were too brave—or too foolish—to use their safety bars. There were other attractions in the vicinity, all with signs that vied almost desperately at times for customers' attention. RIDE THE SPINNING BARRELS, TRY A FROZEN BANANA (THE ULTIMATE TASTE TREAT), DON'T MISS THE AMAZING MOONWALK—IT'S OUT OF THIS WORLD!

Autumn didn't understand how it was possible, but it seemed she was in an amusement park. But the closest one was Kings Island, and that was almost an hour away. The only other amusement park she could think of anywhere near where she lived was Riverfork. It was on the other side of Damara's house, down a hill, and through some woods, but it had been abandoned years ago. So why did she have the strange feeling that *this* was Riverfork?

Images flashed through her mind then— someone holding her hand, helping her over a chainlink fence, guiding her down a tree-covered slope, then through a field of tall grass . . . She wasn't sure who the person was; she (*was* it a she?) wasn't clear in these images, visions, memories, whatever they were. She was a blurry figure, almost as if Autumn had tried to erase her from her mind with only partial success. But even though Autumn knew it was crazy, that it couldn't possibly be true, she felt that this *was* Riverfork, but a Riverfork that had somehow been restored to life. Why would Mrs. Colton bring her here, though? It didn't make any . . .

Mrs. Colton. *That's* who the blurry figure was! *That's* who'd brought her here!

And that realization was the key that unlocked the door where Autumn had hidden the memories of what she'd discovered in her house upon coming home from school, and all the terrible things that had occurred afterward. Her understanding of these memories was imperfect, for they came back to her in a confused, nightmarish jumble, but one thing she was certain of: Her mother was dead. Grief fell upon her like a crushing weight, and it was all she could do to keep from falling to the ground, curling up into a ball and sobbing. But she knew she couldn't afford to take the time to mourn her mother right now, for Mrs. Colton—Emma—would surely be coming after her soon. She needed help, and she needed it now.

Autumn had been taught well by both her mother and her school. She knew not to talk to strangers and not to allow them to lure her into a car. She knew to call 911 in an emergency and that police officers and firefighters were always ready to help kids in trouble. But when no police or firefighters were available, any adult in authority could help. And the nearest equivalent Autumn could think of at the moment were the workers running the rides and manning the various other attractions. And the closest ride to her right now was Bug-Out!.

She ran toward the set of trundling green cars, praying that whoever was in charge of their operation could help her. As she ran, she didn't notice the cloud cover overhead shift colors from purple-black to *all* black. The black of emptiness, of noth--ingness, of death . . .

As artificial night fell on Riverfork, the park's lights came on, their gentle yellow glow doing little to push back the darkness.

"It certainly gets dark early around here," Wheeler said, favoring Damara and Tristan with a tobacco-stained, gap-toothed grin.

Damara glanced upward and saw the sky had become a mantle of solid darkness. The sight chilled her to the core of her being, and though she wasn't sure she wanted to know, she looked at Wheeler and asked, "You said someone else had entered Riverfork?"

"That's right. A friend of yours, though he's not exactly the man he used to be. In fact, you might say he's not a man at all anymore."

"Kenneth," Tristan said.

Wheeler nodded. "Just as Emma's imagination first shaped the park, and then yours, now Kenneth's is having its impact. And let me tell you, the guy has one *seriously* twisted mind."

"We know," Tristan said. "That's why I'm personally scared shitless at the moment."

Tristan's tone was light as he said this, but there was an edge of hysteria to his words. Damara didn't blame him. What sort of nightmare would Riverfork become in response to Kenneth's mental influence?

The air seemed to ripple, as if an invisible wave were rolling through the park. And where it passed, things changed. In the Midway, the game booths no longer featured simple diversions such as tossing rings at milk bottles or throwing darts at balloons. Now the games took on a more sinister and far less innocent aspect. Rings carved from human bone were tossed onto bleached spinal columns, butcher knives were thrown at wriggling fetuses nailed to wooden planks, patrons earned points for seeing how long they could keep their hands inside a meat grinder . . . The prizes the games offered also changed. No more stuffed animals or cheap plastic novelties. Coils of intestines, swatches of flensed skin, severed limbs, eviscerated hearts, lungs, livers, kidneys . . . all hung on meat hooks—fresh, red, wet, and tempting.

The park-goers were altered as well. Few wore clothing any longer, and those who did had on studded leather with openings for their erogenous zones. The males became well endowed, with penises that stretched nearly all the way to the ground, and many had clusters of multiple sex organs. The women's breasts became large and swollen as if massive amounts of silicon were being pumped into their mammary glands by some unseen source. The skin of the breasts stretched tight and tracings of thick blue veins were visible just beneath the surface. Their vaginas widened to become gaping orifices and lubricant dripped steadily from between their legs.

Wheeler wasn't immune from the transformation taking place in Riverfork. His sagging pectoral muscles became large saggy breasts, and his bristly mustache became finer, softer, and curly, until it resembled a thatch of pubic hair. The lobes of his ears became swollen testicles, the skin so lax that it drooped down to his jawline like a pair of grotesque fleshy earrings.

The only ones unaffected by the hideous wave of change were Damara and Tristan—and, Damara noticed, the man wearing a tie and his companion in the white preacher's suit (who were *still* arguing), and the man in the black jacket and his dragonfly-tattooed piece of jailbait. None of the four seemed to be aware of the transformation that had occurred around them, and if they were, they showed no sign. Damara began to wonder if they hadn't changed because, like Tristan and herself, they were real.

But the worst aspect of all these changes was that *she* was powering them; Kenneth was unconsciously directing her power to reshape Riverfork in his own foul image. If only there were some way she could cut off his access to her power . . .

"But there isn't," Wheeler said, as if he'd read her thoughts. Given everything that had happened over the course of the last day, this wasn't particularly surprising or disturbing. In fact, it was among the least of the dark miracles her power had wrought.

"You have no choice in how your power is used. You are the medium, Damara, but you can never be the artist. At least, not so long as you continue to deny your gift."

"What are you talking about?" she demanded. "I haven't *denied* it; I've spent my whole life trying to control it."

Wheeler spit a stream of tobacco into his can, then put it down on the counter and fished a package of chew out of his pants pocket. He pulled out a pinch, stuffed it between his cheek and gum, then put the package back in his pocket. Damara saw tiny slits in the tips of his fingers—slits that resembled the opening in the glans of a penis. Wheeler continued speaking as he began to work the tobacco around in his mouth.

"You haven't tried to control it. Not really. You've tried to *suppress* it, girlie-girl. Big difference. Maybe if you'd accepted your power, embraced it, you'd have gained some measure of control over it by now. Maybe then it wouldn't have built up to the point where it leaked out and spilled over onto your neighbors."

Damara wanted to deny Wheeler's words, to tell him that her power was too strong, too wild to be controlled in the way he was suggesting. But deep down, she knew he was right. She'd never really tried, had always been too afraid to. Instead she'd attempted to lock her power away inside and isolate herself from the rest of the world, to turn her home into a prison. And to what ultimate purpose? Her power had still managed to escape, and look at all the damage it had caused. She hadn't asked to be born with this power, but she had been, and that meant that, whether she liked it or not, she had the responsibility to learn to wield it effectively, if only to know how to *keep* from using it. But she'd denied that responsibility, had refused even to acknowledge it, and that meant everything that had happened—from the disappearance of her little brother years ago up to this very moment—truly was her fault.

"But why would Damara's power flare up so strongly now, after all these years?" Tristan asked.

"Why ask me?" Wheeler said. "You ought to be asking yourself."

Tristan frowned. "What do you mean?"

"I mean that *you're* what set Damara off. Or rather, your returning to town for your mother's funeral. Seeing you—if only from behind the safety of her window—stirred up all sorts of feelings in our pretty friend here. Feelings of longing, confusion, desire . . ." Wheeler leered at Damara. "She became so emotionally unsettled that the control she'd worked so hard to achieve began to slip little by little until she finally couldn't hold on any longer, and pow! Her psychic walls burst like a giant mystical pimple popping, and her power spilled onto those around her. Claire, Autumn, Anne, Emma, and Kenneth."

"What about Tristan?" Damara asked. "My power spilled onto him as well."

"Not exactly," Wheeler said, then spit a fresh stream of tobacco juice into his can. He hadn't bothered to pick up the can this time, and the impact from the tobacco juice hitting the inside of the can nearly knocked it over.

"But Tristan imagined that double of me, the one with butterfly wings."

"True," Wheeler admitted. "But just because you can't consciously direct your power doesn't mean that it can't feed on your imagination by itself. And once Tristan returned home to California, your imagination started working overtime." Wheeler gave Tristan a meaningful look.

Tristan's eyes widened as the implications of Wheeler's words hit home, but he said nothing to refute them.

Damara couldn't believe what she was hearing. "Are you seriously suggesting that I *imagined* Tristan? That he's not *real?*"

"You didn't imagine him the first time," Wheeler said. "He really did return home when his mother died. And he *is* intending to return to clear out the junk his mother collected over the years and then put the house up for sale. But he has not returned to Ohio yet. Poor guy. I wonder how he's going to react when he learns his mother's house has been destroyed."

"No," Tristan whispered, then more loudly. "No, I can't be a fantasy of Damara's given flesh. I think, feel, remember . . . I had fantasies of my own come to life: the gray sludge and the butterfly woman. Can a dream *have* dreams?"

"Dreams and wishes, fantasy and reality . . . the divisions between them aren't as clear-cut as you might think," Wheeler said. "Especially when someone of Damara's abilities is involved. Fantasies can be like nesting dolls, with one hidden inside another. The Damara doll opens and you pop out, then you open and the Butterfly Damara pops out."

Tristan looked pale and he was trembling, but he said, "Of all the insane things that have happened since I got home, this is the absolute craziest! I *am* real!"

"*Cogito ego sum,* eh?" Wheeler said. "Well, it's easy enough to check." He reached into his pants pocket and pulled out a small silver cell phone. He tossed it to Tristan, who caught it out of reflex.

"It's what, after one o'clock in California? Isn't this the time you usually hold office hours? All you have to do is turn on the phone, call your office number, see who—if anyone—picks up. If Professor Tristan Ledford answers, then you'll know."

Tristan looked down at the phone he held in a trembling hand. He made no move to lift the cover, just kept staring at its silvery plastic surface.

"Either he's wrong or he's lying. I'm sure of it," Damara said, though she really wasn't sure at all.

Tristan just kept staring at the phone.

"You imagined me as all-knowing, remember?" Wheeler said. "Thanks to your power, I am. I know exactly what will happen if Tristan makes the call." He gave them an evil grin. "Which is why I want him to so badly."

Tristan looked at Damara as if he were hoping she could tell him what to do, but she had no idea what to say.

"Ever since he returned to town, he's been so loyal, so brave, so kind and considerate. So damn *good* in every way," Wheeler pointed out. "Almost like a dream come true."

"If Tristan isn't real, then why didn't he change with everything else in the park once Kenneth entered?" Damara asked.

"Because Tristan is standing right next to you," Wheeler said, "and because he's so important to you. And perhaps even because Kenneth believes that he's real as well."

Damara was beginning to feel sick. What if it were true? What if Tristan—*this* Tristan—weren't real?

Tristan looked down at the cell phone in his hand one more time before tossing it back to Wheeler. The big man caught the phone easily in his stubby fingers. When Tristan spoke, his voice quavered a bit, but his resolve was firm. "Maybe I'm real, maybe I'm not. That doesn't matter right now. All that matters is getting Autumn away from Emma."

And at that moment Damara knew that real or not, she loved this Tristan.

"So tell us where to find her," Tristan finished.

"I'll be happy to," Wheeler said. He picked up the deck of cards and began shuffling them one-handed once more. But the edges of the cards were razor-sharp now, and despite the man's skill, his fingers were sliced to the bone. Blood dripped from his wounds and pattered onto the counter, but if the pain bothered him, he didn't show it. He just kept on shuffling and bleeding. "All you have to do is play a single game of blackjack against the house." He grinned, and the gaps where his front upper and lower teeth had been now had tiny vaginas in the empty spaces. "*I'm* the house, in case you couldn't guess. Or more accurately, *all* of Riverfork is the house in this game. If you beat me, I'll tell you how to find Autumn."

"And what happens if you win?" Damara said. She tried to keep from looking at Wheeler's hand. He was still shuffling cards, and the flesh of his fingers now hung in tatters, exposing white bone.

"If you lose, you stay here, Damara. In Riverfork—forever."

Damara frowned. "I don't understand."

"It's simple enough," Wheeler said. "A place like Riverfork, which thousands of people visit over the course of many years to enjoy themselves, becomes a repository—or a dumping ground, to put it less elegantly—for the residue of the intense emotions experienced here. Every time someone screams in terror as a roller coaster roars down the first hill, every time a child laughs with delight over an especially wonderful prize that a beloved adult has won for him or her . . . whenever these and a hundred other similar events happen in a place like Riverfork, a small amount of emotional energy is released. This energy seeps into the wood, brick, metal, and concrete and joins with the very substance of the park itself. When this energy eventually reaches critical mass, it can even achieve a kind of life of its own, though nothing that approaches sentience.

"Such was the case here in Riverfork—until a night seventeen years ago when *you* came, Damara. Your power reached out to the psychic residue that Riverfork had absorbed and which had lain dormant for so many years. Your power woke up that energy, Damara. More, it bestowed self-awareness upon it. But you stayed so briefly and left so quickly that Riverfork returned to its slumber once you were gone. But in that all too short a time, the park developed enough sentience to remember and dream while it slept. And what the park dreamed of was your return, Damara, so that it might remain awake and fully self-aware forever."

"You mean you want me to stay in Riverfork and be your . . . your psychic *battery?*" Damara asked.

"Essentially," Wheeler confessed.

A disturbing thought passed through Damara's mind then. "Does this mean that everything that's happened during the last day was *your* doing? That Riverfork was trying to lure me back all along?"

Wheeler chuckled. "Don't be so overly dramatic. If we'd had the ability to lure you back, we wouldn't have waited seventeen years to use it. In fact, we would never have let you leave in the first place if we could have prevented it. No, this current flare-up of your talent had nothing to do with us, though we admit to reaching out to Emma and . . . encouraging her to bring Autumn here." Another gap-toothed, vagina-gummed grin. "Just because we didn't cause this latest episode of your power running amok doesn't mean we weren't going to try to take advantage of it." Wheeler fanned the blood-stained cards from his mutilated hand to the other—slicing the flesh of those fingers in the process—then back again. "What do you say? Is it a bet?"

"Don't do it, Mara," Tristan urged. "Who knows what would happen if Riverfork became truly alive—especially the way it is now? We can find Autumn on our own."

Damara wasn't so certain. Given the way the park kept altering itself to suit the imagination of both friend and foe, they might never be able to find Autumn simply by searching for her. Damara didn't want to remain in Riverfork forever, letting the emotional ghosts of thousands of park-goers feed off her power so that they could maintain some phantom semblance of life. But she couldn't simply abandon Autumn, either. Before she could decide, however, a soft scratching sound came from the inside of Wheeler's spit can.

"What's that noise?" Tristan asked.

"Nothing," Wheeler said, casting a nervous glance at the can. "Just, ah, the tobacco juice settling, that's all."

The scratching sound came again, louder this time.

"Bullshit," Tristan said. "There's something in there." He started to reach for the can, but before he could take hold of it, a green scaled finger covered with sharp black spines—along with slimy brown tobacco spit—poked up over the edge.

"It's Jack Sharp!" Damara said, and her leg wound throbbed as if responding to the nearness of the creature that had caused it.

"And your brother," Wheeler said, sounding irritated. "His spirit merged with Jack Sharp after he was stolen away."

Tristan quickly pulled back his hand. "Why?" he asked.

"Because as Jason Ruschmann died, he imagined that Jack Sharp was going to devour him," Wheeler explained. "And Jack Sharp did; though not quite in the way he feared."

"Some brother," Tristan said. "He tried to kill Damara in the shower."

The finger tapped the side of the can as if to get their attention, then waggled back and forth.

"I think he's trying to say no," Damara said.

Wheeler sighed. "It's true. Jack Sharp had no intention of harming you. Well, no more than necessary, at any rate. As another being fueled by your power, he sensed our presence and our intention. He wanted to incapacitate you, to keep you from coming here and perhaps being trapped in Riverfork forever." He scowled into the can. "Fuck off, junior. We're trying to play some cards here." He aimed a stream of tobacco juice at the spine-covered finger and hit it dead-on. The finger stiffened as if the juice had wounded it somehow, then slowly sank back down into the can. A moment later, Damara leaned forward and peered down into the can, but all she saw was brown slime. She felt a strange mixture of joy, loss, and revulsion . . .

333

joy to know that her brother still existed, loss because he had departed once more, and revulsion at the thing her power had made him into.

Wheeler looked at Damara and fixed her with a penetrating gaze full of excitement and hunger. "Are you going to play or not?"

Damara didn't need any time to decide.

"Yes."

"Are you sure?" Tristan asked. "How can you be certain he won't cheat? Or if you win, that he'll honor the deal? If he's the . . . the spokesman for Riverfork, and the park needs you to remain alive, or whatever it is, then he'll do anything to win."

"I understand all that," Damara said. "But I'm still going to play. It may be the only chance Autumn has left."

A broad grin spread across Wheeler's face. "Excellent!" He shuffled the cards, then dealt them out, one facedown for Damara, then one facedown for him. The next card of Damara's he lay face-up. Seven of diamonds. He dealt his next card face-up. It was the jack of spades. He then put the deck down on the counter and said, "Time to check our hole cards."

Grimacing at the bloodstains on it, Damara lifted the corner of her hole card just high enough to reveal its suit and number. Ten of clubs. She looked up and watched Wheeler examine his hole card. The man—assuming he still qualified as male given the transformation he'd undergone—gave nothing away with his facial expression as he said, "The dealer stays."

Damara considered what to do. She and her mother had played cards sometimes, but they hadn't played blackjack very often. Claire had loved cards, though, much more than Damara, and she often got together with friends to play. Damara wished Claire were here now to advise her, but her poor mother was dead, killed by Emma while giving Damara and Autumn a chance to escape. Damara felt grief threaten to overwhelm her, but she fought it down. The best thing she could do right now to honor her mother's memory and make certain her sacrifice hadn't been in vain was to win this game and same Autumn.

Okay, she had seventeen and Wheeler had a jack showing, which counted as ten. If he was staying instead of taking another card, that meant he was close enough to twenty-one that he didn't want to risk going over. The question was, did he have seventeen or better? Maybe. No, probably. If he had sixteen he wouldn't have been confident of a win—not with five more points to go for twenty-one—so he would've risked drawing another card. Besides, with only a seven showing for her, Wheeler had to know that the highest hole card she could have was one that counted for ten. That meant he knew that his hand could beat hers as things currently stood. She had no choice but to take another card.

"Hit me," Damara said.

Grinning, Wheeler lifted the deck of cards, pulled one off the top with bloody fingers, and placed it face-up in front of Damara.

Chapter Twenty-two

Autumn ran up to the entrance of Bug-Out! and opened the waist-high gate next to a sign in the form of a cartoon caterpillar that said YOU MUST BE TALLER THAN THIS TO RIDE. She hurried inside the metal enclosure that separated the ride from the rest of the park and saw a man sitting on a wooden stool over by a set of controls. The controls were mounted in a metal box sitting atop a metal pole, and a mass of thick black cables ran out from the back of the box and coiled across the ground to where they were attached to the track. Autumn picked her way carefully through the snarl of cables as she hurried over to the ride's operator. She started talking in a rush before she reached him, almost shouting to be heard over the *clackety-clack* of the caterpillar ride rolling around on its endless trip to nowhere.

"Please. I need help, there's a lady chasing me, and she's crazy, she's got shears instead of a hand, and I think she killed my mommy or at least

337

helped her husband do it, and I'm afraid she's going to do the same thing to me!"

Autumn stopped next to Bug-Out!'s operator. He was a small man, not much larger than Autumn, and he sat hunched over atop a long-legged stool. He wore a faded black T-shirt with a logo for something called Led Zeppelin on it, and his jeans had holes in both knees. His tennis shoes were so dirty, it was impossible for Autumn to guess what color they might have originally been.

He looked up at her, and Autumn gasped. The man was bald, and instead of a face, he had a vertical slit running from scalp to chin. As Autumn watched, the man's head began to swell like a balloon, the flesh darkening, becoming a deep red, and a pearl of clear liquid oozed out of the slit in his face and ran down his chin.

Autumn screamed and backed away, but she'd forgotten about the tangle of cables on the ground. She tripped and fell backward onto her butt. She hit hard, and the impact jarred her tailbone and made her teeth clack together painfully. She didn't care about the pain, though. All she wanted to do was get away from the man and his awful swelling head. So far he hadn't done anything but sit on his stool and look at her—if he *could* look without any eyes—but Autumn wasn't about to stick around and wait for him to finally decide to start moving. She got to her feet and turned to run.

But she stopped when she saw that the train of green cars that made up the Bug-Out! ride had started to change. They melded together, metal becoming soft pliant flesh, wheels becoming rapidly scuttling insect legs. But worst of all was the lead car. The top hat suddenly flew off the plastic caterpillar head, and the jolly anthropomorphic face became that of a real caterpillar—large glossy black eyes, an open orifice filled with constantly working mouth parts searching for something, anything to quell its gnawing hunger.

Something like Autumn, for example.

On its next go-round the caterpillar jumped the track and headed straight for Autumn. The girl screamed once more and ran like hell toward the gate marked EXIT.

Damara looked at her new card. It was a deuce.

Nineteen.

Wheeler displayed no reaction, and Damara did her best to maintain a poker face as well, though inside she was thinking furiously.

I've got nineteen, but there's a good chance he's got twenty. The only way I can win is if I get twenty-one, but to do that I need another deuce.

If she got an ace, which could count as either one or eleven, she could tie him, but then they'd just have to play another hand. And the longer she stayed here screwing around, the more danger Autumn might be in. She needed a win, and she needed it *now*.

Sudden inspiration struck her then, and with a grin she turned to Tristan. "I need a deuce."

He frowned in confusion. "Why are you telling me, I don't . . ." He broke off, and she could see

339

sudden understanding in his eyes. "A deuce, huh? Well, that's *exactly* the card I want you to get. Any particular suit?"

"Hearts, of course."

Tristan smiled. "Hearts it is." He closed his eyes and his brow furrowed in concentration.

Damara turned back to Wheeler and said, "Hit me."

Wheeler's face was no longer expressionless. He looked quite nervous as he dealt Damara her card.

And there it was, exactly what she needed: the two of hearts.

Tristan opened his eyes and stared at the card in amazement, the expression on his face making Damara laugh.

"All right," she said to Wheeler. "We've won—now tell us how to find Autumn."

Before the man could answer, a high-pitched scream cut through the air of the Midway. Damara, Tristan, and Wheeler all turned to look in its direction and saw a girl run past the entrance to the Midway, followed closely by an undulating green monster.

"Easy," Wheeler said. "Just follow the giant caterpillar."

Emma pursed her lips in disgust as she made her way through the park in search of Autumn. Since the sky had darkened, the rides and attractions had become nightmarish. The Ferris wheel was now a construction of bone, muscle, and sinew, and it screamed with every rotation as if it were in excruciating agony. The roller coaster was a giant length of oversized intestine; cars of passengers entered the fleshy tunnel at one end and came out as processed waste at the other. The carousel continued spinning, but no longer did horses make the circular journey. They'd been replaced by torsos with no heads or limbs that were impaled on poles running through their anuses and out their open neck stumps. Children clung to the torsos in an obscene version of piggy-back rides, the torsos slowly bobbing up and down in time with the hurdy-gurdy music as the carousel slowly spun round and around.

Like the rides, the *things* she passed (she refused to think of them as people) were surely Kenneth's doing. Nothing so base could ever have sprung from her imagination. Though no two of them looked precisely alike, they all shared a dominant trait of grossly exaggerated sexual characteristics. Giant penises, dripping vaginas, ridiculously large breasts . . . and then there were the ones that had been more creatively designed, with anuses in place of nostrils, or testicles bulging out of eye sockets. Take the one coming at her now, an old man with a vagina instead of a penis. Sickening. And then *it* stopped and spoke to her.

"Hello, Emma."

At first she didn't recognize him, but then she blinked and said, "Kenneth?"

"The one and only. Why do you look so surprised? You had to have sensed I was coming."

"I did. It's just . . ." She wasn't sure what it was.

Now that he was close enough, she could see that what she had at first taken to be a vagina between his legs was instead a ragged blood-encrusted gash, and within it was . . . nothing. Just darkness. No, not even that, for darkness is the absence of light, and that's *something*. But inside Kenneth's gash was absolute and total Nothingness. The sight of it made Emma feel cold all over, as if her blood had turned to freon in her veins. She hadn't been afraid of Kenneth when she'd confronted him back on Pandora Drive, but she was afraid of him now. More than that, actually. She was terrified out of her fucking mind. She had her shears, but what good were they? How could you cut *nothing*?

"You're not looking so good," Kenneth said, his voice eerily dispassionate. "Those black things all over your skin . . ."

"They're nothing, just insect stings. They'll heal soon enough."

Kenneth nodded, accepting her explanation. "It's funny, isn't it? Us ending up like this after thirty years of marriage."

"Thirty-three," Emma automatically corrected.

"You'd think that if we'd wanted to kill each other, we'd have done it long before now."

Emma shrugged. "Maybe we just didn't hate each other enough until now."

"Maybe. Or maybe we loved each other, too. At least enough to balance out some of the hate."

"Maybe," she allowed. "But hate's all we have left now."

"True enough."

Emma snicked her shears nervously. "So, are we going to do this or not?"

"I guess we are."

Emma raised her hand shears and ran shrieking at Kenneth. Her husband—whom she'd already killed once—just stood there, legs spread, waiting for her attack. And then the darkness within his gash reached out for her, and Emma's screams of hatred became screams of an entirely different sort as Nothingness claimed her.

When it was over, Kenneth stood for a moment, alone on the gray brick walkway. He felt something wet, warm, and sticky hit his shoulder. As he reached up to scoop it off with a finger, he felt several more drops hit him, heard some strike the brick. He held his finger up to his face and inspected the viscous slimy substance. It was whitish, yellowish, pinkish, red. He held it to his nose, sniffed, and found it smelled coppery-salty. He grinned then and flicked the goop off his finger as the rain of cum and blood continued falling from the black sky overhead.

Autumn's heart pounded in her ears like thunder, and her lungs felt as if they were on fire. She was having trouble catching her breath, and she feared she wouldn't be able to keep running much longer. The thing behind her wasn't showing any signs of slowing down, though. If anything, she thought it might be picking up speed. Not that she intended to turn around and check. She was terrified, but she wasn't *stupid*. Besides, she didn't need to see it; she could hear the almost hypnotic rhythm of its feet, dozens of tiny insect legs scuttling across the brick walkway.

She passed many people, but she didn't bother trying to ask them for help. Like the operator of the Bug-Out! ride, they'd all been hideously transformed into sexual monsters of one sort or another. And when they saw her coming toward them—with a hungry giant caterpillar close on her heels—they opened their mouths in silent screams and fled in all directions.

She tried to think of a way to escape the monstrous insect larva chasing her—hadn't her mother always told her to keep a cool head in a bad situation?—but she couldn't think clearly. She'd seen too much, *felt* too much today, and her brain was numb and sluggish. She supposed she was in shock, although since she'd only heard about the condition on TV shows, she wasn't certain.

As she ran, rain began to fall. At least, that's what she first thought it was. But the gunk that fell from the black sky was thick and slimy, and it had a funny smell that was nothing like rain. Whatever it was, the stuff was slippery and it was beginning to coat the walkway. Autumn started to slow down so she wouldn't—

Her right foot slipped out from under her, and Autumn slid forward. She fell onto her side and the impact drove the breath out of her lungs. She slid in the pinkish muck, hands scrabbling to find purchase to slow her down, but all they found was more slime. She came to a stop and, unable to get any leverage to push herself up to a standing position, she leaned her head back to get a look at the caterpillar. She saw an upside-down view of the giant insect's mouth parts coming toward her face, and she closed her eyes and waited for the creature to begin devouring her. Several seconds passed, and when she still felt no pain, she risked opening a single eye to take a peek.

The caterpillar was only a few feet from her face, but it was no longer making any forward progress. It thrashed its head back and forth, squealing as if in frustration. Then as Autumn watched, the caterpillar began to slide backward, despite its best efforts to maintain its footing. A strong wind suddenly whipped up out of nowhere, and Autumn could feel it tugging at her, pulling her along the slime-covered walkway after the caterpillar. Frantically, she moved her hands across the path, feeling for some sort of handhold—a crack or irregularity in the stone—but all she felt was warm, viscous sky-gunk.

She looked back once again and saw the caterpillar retreating from her at increasing speed. As the insect pulled away, Autumn became aware that a naked man was standing behind the thing, and her heart seized in her chest as she recognized Kenneth. He had his hands at his sides, balled into fists, and his face was contorted into an expression of supreme effort. The wind tearing at Autumn increased until it felt as if solid hands were dragging her backward. The wind shrieked and howled as the caterpillar fought in vain to resist it. It had continued to rain all this time, and the walkway had become so slick with sky-gunk that the caterpillar could no longer resist. It slipped and its belly hit the walkway, sending splatters of sky-gunk flying everywhere. Now that the creature was no longer able to fight, it slid backward toward Kenneth at a rapid pace and then seemed to pass *into* Kenneth, or rather into an opening between Kenneth's legs. How such a gigantic creature could fit into such a small space, Autumn didn't know, but fit it did. The last thing to be swallowed was the caterpillar's oversized head, the creature squealing in agony as its last piece was compressed, crushed, and devoured.

Then the caterpillar was gone, and all that was left was the naked form of Kenneth standing in the rain of sky-gunk and breathing heavily, as if he'd just fought a titanic battle. The wind still tore at Autumn, but it quickly began to diminish. By the time she had slid halfway across the walk toward Kenneth, the wind died away completely and she stopped moving. Kenneth remained standing where he was for several moments—shadows roiling and seething between his legs. But then he began coming toward her and Autumn, panicked, once more began trying to get to her feet. Between being devoured by a giant caterpillar and being alone with Kenneth, she'd take the caterpillar every time.

She managed to get herself standing again, but

by that time Kenneth was only a couple of yards from her.

"You can't escape me, Autumn. I may not have a cock anymore, but that doesn't mean you and I still can't have fun. I've got lots of tricks left to show you—and not a single one requires a penis. Besides, you know what the experts say . . ." He gave Autumn a ghastly parody of an avuncular smile. "The most important sexual organ is the mind."

Looking at Kenneth had been bad enough when his *thing* had been giant. Autumn hadn't thought there could be anything worse in the whole wide world, but she'd been wrong. The open gash of Nothingness between his legs was far worse. Autumn turned and, being careful of the gunk coating the walkway, began moving away from Kenneth as fast as she could. She knew it was only a matter of time before Kenneth got her and did to her as he pleased. She needed to get away from him, and needed to do it *now*.

"Go ahead and run if you want," Kenneth said. "I can use my Nothingness to pull you back anytime I wish."

Autumn thought of how the giant caterpillar had been sucked into the small dark orifice between Kenneth's legs, and she was determined to avoid a similar fate happening to her. She needed to find someplace where she could hide and rest, someplace that even if Kenneth followed her inside, he wouldn't be able to find her.

And then she saw it: Alacrity's Spectatorium. A

hall of mirrors ... perfect! If she were lucky, maybe she could lure Kenneth inside and lose *him* in there. So, running faster than she should've on the slime-covered ground, she hurried toward the building. Kenneth called out her name again, along with a list of some of the disgusting things he intended to do once he had hold of her. Autumn did her best to shut him out and keep running.

"... coke enema, Autumn. Then I'll take a rubber hose and ..."

Slipping and sliding in the white-red slime, Autumn reached the entrance to the Spectatorium and without hesitation, pressed her hands to the slime-smeared surface of its glass doors and shoved. They opened easily, and Autumn plunged through and into the darkness beyond.

Damara and Tristan had taken Wheeler's advice. They'd fled the Midway in pursuit of the giant caterpillar, but both the creature and Autumn were faster than them, especially with Damara's wounded leg. To make matters more difficult, thick dollops of cum mixed with blood began to fall from the sky, courtesy of Kenneth's diseased imagination, no doubt. The ground soon became slick with the disgusting muck—not to mention what it did to their clothes and hair—and before long they were forced to slow almost to a walk. By the time they managed to get Autumn and the caterpillar in view once more, they saw that Kenneth had gotten there ahead of them. They approached the old man from behind, but before either Damara or Tristan could yell for him to leave Autumn alone, they watched in horrified disbelief as Kenneth somehow drew the gigantic caterpillar toward him and then *absorbed* the creature into his own body.

Kenneth began calling out to Autumn then as the girl fled, voicing a litany of perversions that nauseated Damara and made her more determined than ever to protect her young friend. But she found herself stopping when she saw Autumn head for Alacrity's Spectatorium and dash inside, Kenneth following close behind.

"What's wrong?" Tristan asked, scooping a smear of blood-cum off his face and flicking it onto the ground with a grimace.

"That's the place where my father disappeared, remember?" Damara said. "He thought I went inside, but at the last minute I veered away from the entrance. He didn't see me do that, though, so he . . . he went in. He never came out again." She felt the foul warm stickiness of blood-cum collecting on her body, but she didn't care right then. "I . . . I don't know if I can go in there."

"Not even for Autumn?" he challenged.

Damara didn't respond. She didn't know what to say.

Tristan gently gripped her shoulders. "Don't worry about it. You stay out here, and I'll go in." He gave her a half-smile. "After all, I'm not real. What have I got to lose?"

Before she could say anything to that, he leaned forward and kissed her with lips that felt real

349

enough. And then he pulled away and hurried toward the entrance to Alacrity's Spectatorium. A moment later, he was inside and lost to sight.

Damara stood there, staring at the mirrored entrance to the attraction while blood-cum continued to splatter down around and on her. She imagined darkness, imagined her father finding his way through the hall of mirrors by touch alone, fingers sliding across smooth glass. Imagined hearing him call her name, the sound of his heavy footfalls as he searched for her . . .

Imagined hearing him scream.

She didn't need to imagine that last part, though. She'd heard it seventeen years ago, standing in this very spot or close to it.

Damara could've entered the Spectatorium in search of her father back then, could've attempted to go to his aid. But she hadn't. Instead she'd run, leaving her father to whatever fate had claimed him. A fate created by his imagination, but fueled by her damn power.

Damara stared at the doors, blood-cum *plap-plap-plapping* as it struck the ground. Then slowly, grimacing as her wounded leg protested in pain, she began hobbling toward Alacrity's Spectatorium.

Chapter Twenty-three

When Damara reached the doors, she almost turned away, but she pressed her hands to the mirrored glass and pushed. The doors swung open easily, as if their hinges had been oiled recently instead of neglected for decades. It was dark inside, but then it was dark outside too, in more ways than one. Damara stepped inside and allowed the door to swing shut and seal her inside. She stood for a moment, listening. Autumn, Kenneth, and Tristan were all in here somewhere, and she should have been able to hear them shuffling around and bumping into mirrors as they tried to find their way in the darkness. But she heard nothing. Were they all standing still and listening like her? It hardly seemed likely, but then why was it so damn quiet in here?

She supplied her own answer. *Because it's not just a hall of mirrors anymore,* she thought. *It's changed, like the rest of the park.* But into what, she had no idea.

She decided to risk whispering. "Autumn? Tristan? Where are you?" She strained to hear a reply, but none came. She tried calling their names again, louder this time, but with the same result.

Frustrated and scared, she shouted, "Would one of you do me a favor and imagine a light switch?" But there was no answer and the Spectatorium wasn't suddenly flooded with illumination. She continued standing there in the darkness by the entrance, covered with stinking blood-cum, and thought.

So many of the changes caused by her power were either exaggerations of reality or reversals of it. So how might a hall of mirrors be affected? The curved and rippled glass presented distorted versions of the viewer, making one appear thinner, fatter, taller, shorter and so on. What was an exaggeration of that? To actually *cause* those distortions to happen to the viewer's body? Maybe, but Damara didn't feel any physical transformation happening to her. Besides, it was dark, there was no light for the mirrors to reflect. So how about an opposite effect? Maybe instead of reflecting light, these mirrors reflected darkness. No, what would reflected darkness be but simply *more* darkness? Besides, it didn't feel right.

Then it came to her. Mirrors normally *reflected*. The opposite of that would be to *absorb*.

She reached out with a surprisingly steady hand and felt around for a smooth glass surface. She felt nothing, though, and she began to fear that maybe there weren't any mirrors in here, that there was only darkness and the unseen things that dwelled within it. But her fingertips finally came in contact with cool smoothness and she knew she'd found a mirror at last. She pushed, not hard at first, but with mounting pressure. She thought she could feel the glass surface begin to yield beneath her fingers, but she wasn't sure. And then, as if finally breaking the surface tension of a giant bubble, Damara felt her hand slide forward, and she was suddenly thrown off balance. She stumbled forward and felt a momentary sensation of cold pass over her body as if she'd just stepped through a curtain of flowing water. Then she was on the other side and fighting to keep from falling flat on her face. It was a near thing, but she managed to maintain her balance, if only just.

Wherever she was, it was still as dark as before, but the air felt different. Cooler, cleaner, less oppressive . . . and she could no longer smell the stench of blood-cum wafting from her clothes and hair. She reached up to touch herself, intending to pat her shirt, hair, pants to see if they were dry, but the passage must've numbed her hand because she felt nothing. She tried to lift her foot and stamp it down, but she heard no sound, felt no impact, and she wasn't sure she'd actually stamped her foot at all.

"Hello? Anyone here?"

Her voice sounded flat, as if it didn't travel very far after leaving her mouth.

"I'm here, Dee."

She saw nothing in the darkness, but she heard

the voice clearly enough. It was her father's, and it seemed to come from right next to her. No, rather from *inside* her.

"Daddy?" She reached toward where his voice had seemed to come from, but nothing was there. Nothing she could touch, anyway. "Is that you? *Really* you?"

"Yes, sweetheart. I wish I could touch you . . . hug you . . . but we aren't exactly physical beings in here. At least, I think that's how it works." He sounded slightly embarrassed. "To tell you the truth, even after all these years, I'm not really sure."

That would explain why Damara hadn't been able to feel anything since she'd come here. "But what about our voices? I can hear us speak."

"Do you feel your mouth and tongue move? Your throat vibrate?"

"No," she realized. "I don't."

"We can hear each other's thoughts in this place, but that's all we can do."

"Where are we?"

"Inside a mirror. We're inhabiting a two-dimensional space between a sheet of glass and a silver backing. If there were light, we might be able to see something, but then again, maybe not. I've never had the chance to check. There hasn't been so much as a flicker of light in here since I entered, and who knows how many years that's been?"

"Seventeen," Damara said.

"Seventeen years," her father repeated, his mental voice heavy with both wonder and sadness. "That would make you . . . twenty-eight. My god, my little girl is all grown up. What I wouldn't give to be able to see you right now. I bet you look just like your mother did at your age."

Damara experienced a pang of sorrow. She tried to imagine what it must've been like for her father to be trapped inside a mirror for so long. In the dark, alone, not dead but not truly alive, either. Suspended between one world and another, held trapped and immobile but fully aware every moment, every instant . . . for seventeen years.

"Daddy, I have to tell you something. It's about Mom . . ."

"I know. Not the specific details, but I can sense that she's gone. It was one of the first thoughts I picked up from you once you entered the mirror."

"Then you're aware of what's happening in the park?"

"Yes. I've been here so long, I'm connected to Riverfork now, literally a part of the place. I know about the transformation the park's undergone and how it wants you to stay here and continue feeding on your power so it can remain alive and aware."

"Daddy, there's so much I want to tell you . . . so much that I want to apologize for . . ." Emotionally, she felt as if she were crying, but she felt no tears rolling down her cheeks, no tightness in her throat.

"There's no need to apologize. It's not your fault you were born with your power. If your mother

355

and I had reacted to it better, tried to help you accept it . . . but we didn't. We were too afraid, so we tried to pretend that it didn't exist. Not the best of plans as it turned out, eh?"

"But if I hadn't snuck out that night . . . hadn't come to Riverfork . . ."

"I've had plenty of time to go over what-ifs, Dee, and believe me when I tell you they don't get you anywhere. What if I hadn't followed you that night? Maybe you'd have been trapped here instead of me. Maybe Riverfork would've fed on your power all these years and who knows what it might've become then? What if *my* mother—your grandma—had never read *Alice Through the Looking Glass* to me? Then maybe I wouldn't have been frightened by this place as a child and my adult imagination never would've caused me to be trapped in here. Maybe I would've made it home, been able to be a father to you and a husband to your mom. What-ifs and maybes will kill you if you let them. We are here now, and we have a problem to deal with. How are we going to free you and your friends and return Riverfork to normal?"

"Tristan and Autumn are here, too?"

"And Kenneth," Jerry Ruschmann confirmed. "They're in different mirrors, so we can't hear them and they can't hear us. I've been here long enough that I can sense their presence as well as what they're feeling. Autumn is scared, Tristan's trying to figure out a way to escape, and Kenneth is raging over being imprisoned and separated from Autumn. None of them have the power to break free of their mirrors, just as I don't have the power to break free from mine. Only you have the power, Dee. Only you can set us all free."

"But I can't! It's like Tristan said, I'm a psychic Typhoid Mary, a carrier but not a user. Others can draw on my power and wield it to shape reality, but *I* can't!"

"You haven't tried. You don't want to. But that's not the same thing as can't."

Damara thought then of what Wheeler had said.

You haven't tried to control it. Not really. You've tried to suppress it, girlie-girl. Big difference. Maybe if you'd accepted your power, embraced it, you'd have gained some measure of control over it by now.

"Even if it's possible, how am I suddenly supposed to know how to use my power when I've spend my whole life trying *not* to?"

"You aren't supposed to know. You can't know. There aren't any assurances in life, Dee. All you can do is try and see what happens."

Damara thought about this for a time. When she finally responded to her father, her mental voice sounded small and weak.

"But I'm afraid."

"Of course you are, sweetheart. But you can't let that fear stop you, not if you want to save Autumn and Tristan from a lifetime isolated in darkness."

Damara's fear didn't diminish and she doubted it ever would. But she'd seen too much of what could happen when her power was left uncontrolled. For good or ill, she had to try to learn to use it. For Autumn, for Tristan, and for herself, so that she might—just might—find a measure of peace at last.

"All right, I'll try. Any advice?"

"From your thoughts I can see that over the years you've used a particular image to help you suppress your power. Use it again, but this time adapt the image and use it to set your power free. And don't forget that even if you can't physically feel my presence, I'm right beside you, Dee, and I'll be lending you every bit of mental support I can."

"Thanks, Dad." Reassured, Damara turned her mind to the task of freeing her power once and for all.

The only image that she could think of that her father might have meant was the polar bear in a snowstorm. She'd always used this image, and the field of white nothingness that it conjured in her mind, as a way to close down her imagination so that her power would have nothing to feed on. But her father had suggested she use the image as fodder for her power. But how was she supposed to do that? Maybe, instead of just imagining blank whiteness, she should try to imagine a *real* snowstorm.

She thought of cold . . . cold so intense that your nose hairs freeze when you inhale, and the frigid air hits your lungs like blades of ice slicing into the soft pink tissue inside. She thought of wind . . . wind so fast and fierce that it strikes flesh like a thousand barbed-wire whips, flaying skin and cutting into the bone beneath, blood and marrow oozing forth only to be frozen solid. She thought of snow and ice, crystals so cold, clear, pure, and sharp that they tumble on the air like a flight of miniature shurikens, no two exactly alike in shape, but every single one of them deadly.

Though previously she'd been bereft of sensation in this strange dark place, now she began to feel the cold air caressing her skin, curling down her throat and into her lungs, which tried in vain to warm it. Felt herself exhale and thought she saw a puff of white before her eyes as breath misted out from between her lips. She saw faint white patterns of frost begin to form before her eyes— maybe *on* her eyes?—and she heard a soft cracking sound as if of glass becoming brittle in reaction to the intense cold. The frost continued gathering until what had been a world of unrelieved darkness had become a world of white.

She then began to imagine polar bears. Huge, savage, majestic creatures with shaggy white fur, black padded feet, obsidian claws, feral yellow eyes, and sharp ivory teeth. Dozens, no, hundreds of them, standing upright—twelve feet high or more—on a vast arctic plain, oblivious to the maelstrom of snow, ice, and wind that swirled around them. She imagined the bears opening their great ursine maws and releasing a combined roar. The sound was deafening, easily drowning out the raging fury of the snowstorm, and it seemed to reverberate throughout all existence. Damara felt the vibrations in her body, her mind, and in her soul. She gritted her teeth—though she still wasn't precisely sure she *had* teeth in this placeless place on the other side of the mirror—closed her eyes, and pictured raising her arms over her face to protect herself when all at once Creation shattered.

Damara felt suddenly heavy again, like she was walking back onto shore after a long period of being buoyed by water. She fell forward, and put her hands out to catch herself as she hit snow studded with shards of broken glass. She felt sharp pain as her hands and forearms were cut, but she didn't care; she was too glad to be free. She lay in the snow for a moment, bleeding from where she'd been cut, but not bleeding badly, all things considered. She sat up halfway—ignoring the splashes of crimson in the white snow—and looked around the interior of Alacrity's Spectatorium. The *real* interior. The roof had partially collapsed some years ago, allowing more than enough early evening sunlight streaming in for her to see by.

Sunlight? That meant that Kenneth's black clouds were gone! She felt like cheering, but she held her exuberance in check. What of Autumn and Tristan? What of her father?

She saw no sign of her dad, but both Autumn and Tristan lay several yards away from Damara, both of them motionless. The interior of Alacrity's Spectatorium was covered with mounds of snow, and there were no intact mirrors visible; it appeared they'd all been reduced to glass shards when the polar bears had roared. The snowstorm was over now, though. No more wind, snow or ice. She thought she detected a line of large tracks on the far side of the building, as if a great number of bears had stood up on their hind legs there. But if any bears had been present, there were none now.

Damara was torn about which of her friends to go to first, Tristan or Autumn. Finally, she chose Autumn and made her way across the snow-covered floor toward her, almost slipping and falling a couple times, but she managed to keep her footing until she'd reached the girl's side. Damara knelt next to Autumn and was relieved to discover she was still breathing. Damara sat and cradled the girl's head on her lap while she gently stroked her cheeks. She visually examined Autumn's body and face for lacerations, but she saw only a few shallow cuts, thank god.

"Wake up, Autumn. It's all over."

It took a few more moments of cheek-rubbing and speaking softly on Damara's part before Autumn's eyes finally flickered open.

Damara smiled in relief. "Glad to see you're still with us."

Autumn frowned in confusion. "Where are we? Where did all this snow come from? The last thing I remember is Kenneth chasing me. He didn't . . . get me, did he?"

"No, sweetie. He didn't get anyone." Damara helped Autumn up into a sitting position. "Do you think you'll be okay for a minute while I go check on Tristan?"

Autumn didn't look fully conscious yet, but she nodded and Damara got up and hurried over to Tristan. He had rolled onto his side and was groaning, which Damara took to be a fairly good indication that he was still alive. He had a jagged shard of glass embedded in his left shoulder and a number of cuts on his face, most of them shallow, but one or two were serious enough to need medical attention, if not immediately, then soon. But that glass in his shoulder definitely called for a trip to the hospital.

He sat up as Damara knelt next to him. "Please tell me I don't look as bad as I feel."

She smiled. "That depends. How bad *do* you feel?"

Tristan touched a hand to his shoulder wound and winced in pain. "Like I was hit by a truck and the sonofabitch driving backed up to finish the job."

"In that case, you do look as bad as you feel. Maybe even worse."

Tristan started to laugh, but then his laughter gave way to a series of dry barking coughs. Damara patted his back until his coughing spell was over. Since Tristan was the worst of them, Damara motioned for Autumn to crawl over and join them. The girl did so, though injured, still moving with the ease and confidence that only the young possessed. Autumn took one of Tristan's hands and began patting it gently.

"Do you think he'll be okay?" Autumn asked Damara.

"I think so," Damara said. "But we need to get him to a doctor as soon as—"

Before she could finish, a large mound of snow in front of them burst apart to reveal Kenneth's shivering naked body. He stood up, wrinkly skin blue-tinged, the gash between his legs seething with angry darkness.

"Thanks for getting me out of there, Damara." Kenneth looked down between his legs. "Too bad you didn't dream me up a new cock while you were at it. Oh, well. Maybe next time, right?"

Autumn let out a wordless cry of fright and grabbed hold of Damara. Tristan didn't move, but he said, "You understand what's been happening and that Damara's power was the cause of it all?"

Kenneth nodded. "Once I sucked in the jumbo-sized tequila worm that was going after Autumn, I had a . . . connection, I guess you could say, to the park. I understand everything, more or less."

"And you don't *feel* anything?" Tristan said. "Guilt, remorse, disgust, shame?"

Kenneth grinned. "Why should I? I *like* what I've become, and once I've absorbed Damara— along with you and Autumn, Tristan, just for fun— maybe *I'll* have her power then. Can you imagine all the things I could do with it?"

A wild glint came into Kenneth's eyes, and Damara knew he was picturing a world re-created in his own vile image. She also knew that he was completely and irrevocably insane. She tried to think of a way to stop him, but before she could, he spread his legs wider and the dark vortex at the center of his mutilated crotch began pulling at them. Wind flared to life and snow flew past them and vanished within Kenneth's ebon gash. Damara held tight to Autumn and Tristan, and desperately tried to concentrate. If only her father were here . . .

Above the roaring of the wind, Damara heard a soft tinkling, as if someone were sifting through a pile of glass shards. She turned her head and saw her father standing a few yards away. No, not Jerry Ruschmann, not precisely. It was his image, his reflection cast into hundreds of mirror shards that had joined together to approximate the form of a human being. Each piece of glass contained a different fragment of Jerry's reflection, so that he appeared to be a patchwork re-creation of the man he'd been seventeen years ago.

Damara remembered what her father had told her. *I've been here so long, I'm connected to Riverfork now, literally a part of the place.* That was why he hadn't been released from his mirror like the rest of them. He'd *become* the mirror.

"You know something, Kenneth?" Jerry said, his voice muffled as if he spoke from behind a glass barrier. "I never liked you. You were a lousy neighbor."

And then the glass amalgamation that was Jerry Ruschmann started running toward Kenneth, mirror fragments bouncing and quivering as if they were being held together solely by the force of the man's will. When Jerry closed to within six feet of Kenneth, he leaped toward him, hands outstretched, and his mirror body separated into a hailstorm of deadly sharp glass.

Kenneth shrieked as pieces of Jerry Ruschmann sliced into his body, and the wind pulling at

Damara, Tristan, and Autumn suddenly died. Kenneth, glass shards protruding from nearly every inch of his body, blood pouring from dozens of wounds, turned to look at them, his eyes wide with surprise as if he couldn't believe this was really happening. Then he fell sideways onto the snow and lay still, the white around him absorbing his blood and becoming bright red.

Several long moments passed while Damara, Tristan, and Autumn stared at Kenneth's motionless body. Finally, it was Autumn who gave voice to the question all three of them were asking.

"Is it over?"

Kenneth's body jerked as a pair of metal shears thrust their way out of the opening between his legs.

"Not quite," Damara said.

Huddled together, the three of them watched as Emma Colton cut her way free from her husband's corpse. She pulled herself out, slick with blood and viscera, as if the husband was giving birth to the wife. Once she was finally free, she stood and gasped for breath.

"I thought I'd *never* find my way back," she said. Along with her late husband's gore, Emma's skin was covered with black boils large as clenched fists. She turned to Damara, Tristan, and Autumn, then smiled.

"Now that Kenneth is finally out of the way, will you be so kind as to hand over Autumn? If you do, I'll consider letting you leave here with a majority of your body parts intact."

Damara ignored the woman. "C'mon," she said

to Autumn, and together she and the girl helped Tristan to his feet. Leaning on each other, the three of them started walking through the snow-covered floor toward the exit.

"Don't you *dare* turn your backs on me!" Emma said.

"We're leaving," Damara answered. "We've had enough of this shit to last us a lifetime."

"You'll have had enough when *I* say you've had enough!" Her shears snicked together ominously as she started after them.

Damara didn't bother to turn around. "You know those boils of yours, Emma? Right now I'm imagining that instead of welts, they're eggs."

Damara, Tristan, and Autumn continued toward the exit, accompanied first by the sounds of popping flesh, then by Emma's screams as the newly hatched and very hungry larvae began to feed.

Chapter Twenty-four

Outside the ruined, half-collapsed building that had once housed Alacrity's Spectatorium, Damara, Tristan, and Autumn stood looking up at the sky. It was clear now, and orange blazed on the western horizon as the sun prepared to retire for yet another day. The ground was dry—the blood-cum was gone, if indeed it had ever truly been here—and the park was once again deserted. No happy fifties sitcom families, no S&M mutants . . . just them.

And the park, of course. It might look like nothing more than a collection of abandoned rides and attractions, but Damara could sense it watching them, could feel its need. It didn't want them to go, didn't want to lose its self-awareness and lapse back into a dream state from which it might never again awaken.

Stay! It was Wheeler's voice, and it seemed to come floating to Damara on a gentle but insistent breeze. *You know how to control your power now. You can restore Riverfork to its former grandeur, make it even better than it was, make it into a paradise!*

The park shimmered around them as it came to wondrous, glorious life. Everything was bright, shiny, clean, and beautiful. The rides were larger, more intricate, more exiting, more *fun* than those in any other amusement park on earth. The food and drink were exquisite, so sweet, so delicious, that a single taste would eclipse the high from any drug ever known. The air was filled with music and laughter and the soft whispers of a thousand voices urging them to *stay, stay, stay . . .*

Autumn looked around, eyes wide with joy and disbelief. "Oh, how pretty! I wish we could stay here forev—"

Damara clamped a hand over the girl's mouth, silencing her.

"No, you don't."

With an almost audible sigh, Riverfork shimmered once more and became what it had been and what it was destined to remain. An old forgotten place that had once seen happier times, a memory cast in rotting wood, crumbling concrete, rusting metal, and nothing more.

"Damara, maybe I *should* stay," Tristan said. "I mean, if I'm not real—"

"You're real enough," Damara said. "We'll worry about the details later."

Tristan smiled, nodded, and the three of them

began hobbling toward the exit. They had a long way to go, but that was all right. They weren't in any hurry. Not anymore.

When they finished their meal, the younglings unfurled rainbow-colored wings and took to the air, abandoning the stripped skeleton of the body that had served as both their incubator and first home. Each of them was small, hardly larger than a real butterfly, but they were already growing . . . and growing fast. They circled above the snow-covered floor, the pristine white dotted with mirror fragments, splashes of crimson, and the remains of two people: a gutted corpse that had been split open from throat to crotch, and a skeleton with a pair of long metal shears fused to the bones of its right wrist. Husband and wife, united in death in a way they never had been in life.

And then, one by one, the younglings soared upward and through the open spaces in the partially collapsed roof. They hovered above the abandoned amusement park for a time, listening, as if waiting for something—a signal or sign—to tell them what to do next. Perhaps it came to them, perhaps not, but after a while they began to disperse, some flying east, some west, some north, some south.

Maybe you're right, Mara. Maybe there's no way to completely know what rules—if any—your power operates by. One thing seems clear, though. Once a change begins, it keeps going whether you're present or not. It's like people carry a piece of your power with them.

The younglings scattered in all directions, bearing with them the dark seeds from which tomorrow would be born.

TIM WAGGONER

LIKE DEATH

Scott Raymond is a man haunted by his past and terrorized in the present. As a young boy, he witnessed the brutal murder of his family, but there is so much of the gruesome tragedy that he simply cannot remember. The memories won't come, but the trauma won't go away.

Scott is an adult now, still scarred but learning to deal with it. He has come to Ash Creek to write about another mystery, a missing girl named Miranda. Here, Scott meets another girl named Miranda, who bears an uncanny resemblance to the one who's missing—but she's the wrong age. She will draw Scott into the bizarre hidden world where nightmares are very real...and very deadly.

THE LOVELIEST DEAD

RAY GARTON

To most people it's just a large house, old and a bit run-down. To the Kellar family it's a new start, but soon, it will become a living nightmare. The terrors begin before the Kellars have even finished unpacking. Who are the mysterious children playing on the rusty, vine-covered swing set in the backyard? Who is the figure sitting in the dark corner of the bedroom at night? Who—or what—waits in the basement? They are the dead and they cannot rest. Horror stalks the halls of the Kellar house. And the secrets of the past are reaching from beyond the grave to destroy the living.

P. D. CACEK

NIGHT PRAYERS

Poor Allison. One minute she's crying into her tequila in a country-western bar, and the next she's a vampire. She's fallen for a lot of lines in her time, but she's never had a morning after like this one, waking up alone in a seedy L.A. motel room, dumped again—and suddenly one of the undead. Seth had promised her that things would be different. Then he sucked her dry and left her without so much as a training manual. Now it's up to her to figure out how to survive without a clue in the seamy underbelly of the city at night. But survival is more of a long shot than ever once Allison gets on the bad side of a catty coven of exotic dancers…all of them vengeful vampires.

SÈPHERA GIRÓN
MISTRESS *of* THE DARK

Meet Abigail Barnum. She's new in town, eager to make it big in New York. Hers is the darker side of the city. Her friends are strippers and drag queens, and she works as a waitress in a tourist bar with a back room that's definitely for adults only. But the most important thing about Abigail is…she's deadly.

Abigail has gone insane. Voices and hallucinations are drawing her deeper and deeper into her own world, a world of obsession and pain, seduction and murder. Few suspect just how dangerous Abigail is, but one woman knows her grisly secret. As Abigail descends into madness, can anyone she touches ever hope to be safe?

RICHARD LAYMON
THE LAKE

Leigh is a beautiful girl, eighteen years old, headstrong and rebellious. All she wants from her summer by the lake is a chance to relax and have some fun. And that handsome boy she met certainly looks like fun. But her summer fling will lead to terror. That night in the old abandoned house will haunt her nightmares for the rest of her life.

Eighteen years later, Leigh's daughter, Deana, doesn't know much about what happened to her mother all those years ago, and she doesn't particularly care. She too is looking for fun. What she finds instead is a shadowy figure out for blood—and his own twisted kind of fun. Before he's done, both mother and daughter will be plunged into a whirlpool of fear and madness, from which death is the only escape.
